A LONG KISS GOODBYE

AN OBSIDIAN & MERCURY NOVEL

H. D. THOMSON

AUTHOR NOTE

I've always been into the supernatural, myths, legends, and folklore as far back as I can remember. A couple of my favorite movies are *Jason and the Argonauts* and *Clash of the Titans*. So when I started the *Onyx and Mercury* series, I was thrilled to start something wholly new and different. I wanted to create a world different than anything else and a new legend.

The Greeks had their own legends along with the Aztecs and many other societies. I made mercury a prominent focal point in the series. Its history is fascinating, and many before us used it for thermometers, as a medicine, talisman, and poison. I decided to create a new use for mercury.

Luys' story is pure fiction, just like his brother, Gabriel's, and every other character, other than the historical figures mentioned and the gods from Aztec religion, though I've taken liberty with some of Aztec and Spanish history.

I truly hope you thoroughly enjoy Luys and Avery's story.

CHAPTER 1

> "Faith is but a breath away from fear. Just breathe and
> believe...."
> — *The Book of Stolen Secrets*

Friday, August 16th – 6:15 p.m.

Avery Fleming hurried from her car as heat waves rolled up from the ground, nearly suffocating her with its intensity. Perspiration trickled between her breasts. Almost seven o'clock, and she was sweating worse than a horse after a brutal ride—what fun. The rustle of leaves rattled from nearby trees as a gust of wind thrust her hair into her eyes. She shoved the strands aside and turned her face against the sun's glare. The wind didn't ease the relentless hot air but amplified it that much more.

August. One more month of being subjected to the same hellish conditions.

Sighing, Avery stepped onto the sidewalk of her condo complex and beneath one of several olive trees shading the route to her place. A car door slammed. She glanced over her shoulder, and her hand tightened on the strap of her purse. Even though the parking lot and common areas were in full daylight, Avery couldn't relax.

Last week, someone had murdered a woman less than five miles away. Other than stating the victim had been stabbed multiple times, the press had leaked few details. The news initially reported her boyfriend as the prime suspect, but since he hadn't yet been arrested, there was a chance the sick psycho was out there. She grunted. Just another to add to the many crazies wandering the Phoenix area.

Grabbing her mail key, she moved into the alcove of the communal mailboxes and stiffened. Luys, her neighbor, stood rummaging inside his box. She didn't know anything about him other than his name; she shouldn't even want to. She started to take a step backward, but then he turned, and she forced herself forward. She wasn't about to let him think she was avoiding him.

Straightening her shoulders, she stepped over to her mailbox and three feet from his own. His aftershave drifted toward her, a supple scent of cedar or pine with maybe a hint of orange.

Avery tightened her jaw. So he smelled nice. Lots of men smelled nice. So what if he was over six feet and looked gorgeous in his tailored slacks, white button-down shirt that contrasted with his dark brown, almost black hair. Lots of men in Scottsdale were drool-worthy. She'd even dated a couple. Granted, they hadn't exactly been keepers.

This guy didn't know how to do anything but frown. Not once had she seen him crack a smile.

She liked friendly people. She liked people who smiled. She liked someone who didn't frown all the time. Life was too short.

After unlocking her metal cubicle, she found a couple of fliers inside. Most of her bills came via email, but she checked once a week in case she might have missed something important.

"Excuse me."

She blinked. With her hand inside her mailbox, she turned to her neighbor, forcing a bland expression on her face.

Then she realized he was—of course, frowning at her—expecting some type of response. "What?"

"You're stepping on a letter of mine."

She glanced down and recognized he was right. It must have slipped from his mailbox and landed on the ground. She stepped off the letter or tried to. Great. The envelope was attached to the sole of her shoe.

A distinct and impatient sigh passed his lips.

After shaking her foot a couple of times, she found the blasted thing stuck. She rested a hand against the wall, but he beat her to the envelope.

He caught her ankle. "Here, let me."

The cool pressure of his hand on her skin shot a tremor of shock up her leg. Before she had the thought to respond, he deftly peeled the envelope from her sole and released her ankle. She had a brief glimpse of her footprint and gum on the once pristine white paper before he stuffed it between his junk mail.

It was her turn to frown. She stepped backward, widening the space between them.

That's when she noticed something by his feet. "What is that? I can't tell. There's so much fur—"

"A kitten." He scooped up the animal with one hand.

"I didn't know you had a cat." She avoided meeting his gaze to stare at a long-haired tortoiseshell kitten. The last time they'd had eye contact was when he'd gotten a full-frontal view of her partially naked body as she came out of the community pool. She hadn't intended to flash him; she'd thought her swimsuit top was on. He'd acted as if she'd intentionally given him an eyeful.

"Well, it seems I've inherited one today." He turned his back and walked toward his condo.

She crinkled her mail beneath a fist, waited a minute, and moved from the mailbox to her condo. As she rounded the corner to her home, the neighbor disappeared into his place next to hers before closing the door behind him.

Once inside, she quickly stripped and showered, washing away the day's stresses from her auburn hair and body. She was meeting Cristina and her husband, also relatively new neighbors who lived two buildings away in the complex. She loved this area in Scottsdale, Arizona. A bit of old town but still safe compared to other neighborhoods in the greater Phoenix area.

The last two weekends, she'd joined her neighbors for drinks. She usually met them instead of going together. That way, she could leave when she wanted or needed to. She wasn't one to stay out past midnight, and they seemed to like the nightlife, at times going to another bar and not getting home until after three am.

After changing into a long flowing white sleeveless dress—anything more and she'd be sweating the second she was outside—she walked the short distance in a pair of flats to *The Thing*, a restaurant and lounge that opened last month and was considered *the* place. Give it a month, though, and the next craze would replace it. She reached the entrance of the restaurant then maneuvered through the crowd to get to the hostess.

Her phone dinged with a text. Cristina.

Perfect timing.

We're in the back right corner. I'm wearing bright pink. You can't miss me.

Avery broke free from the lobby to get to the bar, feeling like a pinball as she bumped shoulders and bodies to get through the crowd.

"So, how goes it?" Cristina greeted her with a grin.

"Great! It's the weekend, and a drink sounds pretty good about now." She dropped into a plush lounge chair opposite Cristina and her husband. "Hey, Stephen."

Slouched in an overstuffed chair, Cristina's husband straightened, leaned forward, and set his drink on the low-slung copper coffee table. Dark brown hair, thick and wavy, reached past his shoulders, while his equally dark brown eyes, prominent jaw, and brow added to a handsome, sexy picture. He was just as attractive as her neighbor, but unlike her neighbor, Stephen knew how to smile.

"Glad to see you made it." He flashed a set of perfect white teeth. "Cristina was telling me your new job's been challenging."

Avery shrugged. "Yeah, but it's not something I wasn't expecting."

"If it involves too much mental or physical effort, I'm gone." He tapped a finger on the arm of his chair and shook his head before he waved down a server. Once the waiter took their drink and appetizer order, Stephen urged, "So tell me about your new position. Not sure I could do what you do. Sounds like work."

"That's why they call it a job."

"Funny." Cristina laughed before throwing an odd look at Stephen.

"I promised myself I wouldn't complain. Compared to my last job, they offer far better insurance, which kicks in next month." Then Avery admitted, "But it's going to be challenging. I won't lie. I'm just going to have to learn to compartmentalize better than I ever have being a social worker. I can't let my clients' lives emotionally cripple me. Otherwise, I won't be a help to anyone."

Cristina wrinkled her nose. "I'd be too depressed working with the mentally and physically challenged, especially when you can only do so much with your job. I can't imagine living on the street, and I surely couldn't handle knowing a mother and her autistic child were living in their car..."

"Hey, I thought we came out to have fun? Not talk about something maudlin and depressing." Stephen arched a brow at his wife. "Wasn't that the purpose?"

"Yes, of course," Cristina agreed as the waiter came with their drinks and food.

"Good." Stephen took a deep swallow of his whiskey and club soda. Ice cubes rattled when he planted his glass on the coffee table and eyed Cristina.

Cristina gripped her fingers around her wrist and circled them back and forth as she stared at her lap and didn't touch her food. "It's good to get out. Being behind a desk all day with ledgers and numbers can get a little mind-numbing even when I enjoy accounting."

Avery frowned and shifted in her seat. Cristina's mood had just done a nosedive. But why? Had Avery missed something? Stephen didn't look upset, but there was definite tension around the coffee table. Unless Avery's mood detector was out of whack...

Cristina tugged the strap of her purse from the arm of her chair, strung it over her shoulder, and rose. "I'll be back in a bit. The restroom calls. Not a good sign when I haven't even had a drink yet!"

Stephen caught his wife's wrist and teased, "Do you have to? I'll miss you."

"I'll miss you too."

"Do I get a kiss, at least?" Stephen asked with a half-grin.

"Of course." Cristina quickly leaned down and kissed him. As she turned, the curtain of her dark chocolate-colored hair obscured her expression.

"I might as well join you." Avery swiftly rose and followed her friend to the restroom.

In the bathroom, Avery blinked at the harsh fluorescent bulbs, a drastic shift from the muted lighting in the main bar and dining area.

Once done in the bathroom stall, she joined Cristina at the sinks and washed her hands. When Cristina lifted a hand to brush her hair away from her brow, her long sleeve slid backward to expose several black and purple bruises.

"What happened?"

Cristina dropped her hand and brushed her sleeve back down. "Nothing. I fell. Going down, I hit my arm on the counter."

"It looks awful." Avery stepped closer and lifted the hem.

Her friend sidestepped, but not before Avery caught sight of four distinct marks, similar to a hand's brutal grasp.

She opened her mouth to argue but closed it at the belligerent gleam in Cristina's eyes.

"Let's go," Cristina murmured, then slipped from the bathroom, not waiting to see if Avery followed.

The wontons, edamame, and sliders were tasty and still warm when they returned to their chairs. For the next hour, Avery struggled to keep her expression neutral. But she couldn't stop thinking of Cristina's bruises.

Stephen must have grabbed Cristina hard enough to leave marks. It must have hurt like hell. Avery didn't have any proof it was her husband, but who else would it be? The abuser was always the spouse, right? Cristina wasn't having an affair—at least Cristina never mentioned it. And those were finger marks, not some light bruising from hitting the corner of a counter. Avery wasn't that naïve. She'd seen too much abuse over the years.

When Cristina sank into the chair next to her husband, Stephen grabbed her hand and brought her fingers to his lips in a brief caress. Her fingers curled into his before she slipped them from his grasp—too quickly? It seemed like it—and reached for her drink on the coffee table. Avery briefly made eye contact with Stephen, unable to read beyond his bland expression. But something in his eyes made her take a deep swallow of her drink. The smooth and smokey texture of her wine didn't soothe her growing agitation. Her hand tightened on the glass. She shifted uneasily in her chair.

Avery stared down at her half-empty drink. She hated the idea that Cristina might be in an abusive relationship. Ugh. She could offer help and direct her to various available resources, but she couldn't force her friend into doing anything.

The evening had lost any pleasure she might have found in it. She glanced at her phone by her elbow on the armrest of her chair. A little after nine. She placed a hand against a pretend yawn. "I think I'm going to head on home. It's been a crazy, busy week."

"How about we drive you home?" Cristina asked. "We can drop you off on our way to the *Dirty Buffalo*."

"No. No. I'll be fine."

"What about a taxi or Uber?"

Avery arched a brow. "To drive me two blocks?"

Cristina shrugged and made a face. "Well, you never know. You heard what happened in North Scottsdale, right?"

"Yeah, I should be safe. They're saying it's the boyfriend and not a serial killer."

"The suspect's always the boyfriend." Stephen reached for Cristina's hand again and chuckled. "Well, I guess it's a good thing I'm your very boring husband and not your boyfriend."

Cristina groaned with a laugh, but Avery found nothing funny about the topic. Then her friend frowned. "I hear the scene was pretty gruesome."

"When it gets personal, it usually is," Avery said.

Cristina made a face. "Well, I hate to say this, but I hope it really is the boyfriend. I don't think I can handle another serial killer in the Phoenix area. The last one had everyone driving on the freeways, terrified."

Stephen let go of Cristina's hand and leaned toward the table. "I guess the serial shooter didn't think of his victims as people."

"That's crazy." Cristina wrinkled her nose. "I don't know who gets off by killing some random person.

From what I heard, the serial shooter thought it was some type of game. I'll never get it." Cristina shook her head, her lip curling. "Using people as target practice. How low can you get?"

"They're sick." Avery set her glass on the table.

"Or evil," Stephen argued.

Avery cocked her head to one side. "You think there's such a thing as evil? What about a person being mentally ill?"

Stephen shook his head. "There are too many people who are mentally ill." He waved a hand around the room. "Take this place. I'm sure if we counted everyone here, I'd run out of fingers. Lots of people have mental health issues. You don't see them shooting down people on the freeway."

"True." Avery shifted in her chair. "But there are degrees of mental illness. Many people can function easily in society and mask their pain and psychosis. Most people don't like their illness to become common gossip. Even now, with public figures coming out with their depression or other disorder, I think it's still a big taboo. Society is still too apathetic with snap stereotypes." She didn't know how the conversation had turned this dark and morbid.

"Interesting point." Stephen leaned further toward the table between them and rested both elbows on his knees. "If you say there's a large percentage of mental illness in the general population, and evil has nothing to do with it, then the country would be inundated with shootings, stabbings, and continuous violence because of some mental incapacity. The police wouldn't be able to get a handle on it. Society would turn into pure chaos." Stephen's mouth turned into a thin line. "No. I'm not buying that. There's evil. It's called choice. A person chooses that fork in the road, they justify their behavior, they pursue self-gratification, and to hell with the ramifications and the ruin they leave behind. And if it becomes personal, it gets even messier."

"Okay, this has gotten way out of control," Cristina broke into the conversation, waving a hand as if in surrender. She laughed, but the inflection sounded hollow.

"I'm not going to argue," Avery said, shaking her head. "And before the evening gets even more depressing, I think it's about time I took myself home. I hope I didn't completely ruin your evening." She smiled at Cristina. Right now, she didn't care if she dampened Stephen's night. He'd been way too argumentative and sanctimonious.

"Are you sure you're not too tired to hang out longer? Stephen's younger brother is visiting, and we don't want to go home just yet. He can be a bit much at times." Cristina's eyes crinkled with a smile. "You can join us if you want to at the *Dirty Buffalo*. We're going to head on out there in an hour. You know you're always welcome. Right, Stephen?"

"Of course!" His lips curved into a genuine smile.

Avery paused with a reply but already knew her answer. Until tonight, she'd considered Stephen fun to be with. But now, she wasn't so sure, not with Cristina's bruises. Yeah, she might judge him with no proof, but she couldn't shake her feelings. Right now, she found Stephen unnerving. Talking about evil sure hadn't helped.

She shook her head, grabbing her phone to slip inside her purse. "Thanks for the offer. Home is sounding pretty good after the day I've had. A walk and some fresh air will do me some good. Plus, it's just two blocks away."

When she pulled her wallet from her purse, Stephen lifted a hand. "Hey, I've got it."

"Are you sure?"

"Of course." Stephen smiled, humor dancing in his dark eyes.

The softening in his face made Avery wonder if she was getting way too reactive and spinning tales where there were none. The couple could be into rough sex.

She nodded and smiled back. "Thanks!"

She slipped from their table with a wave. Once outside, the quiet of the night shouted at her, making her realize how loud the bar had been. The abrupt silence made her suddenly aware of her solitude. So she was alone. Millions of people were alone. But they had other people in their life. Family. Friends.

She didn't have family, but she did have a few friends.

But no one close to her, another voice argued inside her head. *Because you've let no one get that close... Because you're chicken. A scaredy-cat...*

She mentally shook her head. She wasn't scared. The opportunity just hadn't been there yet. That was all...

Yeah, right.

Several cars sped past as she walked down the sidewalk. She felt safe. The street had a good amount of traffic, and there weren't really any areas without lighting other than a couple of large paloverde trees throwing shadows in places.

The heat, though, hadn't abated. After walking fifty feet from *The Thing*, she felt sweat cling to the small of her back, beneath her breasts and hairline. She'd be drenched by the time she got to her front door.

When her one-story condo came into view, she pulled out her key ring and quickened her step. The light by her front door beckoned. The neighbor's windows were black. Maybe he'd gone to bed already. Probably alone. She hadn't yet seen him with a woman or man. Avery frowned. She shouldn't be thinking about what he was doing or with who.

A scrape of a foot against asphalt broke into the night behind her. She looked over her shoulder. Nothing other than the trees rustling in the wind. No sign of another person behind, to the sides, or in front of her. The lights in the parking lot illuminated all the cars except for the ones beneath the overhang along the brick fence.

Shivering, she left the sidewalk and cut across the decomposed granite toward her condo, slipping a hand into her purse for the pepper spray tucked away in a side pocket. A flash of movement entered her peripheral vision. She pulled her hand from her purse, her finger on the nozzle.

Laughter. A voice, the words indistinguishable and unidentifiable as a male or female.

Pain, savage in intensity, crashed against her skull. Then she fell into blackness.

CHAPTER 2

Sunday, August 17th – 11:23 am

Pain. It throbbed around and inside Avery's skull and seared her chest. She shifted, then cried out at the deepening pain. She clutched onto some type of fabric and twisted the material between her fingers.

Slowly, so she didn't make the pain worse, she eased open her eyes. The ceiling stared back at her. Something was wrong. Nausea rolled through her stomach, threatening to rise up her throat.

Calm down.

She didn't dare move until the urge to vomit subsided.

This wasn't a hangover. The pain was too intense.

She lay flat on her back for several minutes as she grew conscious of her surroundings. She slid a hand across a bed and touched a pillow beneath her head. Just as slowly, she turned her head but didn't relax at the familiar sight of the Arizona desert watercolor painting on her bedroom wall and her nightstand with her e-reader, sandalwood body lotion, earplugs, and girly lamp.

A thin sheet covered her naked body up to her neck.

How? She didn't remember getting to her condo, never mind undressing. She usually slept in her underwear and a t-shirt.

Panic roared through her body. No. Please God, no! She touched her hip and between her legs with a trembling hand. She didn't feel violated. She would know if she'd had sex with someone, never mind being raped, wouldn't she?

She struggled to remember. She'd walked from *The Thing,* crossed the complex's parking lot, and had started cutting across the property toward her condo. But she didn't recall getting to her front door…

Then the pain had hit, exploding against her head. Something or someone must have struck her from behind before she'd blacked out.

That someone must have dragged her inside and attacked her. Rape. They must have. Why else would she be naked? There was no other logical reason she could think of.

She jerked upright. Pain cut into her chest and skull. She cried out and quivered against the onslaught as it crashed then swept through her. Gasping, she sat frozen in the middle of her bed, the top sheet pooled around her hips, grappling for strength as darkness closed in around her. She struggled to keep from fainting.

Daylight streamed through the blinds and into the bedroom window, spearing horizontal lines across the carpet. From the sun's position, it was late morning or early afternoon. How long had she been asleep? Had she been drugged?

She touched her chest and recoiled. Her fingers had swept across something unfamiliar against her skin.

Choking back a sob, she fumbled from the bed. Her legs buckled, and she grabbed onto the mattress before she pitched forward. After taking a couple of slow, measured breaths, she regained some strength and stumbled into the bathroom. Grabbing onto the lip of the sink, she snapped on the bathroom light. The room flooded into bright, near-blinding light. She blinked until she could focus.

She stared at her naked reflection. Her red hair, thick and unkempt, tumbled down past her shoulders. Half circles stamped dark shadows beneath her blue eyes. A bruise stained her temple from probably pitching forward when she fell.

Her gaze traveled lower, past her face, her neck, and froze on her chest.

She gasped. Then a keening noise erupted from her mouth and echoed against the walls and bathroom tile as a fresh wave of panic slammed into her.

No. Impossible

Shuddering, she lifted a hand in horror and touched her skin between her breasts. A horizontal cut, looking as if a high schooler had stitched the skin closed with a thick black string, crossed several inches below her breastbone, while another vertical incision cut across it. Dried blood covered both lacerations.

Oh, my God. No. No. No.

The ruin of her chest wasn't some mirage or figment of her imagination. Someone had cut her open, operated on her, and stitched her up afterward.

Luys Martinez grabbed his wallet and stuffed it in the back pocket of his jeans. After a quick look over his shoulder to make sure the kitten hadn't moved from her spot under the coffee table, he scanned the list of errands on his phone, then grabbed his keys, stepped outside, and closed the door. A wall of heat hit him, a shock from his condo's air conditioning.

The door closed to his left. Movement, a flash of copper hair along his peripheral vision. He stiffened. His next-door neighbor. Avery, the sexy-as-hell redhead. She was usually out doing errands or whatever she did by this time of day. He liked to avoid her. Sometimes he did a pretty good job of it, but this week wasn't one of them.

He didn't like being anywhere near her. She reminded him of what he didn't have. He'd been single for... It didn't matter how long.

Realizing Avery was walking down the same sidewalk and headed in the same direction, he started to cut across the yard to use a different path to his car but paused when he fully noticed her.

Dressed in a pair of flannel shorts and a large black t-shirt bunched around the waist, she stumbled forward, then weaved back and forth on the sidewalk as if drunk. One of her thin flip-flops threatened to come off as she lurched forward. Then as she turned slightly, he realized her shirt was bunched up because she was clutching the hem to her stomach.

"Hey." He hurried to her side. "Are you okay?"

"Yeah." She looked down at the ground, her matted red hair falling forward and shielding her face. "Sure. Just n-need to get to my car."

"You don't look fine." Was Avery roaring drunk in the middle of the afternoon?

He should turn around and walk away. He should mind his own business. He should...

Luys touched her shoulder.

She flinched. Her hair shifted again, this time finally revealing her face. Tear tracks stained her cheeks while the color had leached from her skin, leaving it a sickly gray. A bruise stained her temple. She looked like she might pass out.

As Avery took a step back and away from him, her flip-flop caught on the sidewalk. She pitched sideways, and the purse strapped over her shoulder swung wildly. He grabbed her around the waist before she tumbled to the ground.

She cried out. Sensing he might have hurt her, he almost let go but thought she was better off standing with his help than landing on the decomposed rock by the walkway.

She listed against him. "I've...I've got to get to the hospital."

"I'll call the ambulance."

"NO. I can take myself."

He'd been avoiding people for as long as he could remember, and now in his arms, he had a woman ready to faint, for God only knew what.

"You're not in any condition."

She pushed him away and took in a shuddering breath as she glanced over to the parking lot. A look of embarrassment cut across her features. "I can't-I can't afford the cost of an ambulance."

"I'll take you," he found himself offering.

"I—" She looked up at him and searched his face. She closed her eyes as if she could fight off the pain with sheer willpower. Wavering on her feet, she clutched at his arm to steady herself and looked as if she might fall to the ground at any moment.

He realized she wasn't in any condition to think clearly and someone needed to do something. It looked like that would have to be him.

"Here. It's a quick drive to the hospital. Three miles at most." He picked her up and found her surprisingly heavy. Her muscles slackened beneath his hands, and she slumped against his chest. She'd passed out.

After some struggle, he managed to set her gently on the passenger seat of his sporty Subaru. Then he reached for her seatbelt, accidentally brushing his arm against her chest.

She jerked awake and pushed feebly at his arm. "No! Please. I-I can't handle the pressure against my body."

"Ahh, sure." He quickly retreated, shut her door, and slipped behind the wheel of his car. "Do you want me to contact anyone?"

Silence hung in the air, and he thought she might have passed out again. Then finally, she admitted, "I don't have anyone."

"What about out of state?"

"There's no one." With both hands balled into fists on her lap, she rested her head back against the headrest. Her throat contracted with a swallow.

He wondered what was wrong with her. She looked fragile and lost. "Did someone hurt you?"

She turned her head and looked out the window in the opposite direction, not answering. Silence howled through the interior of the car for the rest of the drive. He stuffed his thoughts away for another time. If he didn't ask questions, she'd remain a stranger, someone he couldn't connect to, wouldn't feel for.

When he pulled into the parking lot, for a wild moment, he thought she'd died until he caught the gentle rise and fall of her chest.

After a faint protest from her, he carried her from the car, through the entrance of Desert Valley General Hospital, and into the emergency room. This close, he noticed the abrasion on her temple, the dried blood on her upper chest where her t-shirt gaped open. A scent he couldn't decipher radiated from her. Blood and something else. Something familiar, but he couldn't distinguish the smell.

At the receptionist's window, the woman pushed at his shoulder. "Please put me down."

"Are you sure?"

She closed her eyes briefly, then nodded. "I'll be fine."

He eased her gently to the ground. She sank against his side but remained upright.

The receptionist blinked at them from behind the window before turning her gaze on him. "Are you her next of kin?"

"I—No," he replied after a pause and shook his head, momentarily disconcerted at the question.

"I need you to fill out the first four screens to the best of your ability." The woman offered an electronic pad.

He took the pad for his neighbor and frowned at the first line. Last name? Emergency contact? He had no idea on any of it other than her first name.

From beside him, Avery slumped. Before her knees

hit the floor, he dropped the pad in a nearby chair, caught her around the waist as her purse fell and its insides scattered across the linoleum. Legs braced, he swept her up against his chest. Her hair caught against the stubble of his chin and cheek.

The receptionist jumped from her chair and disappeared around the doorway behind her. Before he had the chance to decide what to do next, two techs or nurses with a gurney came through another door.

He helped them ease the woman onto the gurney. Her flip-flop slipped from her red-polished toes to land on the corner of the stretcher while her head slid to one side. He swept several strands of hair from her parted lips. She looked like a doll tossed to the road and run over. For months now, he'd secretly wanted to know everything about her: what made her laugh, made her cry, who touched her life, what she believed, and whether or not life had been kind to her. But today, kindness didn't exist in her world. Hopefully, only momentarily. After all, the only constant was change. At least for most people.

He reached over to touch her one last time, having this crazy idea that he could will his strength into her, but the staff opened the door to the restricted section of the hospital and swept her down the hall before he could feel her skin.

"Sir?"

The door closed, and his neighbor disappeared from view.

"Sir?"

He turned to the receptionist back behind the glass panel. "Yes?"

"Do you plan on waiting?"

"I—" He stood between the hallway and waiting room, feeling as if he hung between two worlds. He didn't want to get involved. The idea terrified him.

The woman nodded to the pad visible in the chair near him and the woman's purse on the floor by his feet. "I'm going to need her insurance information, social if you know it, name, and address." Her gaze softened. "If she doesn't have anyone to contact in case of emergency, she might need someone."

"Yes, I'll wait," he said in a hoarse voice.

He sat in the waiting room, her purse in his lap, her wallet in his hand, and wondered how the devil he got into this situation. For someone who didn't involve themselves in anyone's business, he seemed to be getting in quick and deep. He snapped open her wallet and pulled out her driver's license. Avery Fleming. Auburn hair, blue eyes. 5' 6" 138 pounds. Her picture stared back at him. It didn't do her justice.

From the moment he first saw her step out of her condo last year, he'd been gobsmacked. She was beautiful with her thick auburn hair, bee-stung lips, and classic nose. Other than today, she moved like a dancer, smooth, confident, and with a grace he couldn't help but admire. But there was something more than beauty that drew him to her. An aura radiated from her. There was a worldliness in her face, but also a kindness, as if all the hurt and disappointment she might have suffered hadn't stopped her from having hope, of believing in something good. He'd ignored her overtures of kindness. He'd made a point of being cold, unapproachable whenever they inadvertently met by their respective front doors or mail alcove, and it had worked perfectly: she'd kept away.

He'd hated causing her to feel uncomfortable, but if she found him obnoxious, he'd be safe. He didn't dare let anyone into his life.

It was too dangerous.

CHAPTER 3

Sunday, August 17ᵗʰ – 3:12 pm

Lying on a hospital bed and waiting for the results of her CT scan, Avery stared up at the ceiling and tried to stop her racing mind. After the nurse had wheeled her into the hospital room, she'd had a good half an hour with only her thoughts and nothing else. It wouldn't take much to push her over the edge. She couldn't seem to stop the image of someone standing over her naked body, their hands on her, probing, touching, cutting. No! She needed to stop. She didn't dare go there. Otherwise, she was liable to have a panic attack.

Why do this to her and nothing else? No one had robbed her. She'd found nothing missing or out of place in her condo. She had found her purse on the coffee table in the living room. Who cuts someone open but makes sure the person's belongings are safe?

A knock sounded on the door. The doctor, a woman with salt-and-pepper hair, pulled up into a messy bun, stepped into her hospital room. Avery hit the remote by her hand. The bed hummed and lifted her into a seated position.

"Do you have the results?" Avery plucked at the bedsheet at her waist, then pressed her palm against her stomach to quiet the tremor in her hand. She was afraid to know.

When she'd woken up, she'd been in another room with a nurse and doctor peering down at her. After they'd done a quick check of her vitals, the questions had started. The nurse hadn't done a very good job at hiding the horror on her face when she'd seen Avery's chest. The doctor had likely seen worse situations because she'd only nodded with a light of sympathy shimmering in her eyes, which only made Avery want to break down and cry.

Dr. Clark rolled a gray-topped cushioned stool over to the side of the bed and sank down on it. She sat for a moment in silence as if trying to find the correct words. Then she met Avery's gaze with gentle green eyes. "I don't know what to tell you. We did a complete scan, and everything looked normal. All your internal organs look fine. There's nothing to explain the rationale as to why someone cut you open and stitched you back up. The stitches are a mystery in themselves. They don't consist of any of the material you would find from a hospital or medical center, and they look like thread someone would get at your typical fabric or craft store."

"And my heart and other organs? There's nothing wrong with them?"

"So far, everything looks and sounds good. The EKG found nothing unusual. The x-rays showed nothing out of the ordinary. I'll know a lot more once I look at the CT scan." The doctor brushed a hand along the length of her thigh as she pressed her lips into a thin line. "The police were notified."

Avery stiffened. The hand against her stomach balled into a fist.

"What this person did is sick and deserves to be apprehended and arrested," Dr. Clark said. "They'll have some questions for you."

"When?" She didn't want to talk to anyone, never mind the police with all their intrusive questions.

"Probably in a couple of hours. I want you to get some rest first. No doubt you need it. Your health comes first." Dr. Clark rose. "I'll be back in a bit."

They must have given her something to calm her anxiety because she nodded off. She woke up when the door to her room swished open and Dr. Clark reappeared.

Avery rubbed at her eyes and face, trying to get the cobwebs from her thoughts. Dread and the need to know vied with each other. "So?"

The doctor resumed her seat on the stool by Avery's bed. She held a tablet and swiped it several times and then typed something before turning the computer's screen toward Avery. "A CT scan can help show the heart's structure. That includes valves, chambers, and the muscle itself. It also can tell me how well your blood flows through your heart and major vessels. Going through numerous image slices tells me there isn't any damage from your attack, and there's no sign of a lack of blood flow from the muscle. The heart and surrounding area are healthy and typical of someone your age."

The doctor shook her head. "I'm baffled. Are you sure your attack happened yesterday?"

"Yes."

"Strange. I would have guessed much earlier." The

doctor frowned. "There doesn't seem to be any motive. I also can't find any evidence that reveals your attacker did some medical procedure other than cutting through your tissue to get to your chest cavity. They didn't break your sternum, but it looks like you might have fractured it at some point when you were younger. There's no damage inflicted to your muscle, tissue, or any major blood vessels." The doctor's lips narrowed. "I don't know what to tell you. Someone is playing some sick game with you, for only God knows why. If I didn't have visible proof of the incision and sutures, I wouldn't believe it. The stitching can't be from a surgeon or, for that matter, an experienced seamstress. The person didn't know what they were doing the way they threaded your skin together. It boggles my mind that you didn't die. We still need to keep an eye on you. I'd like you to visit your primary care physician in two days to make sure you're healing fine. There isn't any sign of infection, but I've prescribed an antibiotic and pain medication for you to take home with you. Actually, I'm amazed by how well you're healing under the circumstances. It's quite extraordinary."

"So I'm free to go home?"

"Yes, all your vitals are normal. I'll have the nurse start the paperwork for your release. I have two detectives waiting in the hall to talk to you, though. I warned them to keep it quick."

"Have they caught the person?"

"I'm not sure."

She didn't like the idea of talking to the police, of their knowing looks, their curiosity. Ugh. Like she was some type of lab rat. She was sure they hadn't come across an attack like hers. Who wouldn't be curious? She would have been the same. She grabbed the metal bar along the length of her bed. But if she didn't help them…

"So this person is out there right now? He could come back and do it all over again?" The idea of looking over her shoulder the minute she left the hospital left her reeling. "They could be a stranger or someone I know, and I wouldn't have a clue."

Dr. Clark winced. "I can't help you there. You'll have to talk to the police. Maybe they know something I don't. All I can say is that you're lucky you survived this." She patted Avery's arm. "You'll be fine. You're young and healthy, and you should heal quickly."

"I'll be fine?" Avery's lips thinned, unable to crush the sarcasm from her voice and the growing wave of self-pity roiling through her. "I don't think so. Some sick person cut me open, and I have no memory of it. And I have no clue why!"

"I apologize. I didn't mean to sound like I was making light of your situation. I do have resources for victims of violent crime if you feel the need to talk to someone. And I'm sure the police will uncover something."

"I've never heard of anything like this happening to someone else except for horror movies. Have you—" Avery was afraid to ask.

"Have I what?"

"So someone cut me open, left my organs and everything else alone, and stitched me back up. It doesn't make any sense. Have you heard of other people being operated on for no reason? Not just in this state but other places?"

The doctor looked down at her chart briefly before shaking her head. "No, sorry. This is a first for me. I've asked the medical staff in this hospital and the surrounding hospitals. I haven't heard back from everyone yet, but so far there's nothing anywhere similar to your attack. I also did some research and asked several of my colleagues with no success. This is very new to me and the staff here. I would think the police are going to want to keep this quiet. I know I wouldn't want the public panicking."

Avery grunted. She tried to blink back the tears blurring her vision, but it was a vain attempt at best. The idea of her neighbors or co-workers finding out about what happened to her was horrifying. She wasn't about to open her mouth to anyone. But there were other people. People in the hospital—nurses, doctors, or technicians might talk. It was bound to get out. Yeah, there were HIPAA rules, but the attack was too tantalizing and bizarre for it not to, especially if there was a chance of profiting from it through the newspapers.

Angry at herself for feeling so helpless, Avery rubbed at one eye with the back of her hand and shifted on the bed. At the sudden wave of pain, she bit back a gasp. On top of it, her head throbbed like crazy.

"Sorry. It's going to hurt for a time even with the painkillers, and it's normal to feel emotional after such a trauma," Dr. Clark quietly assured. "Don't feel like you're being weak. Your body needs to recover, and you should take several days off work, preferably a minimum of a week. The nurse will go over your home recovery in the discharge papers and answer any questions you might have. Your primary physician should be able to remove the stitches. I've contacted their office, but right now, I want you to stay home tomorrow at a minimum. Don't lift anything over twenty-five pounds, and if you can, have someone with you or at least check in on you."

She couldn't take time off, never mind an entire week.

Her answer must have shown on her face because Dr. Clark smiled gently and said, "Nuh-uh. I can see you want to argue with me. Absolutely no working at the office tomorrow. You need to stay home Monday."

"Monday?"

"Yes."

The doctor had to have it wrong because that would mean... Panic swarmed through her insides. "But tomorrow can't be Monday. That's impossible."

"Why?"

"That would mean I lost two days. I thought today was Saturday. I never thought of checking the day or anything. I didn't pay attention to the dates..."

"I'm sorry." Dr. Clark frowned and glanced down at her iPad for the longest time. Finally, she looked up and met Avery's gaze.

Avery pulled at the hem of her sheet and looked away from the compassion in the doctor's eyes. It would only make her want to cry that much more. She needed to get angry; she needed to feel outraged, but right now, she was drowning in pain and shock and self-pity and couldn't find it within herself to break free from those emotions.

"I'll leave you now unless you have any more questions? The police have been waiting patiently in the hall. What happened to you is a crime, and we, as a hospital, must report it. I hope you understand."

"Yes, yes, of course. I can't think of anything more right now." They were going to ask questions she didn't have answers to. And some of those questions she knew were ones she didn't *want* to answer. She'd never been one to share her life, her thoughts, her feelings. Most of the time, she tried to keep to surface relationships. They were easy and required little thought or feeling.

But now an officer was going to pry into her life and probably ask her the most intimate questions...

"Oh, I forgot to mention there's also a gentleman in the waiting room wanting to see you. Did you want him sent in after the police are done?"

Avery's eyes widened. She'd completely forgotten about her neighbor. The trauma and drugs the hospital staff had been giving her for the pain were clouding her mind. She vaguely remembered Luys helping her to the hospital. When he'd first approached, she'd been afraid of him, suspicious he might have something to do with her assault, but fog had filled her brain to the point she hadn't been able to think, and it had been near impossible to stop herself from falling on her face. The ground spinning and nausea hadn't helped. She couldn't have fought him off if she'd tried. A couple of times she'd even passed out.

But if he had been the one who attacked her last night, he could have easily overpowered her in her weakened state and finished her off. Still, she didn't like the idea of him coming in, but at the same time, turning him away was beyond rude. He'd not only helped her but had been waiting for hours. She'd never have been able to make it here on her own. He deserved some answers. Or lies...or whatever words would ease his mind and make him not ask questions. "Ahh, yes, I'll talk to him."

"I'll let the desk know then." Dr. Clark rose from the stool and slipped from the room.

Even after the door closed behind her, the doctor's voice filtered into the room from the hall, "She's somewhat confused, which is normal under the circumstances. But I do think she's confused as to the timing of her attack. I'm thinking from the condition of her wounds, it happened well over a week ago. Try to keep your questions brief. She's had a traumatic experience."

"I'm sure she has," a man answered.

Then the door opened, and two plainclothes officers stepped into the room. The older, stockier of the two with short graying hair stepped to the side of the bed. "I'm Detective Hatcher." He nodded to the other man. "And this is Detective Atkins. I'm sure you know we've got some questions for you. Hopefully, we won't take much of your time."

She glanced at his ID badge pinned to his light blue dress shirt. "Have you found the person who did this to me?"

Hatcher shook his head. "We don't have any arrests."

"What about suspects?"

"We're working on it. That's one of the reasons why we're here. We need to ask you if you know of anyone—neighbors, co-workers, acquaintances, anyone you can think of, even if it might sound strange—who would attack you?" Detective Hatcher asked, with one thumb hooked around his belt and his watery blue gaze unreadable.

She didn't like his smile. It felt forced or insincere. Or it could be just her feeling edgy and unsure. "No. Not at all. The people I know wouldn't even dream of mutilating me like that."

"Are you sure? Maybe you had a conversation with someone. Maybe they thought you wanted to have something fixed. Say they started working on you and realized they were over their head." He rocked back on his heels. "Some women value their appearances, and a good many get certain procedures done."

It took her a moment to realize what he was saying. The anger that flooded through her drowned her pain. "Are you serious? You think I willingly had someone operate on me for no good reason? Oh, excuse me—for a breast augmentation?"

"I didn't say that."

"But you implied it just the same."

Hatcher's expression didn't alter. "I'm trying to be thorough."

"Well, this was against my will. I'm sure there is bruising on my head where they hit me. I don't know what type of *proof* you need!"

"I'm doing my job. I have to ask questions. Most of them are uncomfortable. I'm sure none of this is easy. We'll make it as painless as possible. Same with the pictures of all your injuries. But for now, I need to ask you some more questions—like about any enemies. Do you have anyone you might know who could have a motive to want to hurt you?"

At her side, her fingers curled into the sheet. They were only doing their job, Avery tried to tell herself. They needed to pry into her life and eliminate any suspects, including herself. She needed not to take it personally. But damn it! This was so freaking hard. And this detective was an insensitive ass. There was no going around that.

After taking a slow, calming breath, Avery tried to rein in feelings of self-righteousness. She frowned and made a point of thinking over the last several months. Cobwebs clouded her thoughts. The harder she searched, the thicker the strands twined through her memories and obscured the past. The drugs... She couldn't focus well. Shifting, she sat up straighter. Her stitches protested at the movement, and she sucked in air between gritted teeth.

"Are you all right?" Detective Atkins stepped away from the door and toward her bed.

"Yes." She curled a hand into a fist to stop herself from touching her stitches. She didn't want to bring more attention to her disfigurement.

Oh, God. She hated the idea. "The doctor... She seems to think I'm the only person this has happened to. There must be someone else, right?"

"No, not that we're aware of in Phoenix or surrounding cities." Beneath his dark brown brows, the pity in Atkin's eyes shredded her nerves. "The department is doing a further search in their database for any similar cases, but right now, we're not at liberty to discuss any findings."

"Well, that's just wonderful." She didn't bother masking her disgust. She struggled to hang onto her anger. Anger would give her the strength, the energy to fight back, to rise above this. She hated self-pity. Always had. She found it debilitating and useless, but that didn't stop it from sapping her energy, her thoughts.

She tightened her jaw and struggled to focus. She would not fall apart. She'd let it happen when she got home and no one was looking. Right now, she needed their help, and they couldn't do that if she were a mental mess. "Why single me out? What could I have possibly done to have someone do this to me?"

"That's what we need to find out. What about neighbors? Anyone new you've come into contact with? Do you know of anyone with some type of medical background or who's fascinated with television shows on the subject?"

"No."

Detective Hatcher folded his thick arms against his stomach. "So, you didn't see anything unusual that night?"

"No. It's a pretty quiet place with little crime compared to areas south of me. At least I thought so."

"I'm familiar with your complex, and it's relatively safe. I guess as safe as you can get nowadays." Detective Atkins moved to the side of her bed. His smile, bright white against his olive skin, subtracted years from his face, and he didn't look much older than her. She suspected not even thirty.

Hatcher threw him an annoyed expression. "Well, obviously it's not that safe if Ms. Fleming was attacked and left for dead."

But Avery didn't think she'd been left for dead. Why clean her wound? Leave her lying naked in her bed? They could have easily left her in an alley or a dumpster. Then there was her purse.

"My purse. I'm sure when I was initially attacked, I dropped it outside, but the next day when I came to, I found it in my living room with nothing missing."

"Do you have it with you?" Hatcher asked.

"Yes. I'm sure someone at the hospital has it."

"We'll check and see and have it dusted for prints just in case," Detective Atkins answered.

"Thanks."

"I have a department photographer here to take some pictures," Hatcher said.

"What?" She couldn't keep the horror from her voice. He'd mentioned pictures, but it hadn't clicked that they planned on taking photos of her ruined chest.

"Sorry, but it's something that needs to be done."

Avery backed down. She could say no, but then what would they think of her? Would they put her case below all the others if she didn't cooperate?

Hatcher asked several more questions. Then he pulled a card from his back pocket and offered it to her. "If you can think of anything else that you missed, don't hesitate to give me a call. We'll also make a point of having an extra officer in the neighborhood."

She took it with a tentative hand. "Thanks."

"Even if you remember something more and you think it's trivial, still call us. It might be significant from a different perspective. Our priority is to find the person who attacked you," Detective Atkins added with a comforting smile. Then both men left the room.

Before she even had time to get her bearings, a knock sounded on the door. A woman entered with a digital camera strapped over her shoulder. A tag on her chest revealed her credentials and the name of Brooke Campbell.

Stiffening, Avery eyed the other woman. Her cap of chestnut hair clung to her head in a bob and framed an angled face. She looked about twenty-eight, the same age as Avery. But unlike Avery, her eyes seemed far older. No doubt she'd seen some gruesome scenes. Well, the idea of the woman seeing another gruesome scene when it came to her chest made Avery want to pull the sheet up to her neck. Of course she didn't. She'd have to grit her teeth and pretend that baring her mutilated body to a stranger didn't bother her.

"I'll be quick," Brooke offered as she pulled the strap from her shoulder, adjusted her camera, and moved to the side of the bed. "I can only imagine how uncomfortable this is for you."

Avery bit her inner cheeks as she struggled into a better position. Pain seared her body, and she bit harder to keep herself from crying out. With a hand on her upper arm, Brooke helped her with the gown's back ties and stepped back when Avery shrugged out of her gown until it pooled around her waist. She turned her head to the side as Brooke lifted her camera. She couldn't handle meeting the other woman's gaze. Feeling like a specimen pinned to a cushion under glass, she waited, forcing air in and out of her lungs at a slow, measured pace. She felt violated all over again. When she looked over to the window, she only saw the blue sky and nothing to distract her as the woman snapped several shots of her chest.

"All done," Brooke murmured and helped Avery awkwardly get her gown back on and tie the clasp behind her neck. "Thanks for your patience."

With her gown back in place, Avery slumped against the back of the bed with a groan. To hell with being brave and acting like nothing was wrong with her.

She was flat out mentally and physically exhausted. The pain, police questions, and submitting to getting pictures taken of her naked chest were too much. She blinked back tears.

As Brooke pulled the camera strap back onto one shoulder, her green eyes flashed with some undefinable emotion before she masked it. Her wall of professionalism made Avery wonder what she was thinking. Was she thanking God she wasn't Avery? Or judging how she'd gotten herself in such a freaking mess? People judged no matter how much they told themselves they didn't, and Avery was as guilty as the next person.

Did she think Avery was running with the wrong crowd? Somehow did it to herself because of her rash behavior? After all, she was walking home alone at night. Maybe she thought Avery had it coming to her.

"Thank you," Brooke murmured before she backed out of the room to leave Avery wallowing in her self-pity.

Closing her eyes against the world around her, Avery hit a button by her hand, and the bed hummed as it lowered her to a more comfortable position. Not even a minute passed when someone else knocked on the door. She jerked at the sound and muttered under her breath. Hospitals weren't the best place to get any rest.

She snapped open her eyes, expecting someone else to make her feel small and insignificant. When her neighbor stepped into the room, she didn't relax. She suspected the only time she'd be able to find some solace was when she escaped into her condo, but even then, she didn't think she'd get any sense of peace. Until they caught the person, she'd be on constant high alert, scared of someone else's shadow, including her own.

Avery met her neighbor's dark, concerned gaze and fumbled for words. She owed him a lot. She plucked at the edge of the bedsheet, thought of her bedhead hair, the tent of a hospital gown, and was disconcerted at how concerned she was when it came to her appearance. She shouldn't care, and it was stupid to worry about what he thought of her looks, what with almost dying.

"Thanks for helping me…earlier. I'm not sure I would have been able to make it to the hospital without you."

"Anyone would have done the same." He sat down on the stool the doctor had used earlier. "So you will be all right, then?"

His broad shoulders, long legs, and masculine frame took up far more space than Dr. Clark's slight figure earlier, while the genuine concern in his dark brown gaze made her realize maybe he wasn't such an ass. Maybe she'd misjudged him.

"Yes, I'll be fine. I just need a bit of rest." She clasped her hands in her lap, telling herself he didn't have a clue what had happened to her, that he didn't know about the ugly disfigurement on her chest, of her attack, of her inability to think… And she wasn't about to tell him the truth of what had happened. It was too personal, too raw.

Thank God he didn't ask any more questions. She didn't have the energy to field them.

"Louis." She cleared her throat in embarrassment. "I'm sorry you had to wait so long to see how I was doing."

"It's Luys."

"I'm sorry?"

"Yes, but it's spelled LUYS, not the usual LOUIS. The spelling goes back centuries and originated in Spain."

"How unusual." His accent hinted at a different country, but she hadn't been able to place it until now.

He smiled, but Avery sensed his forced expression as a sudden stillness radiated from him. Or was that her imagination?

He rose to his feet. "The nurse at the desk said you're ready to check out of the hospital. They need to finish up their paperwork. I'll be in the hall when you're ready."

"Oh, no." She tried to breathe through the pain. "I…I can take a taxi. Or Uber." He'd done too much already.

He shook his head, his expression gentle. "I'm already here. It is no trouble. Seriously. And I could not leave without knowing your condition. I wanted to see for myself that you were okay."

"I'll be all good in a couple of days." She made herself smile. It would be stupid to turn him down. He was making things easy for her. *Just take the freaking offer.* Hadn't she learned pride never helped anyone? "Sure. That sounds great." She wrinkled her nose. "I'll be out in a bit. At least I have a set of clothes. Hospital gowns are not exactly street clothing."

When the hospital attendant finally wheeled her from the room after getting dressed and checked out, Luys was waiting in the hall. He smiled again, his white teeth once again a sharp contrast against his dark skin.

Avery frowned. She was beginning to wonder if

she'd completely misjudged him. She'd always considered him unapproachable, even surly when they crossed paths at the complex's mailboxes, in the parking lot, or walking back and forth from their condos.

After stepping from the wheelchair, with the attendant standing by, Luys cupped her elbow. "I pulled the car up to make it easier while you were finishing up with the hospital's paperwork."

Avery didn't have the energy for small chatter on the way home and thank goodness Luys must have realized that. She was exhausted by the time they pulled up into the parking lot.

Once he helped her from the car and followed her to her condo, he said, "I'll check on you after you settle in." He frowned. "You had me worried there for a bit. No one would tell me if you were going to be okay or not for the longest time."

Now she was starting to feel bad about all the nasty thoughts she'd had about him. She couldn't remember the last time someone had taken care of her. It made her feel uncertain and awkward.

When she reached the entrance to her place, what little energy she'd had drained from every pore of her body. Sleep. She hoped when she hit the bed, it wouldn't be elusive or, for that matter, she'd be plagued with nightmares and worries of her attacker coming back and this time killing her or doing something even more gruesome and deviant.

At the door, Luys' brow drew together into a dark slash. "If you need anything, I'm minutes away. What is your phone number in case you need someone to get to you quickly?"

She wanted to argue, but she was too tired. When she gave it to him, he punched the number into his cell, and her phone dinged in her purse with his text.

"I'll be fine." She hung onto the door jamb.

He hesitated, looked about to say something, but then nodded, turned around, and walked to his door only yards away from her own. Not waiting to see what he would do next, she stepped into her place and closed the door behind her. After dumping her purse on the floor, she dragged herself through the living room and into her bedroom. She carefully pulled her shirt off. She hadn't put on her bra for fear of hurting herself but had stuffed it into her bag. She avoided looking down because she was afraid if she did, she'd break down and start crying, or worse—she'd crack.

Next came her shoes, socks, and the rest of her clothes. She crawled into bed and lay on her back to stare up at the ceiling. The window blinds didn't entirely block out the daylight. She stared up at the ceiling until it blurred from her tears.

She wiped at her eyes with both hands, but her vision blurred again.

Sounds from outside cut into the room. She swore the murmur of the neighbor's television filtered through the thick walls. That and someone whispering.

She frowned, struggled for anger, for some emotion to keep the tears at bay, but her struggle fractured, then completely ruptured, and the tears came in a torrent, and, for the life of her, she couldn't stop them. She cried until she'd drained herself of every teardrop.

As she stared up at the ceiling, she knew she should

feel outraged or any number of emotions. But right now, she felt bereft, even empty inside.

Tomorrow.

Things would look better in the morning. Somehow, she'd bounce back. After all, she'd been on her own since she left the foster system at eighteen. She'd struggled with homelessness, lack of a family, her health, and a system that didn't do her any favors. She'd get through this too.

Tomorrow.

Then a sudden and unexpected wave of rage roiled through her, and she clung to it.

Some sick, deviant person had attacked her for no reason. For fun? Just because they could? Her nostrils flared. She would not be a victim. Not on this. The bastard wouldn't make her crawl into a hole. He'd pay for this. Her fingers twisted the bedsheets in her hands.

The police would find her attacker. They had to. She wouldn't allow for anything less.

CHAPTER 4

Wednesday, August 20ᵗʰ – 7:05 am

As Luys combed back his damp hair from a recent shower, a knock at the front door resounded through his place and into the bathroom.

Avery. Maybe something had happened? He'd called last night as he had every night since she had left the hospital. When she hadn't answered on his second try, he had shown up at her door and found her well but tired. Reassured she wouldn't pass out on him and would be fine until the next day, he had left.

Why in the name of God did he continue to worry about her? He should not be concerned about Avery. He should have let her get a taxi or had someone else drive her back home. And he should have left the hospital the moment he drove her there yesterday. She was not his business.

Don't get involved...

His jaw tightened. Hadn't he learned that years before?

Barefoot and in dark gray slacks, he grabbed a shirt from the closet and quickly shrugged into it as he strode to the front door. With his shirt unbuttoned, he opened the door, not thinking of checking who it was first. He sucked in a breath. God's teeth. He forced his features into a bland expression and hoped his shock didn't show.

A man with short, salt-and-pepper hair, large brow, navy pants, and a white shirt stood at the entrance. Luys glanced at the badge the man shoved in front of him. Detective Hatcher.

"Do you have a few minutes?"

"I—" He didn't want to talk to anyone, never mind someone related to the law. "I'm in a hurry. I have to leave for work soon."

It was the truth.

The detective didn't move from his spot in front of his door. "It's either now or later. When do you expect to be back from work?"

"No, now's fine." He might as well get it over with. "Is there a problem?"

"A neighbor of yours was attacked here in the complex. My understanding is you were the one who drove the victim to the hospital."

"I—" His hand tightened on the door's edge. The sun-heated metal burned his palm, but he only tightened his grip on the door, hoping the pain would sharpen his mind and keep him from reacting instead of responding. "Avery? She was assaulted?"

"Yes, she didn't tell you that?" The surprise in the other man's hazel eyes was unmistakable.

"No. I was outside when she was trying to get to her car. She was planning on driving herself to the hospital. She looked far too sick, and I thought it only natural to offer to drive her."

"And you didn't call an ambulance?"

"She wanted nothing to do with one. She was worried about the added expense."

"And your name?"

Luys almost lied but realized the detective could easily learn the truth through the leasing office. He didn't dare create trouble. He couldn't afford it.

"Luys Martinez." He opened the door wider and stepped to the side. "Come in."

"No need. Right now, I'm getting preliminary information." He looked behind Luys' shoulder to the living room, his expression inscrutable.

"And your place of employment?"

"The Horizon Center."

The detective's eyes narrowed.

"Is that a hospital?"

"No. Not really. I work for a research facility connected to the Horizon Community Hospital. We—"

"So, you're a doctor?"

"Yes."

Luys sensed a complete shift from the detective even though nothing changed visibly in Hatcher's expression or the way he held his body.

"Do you work on weekends?"

Tension cut a swath across Luys' shoulders. He did not like all these questions. Something wasn't right. "Not usually."

"This last weekend?"

"No."

"Where were you Friday night?"

"Home."

"And did you have company at all, or were you alone?"

"Alone."

God's teeth. He did not have an alibi. "I don't know the woman."

"Yet, you're neighbors." The detective shifted impatiently on his feet.

Luys' phone started ringing from the living room. He glanced over his shoulder, and when he turned back around, Hatcher lifted one thick gray brow. "Did you want to answer that?"

"No." He wanted to get this Hatcher to leave, to stop him from asking questions. But Luys feared it was too late. Soon, Hatcher would be back once he searched the police database.

"I haven't had time to get to know her or anyone else in the neighborhood," Luys explained.

"So how did you know she was your neighbor?"

Now the man was acting like an ass. "Because she lives next door to me. Also, we've crossed paths at the complex's mail center."

"I'm sure you couldn't help but notice her. She's a looker. I bet you'd like to get a little something there." Hatcher's gaze narrowed. "Did she say no? Did that get you angry?"

The hand at his side fisted as he forced himself not to react. Something Luys suspected the detective would relish. He wanted to wipe that bland expression from the detective's face, but, of course, he didn't, not because he considered himself civilized, but because he did not want to be hauled off to jail for assault. Getting violent would only make him a probable suspect in Avery's attack.

"Are we done?" Luys asked between gritted teeth.

"For now." Hatcher's lips peeled back into a smile.

Luys shut the door with deliberate calm. After taking a slow breath, he twisted his neck back and forth, sending his vertebrae cracking as he pivoted and walked into the living room.

He picked up his phone from the coffee table. Gabriel's telephone number appeared on the screen after a swipe. He quickly returned the call.

Gabriel answered on the first ring and immediately asked, "Are you okay?"

"Why?"

"It hit the national news. The victim was some type of social media star."

Luys frowned. "The police were just at my door asking questions. Why would an assault hit any news feed?"

"I'm not sure what you're talking about. I'm talking about Mayor," Gabriel murmured. "She's turned up."

"What? Are you sure? I had hoped she'd disappeared if not for good, at least for several years—"

"I had hoped the same, but apparently not."

"Has there been a murder?"

"Yes. Haven't you read about it? We both know it's only a matter of time before people end up dead around her. Ever since she disappeared from Spirit Lake, I've searched the Internet for any keyword that might be remotely tied to Mayor."

"Where was the murder?" Luys whispered.

"In Phoenix. About five miles from you. I would have thought you knew."

"I've been distracted."

"The papers are saying a stabbing, possibly the boyfriend as the killer, but my sources through the police department are saying something different. The murder was far more brutal than what's been reported. I'm sure the police don't want the public to panic."

"It could be someone other than Mayor. Someone equally sick and twisted."

"True. But the killer ripped open the chest cavity."

Luys sank down hard on the edge of the sofa. This wasn't looking good. "A woman? Do you have the name of the victim? Mayor has always gone after men."

"Jennifer Stewart. I might find out more about her given time—"

"Time? We might not have much of it until the next attack. Once Mayor starts…" Luys whispered.

After a couple more minutes of talking, Gabriel urged, "Keep me posted. And if it's an experiment gone wrong, I thought Mayor knew better. No one has ever lived long after one of Mayor's experiments. Think of Hector."

Luys winced. Gabriel had been the one who had tried to stop the horror of that day. "I remember. I would like to forget. The poor bastard did not deserve that end. No one does."

"Maybe you can talk some sense into Mayor."

"That's impossible. Mayor won't listen."

"It might happen with you."

Luys sighed. "First, I have to find Mayor."

"All you have to do is wait. Mayor will come to you. It is only a matter of time."

"But in the meantime, while I wait? You know there will be carnage, innocents dead. I need to find Mayor before it goes further. I can't live with the guilt if I stay silent and blind."

"Holy Mother." Gabriel's voice dropped, then steadied, though the sadness and regret in each word were unmistakable. "I was lucky to come out of it alive this last time, and it could have been much worse. Amanda could have died along with her daughter."

Luys was at a loss for words. They had all suffered. Too many years, to the point he did not know what it meant to live, to believe in the possibility of happiness or hope.

He needed to remain calm. He had survived worse than this.

He needed to stop Mayor.

After Luys hung up with his brother and finished dressing, he called into work to let Baxter know he'd be in later in the day and ran a couple of errands. One of them included checking on Avery one last time. And if she was on her way to being completely healed, he'd make a point of avoiding her after today.

He walked out of the bedroom and into the living room. He paused. The air stirred around him. The back of his neck prickled with unease. Something was off. He eased further into the room, peered into the kitchen, and then backtracked to the second bedroom. It felt like someone had been in his place. But how? The door was locked.

His lips firmed. The need to check on Avery escalated. He rolled his shoulders and stepped outside, walked the short distance to Avery's front door, knocked, and waited for her to answer.

The door opened to Avery's condo, and Luys froze. His thoughts scattered into fragments, and it took him a moment to get his bearings. The last person he thought to see stood at Avery's front door.

CHAPTER 5

uys finally found his voice. "What are you doing here?"

The woman smiled, a wicked gleam in her silver-blue eyes. "You are here for Avery, yes?"

His hands tightened into fists. At the sight of Mayor standing inside Avery's home as if she belonged there, Luys fought back his rage.

"What have you done to her?"

"Calm down," Mayor murmured in a throaty whisper. "We don't want her getting alarmed for any reason." Her voice rose as she glanced over her shoulder. "Are you well enough for company?"

God's teeth. What was going on?

Mayor opened the door wider to reveal Avery sitting on the sofa in the living room.

He brushed by Mayor and strode into the condo. "Are you okay?"

"Yes, much better. Thank you." With her legs curled up beneath her, she stared back at him with curious blue eyes and with a glass of iced water in one hand. He knew he was acting intense, probably looking paranoid. He hoped he wasn't visibly shaking, but he was having difficulty recovering from not only coming face to face with Mayor but having his sister in the same room with Avery.

Avery could not know the danger Mayor embodied.

He sat down in a chair adjacent to Avery and searched her face. Color had returned to her cheeks, along with a sheen to her long auburn hair.

"You do look better," he whispered, conscious of Mayor standing behind Avery and the sofa, though he didn't look up to acknowledge her. "I'm glad."

"Yes, well, thank you again for everything you did the other day and, of course, continuing to check on me."

In the beginning, he hadn't wanted to help, had hated the idea of getting to know her for fear of precisely this. Somehow Mayor knew what he thought of Avery. How he didn't have a clue. It was almost like she could dig into his brain from some remote location and read his deepest fears and aspirations. "I'm glad I was there to help."

Feeling impotent, Luys sat stiffly with both hands gripping the arms of his chair as Mayor drew closer to Avery and placed a hand against the top of her chair and inches from her head. He recognized her subtle move. If he lashed out at Mayor now or reacted in the wrong way, Mayor would retaliate, and Avery...he hated to think what could happen.

Mayor could be savage and unforgiving. In her sick mind, she could always justify her horrendous acts.

Avery glanced at the iced water in her hand, growing decidedly uncomfortable with the intensity of Luys' gaze. Before their lives intersected the day he found her trying to get to the hospital, she was guilty of judging him incapable of deep emotion. Cold would be what she would have described him. The blank looks turned her way as they crossed on the sidewalk, the lack of a cordial greeting in the parking lot or by the condo's mailboxes. They were neighbors, for goodness' sake. A 'hi' would have been nice, polite, the thing to do.

She suspected he worked a steady job; he left and returned from his condo about the same time she did. But that was all she really knew about him.

Avery forced herself to meet the potency of his gaze. She pulled the glass closer to her chest, disconcerted at the strength of the attraction that roiled through her. She shouldn't care what he thought of her or if he found her attractive, and it was probably best not to dwell on such crazy speculations.

Right now, she looked a mess. Black workout leggings and a turquoise t-shirt, her hair scraped back into a ponytail, and no makeup. She felt vulnerable because of it, never having expected company today. First Mayor and now Luys.

Earlier in the morning, she'd tried a shower but had settled on a sponge bath. She'd been too tired to do anything else. The doctor had been right. She hadn't had the energy or ability to get herself to work the next day. She'd called in for the week. Surely that would be enough time to return to what she now considered normal.

She hadn't bothered seeing her primary care physician on Tuesday for a follow-up appointment, as Dr. Clark suggested. She'd wait another week when her stitches were probably ready to be removed. That way, she'd only have to pay the one office visit.

While in the bathroom today, she'd avoided the

mirror again, but she hadn't been able to stop herself from looking down at her wound. The skin around the stitches didn't look near as angry, and she found them not as bad as she'd first envisioned. Still, she cringed. It was the idea of someone touching and violating her she found unsettling more than the incision itself.

Luys leaned forward in his chair, dropping an elbow on one knee. "Is there anything I can do to help? I can—"

"She is fine," Mayor murmured.

He glanced over at the woman, his face expressionless, but an emotion Avery couldn't decipher radiated from him.

Avery frowned as she took a sip of iced water and let an ice cube dissolve in her mouth. The moment Luys had stepped into the room, tension had thickened the air, but she had no clue why. "Do you know each other?"

"No."

"No."

She then realized they were lying. Hostility. Yes, that was the only word she could describe the feeling between them. How did they know each other? Lovers? A bad break-up months before? She inwardly sighed. It wasn't her business, now was it?

She knew little about Mayor. They both frequented the coffee shop down the road and, over time, had started talking while waiting in line. After a couple of months, Mayor had invited her to a gathering at her home. She persisted until Avery finally gave in. She'd actually enjoyed the evening, meeting an eclectic group—a couple of artists, CEOs, a retail clerk, and an engineer thrown into the mix. So far, the other woman hadn't talked much about herself, but Avery considered Mayor, a distinct accent to her voice, sophisticated and well-traveled.

Mayor squeezed her shoulder and moved toward the front door. "I will go. I'll check on you another time, though, yes?"

"That's nice of you." She glanced up and met the other woman's gaze. "But I'm sure you're busy."

"No. Not at all." A smile broke across Mayor's face. "No doubt, you will feel far better and be full of vigor by tomorrow. Mark my words." She clapped her hands and laughed before she pivoted and stepped from the room, the door clicking softly closed behind her seconds later.

A silence—definitely an awkward one—filled the distance between her and Luys. Avery thought about asking how he knew the other woman but decided now wasn't the time. Plus, again, she had to tell herself their relationship or lack of wasn't her concern. She didn't know him well enough to start an interrogation. And she had an idea he would probably lie about how he knew Mayor. He'd already lied about it minutes before.

Luys rose, pushing abruptly off his chair's armrests with both hands. "I forgot my phone. I'll be right back. I'm expecting an important call."

Before Avery could respond, he disappeared out of the door too. She cocked her head to one side. She didn't hear his door opening and closing. How strange.

Frowning, she closed her eyes and listened. Voices. A man's and a woman's. Yes. Mayor and Luys talking. No arguing. Frowning harder, she concentrated on their words. Then, suddenly, other noises interfered. The refrigerator's motor growled from the kitchen. The air conditioner clicked on, the hum drumming loudly into her head. The leaves from the trees outside rustled as a monsoon approached from the west. Her eyes snapped open. Before she had time to wonder why she could hear everything so clearly, a knock vibrated on the door, and Luys stepped back inside, waving his phone in one hand before slipping it into his back pocket.

"Have you eaten today?" he asked.

These last couple of days, he'd dropped by without asking questions. Instead, he'd supplied her with food, drinks, and magazines, staying long enough to ensure she wouldn't land on her face from the kitchen to the sofa or bed. She'd started to hope for his company, which she wasn't about to admit to him. Not yet anyway.

"Ahh, a little."

He arched a brow.

She wrinkled her nose and uncurled her legs from beneath her. "Some crackers earlier today, but I haven't had much energy to go out or cook something for myself. I know I should have something a bit more substantial..."

"You should have told me earlier today when I called to check on you. I would have gotten some takeout. Do you have a lot of groceries?" He stepped into the kitchen, where Avery could easily see him across the counter because of the open floor plan. He opened her refrigerator. "Oh."

She made a face. "I'm not much of a cook."

"Yes, I can see that. I'm glad I didn't listen to you and brought over some to-go meals from a nearby restaurant the last couple of days." Humor lightened his voice. "Orange juice and eggs. Not sure I can whip anything up with that. I guess I could fix you an omelet with egg as your only ingredient."

He stepped back into the living room and sank into the cushion beside her. His brown gaze filled with obvious concern as he searched her face. "How about I run to the store and get something to make you a meal? You must be getting tired of the restaurant food I have been bringing you."

"Oh, no. There's no need for that. I'm really not that hungry." Her stomach protested with a loud grumble. Great. Her body was exposing her for the liar that she was. She wasn't used to people taking care of her. Usually, it was the other way around. And she really shouldn't let him get too close. It wouldn't be smart. Or the right thing to do.

"See? You're hungry." He leaned closer and lifted a hand as if he was about to touch her hair or face, but he dropped it back down and abruptly straightened. "No arguments. I want to help by making dinner. You can thank me later."

"I... okay." She was getting decidedly uncomfortable at his nearness.

His too-close body made her realize how long it had been since she'd been alone with a man, never mind having one in her bed.

"I make a great pasta dish. Does shrimp work for you?"

"That would be lovely." Her heart skipped a beat from the warmth in his eyes and voice. She liked the feeling of being cared for, but it terrified her at the same time. But wouldn't it be amazing if she found love or even a fleeting infatuation? The familiarity of a lover, of bodies bound in the heat of passion, the deep resonance of someone else being a witness to your life...

Impossible. Stupid. Crazy. She'd watched and read too many romances over the years and ruined her teens and early twenties by believing in some grand love, of a passion that eclipsed everything else. They'd been fantasies she'd lost herself in to keep her going, to keep her from failing, to keep her from giving up on herself.

She was a fool to think beyond the fantasy. Even if romantic love was real, she didn't dare let a man's kindness over cooking dinner for her overshadow the reality of her life.

Some sick psycho out there had carved her up for some crazy reason. Next time they might decide to kill her.

He rose. "I'll be back. Don't open the door to—" He shook his head.

"Yes?"

"Nothing. Just be careful. I'm sure you are."

She frowned at the closed door once he had left. Was this the same man who pointedly ignored her at every opportunity after she'd moved in? Some things didn't make sense. Unless... he was being nice now so she wouldn't suspect he was the one that cut her open.

At the idea, she cringed. That would make him a psychopath. But another part of her quickly discounted the thought. She knew he'd lived in the complex as long as she had, which was over a year. Why wait all this time and then decide to target her? It didn't make sense.

Not about to have him see her again with a bed head and ratty clothing, Avery pushed off her chair, locked the door behind him, and decided she needed a shower. Not that anything between them would happen. Not now, not with the ruin of her chest. She hadn't wanted to take a really good look at her naked body in the mirror since the hospital; she hadn't wanted to cry again.

Mindful that she needed to hurry before Luys returned, she grabbed some fresh clothing from the bedroom, stripped, and clicked on the shower. She winced as the shower door creaked open. The noise of water hitting the stall's floor sounded exceedingly loud. Maybe the hit on her head was making her sensitive to sounds.

Lathering her hair, she closed her eyes and let the water wash over her. Once she had the shampoo rinsed from her eyes, she grabbed a bottle of shower gel. Soaping up, she looked down and paused, her hand squeezing around a bright pink sponge she'd grabbed from the shower's shelf. Her chest... The red welts between the stitches had disappeared. She quickly rinsed off and grabbed a towel.

Turning off the shower with a snap, she then stepped toward the full-length mirror and turned on the other light above the counter. Leaning closer, she stared at the flesh between her breasts.

"Impossible," she breathed, turning from side to side.

She patted the area, shivering as the air from the conditioner brushed across her naked skin. With a trembling hand, she rummaged in a drawer to pull out a pair of manicure scissors.

After clipping the first stitch, she pulled it free. The scar looked like the injury had occurred months, even years earlier. Carefully, afraid she might be hallucinating but unable to stop herself, she snipped at the rest of the black, ugly stitches and eased them from her flesh, cringing as several black rope-like spider webs clung to her skin.

Once done, she ran a hand across the skin below her collarbone and between her breasts. She'd had an appointment next week to remove her stitches, but going back to a doctor's office seemed pointless.

This was crazy.

It looked like she'd had an operation years before, not days ago.

She grabbed the counter and closed her eyes. Sounds swirled and rolled around her. A car door slamming. Yelling from somewhere in another condo, the words clearly distinguishable filtered through the walls. "I'm tired of this bullshit!"

She pressed her hands against her ears.

The noises wouldn't go away.

She took in the sound of a fly or bee buzzing, the wings batting rapidly in the air. Then a cough. The hum of the highway. All merging and building inside her head.

She squeezed her palms harder against her ears.

She was going crazy. The noise. She was drowning in it!

"Stop!"

She mentally forced the sounds away.

Sudden silence hit her from all sides, almost as deafening as the noise had been.

She gasped in surprise.

Someone knocked on her door. Luys' muffled voice came through from the outside. "Are you okay?"

Shit.

She grabbed a towel and dried herself. "I'll be right there!"

She pulled on another pair of workout leggings and a shirt, brushed her hair, and added a bit of foundation and mascara. She didn't pull her hair back into a ponytail but let it fall past her shoulder to air dry.

With a hand on the bathroom doorknob, she took one more look in the mirror. She didn't look any different. From all appearances, she looked normal. The same blue, too large eyes, auburn hair, high cheekbones, and pointed chin. But no normal person healed this fast. No normal person could hear things like she'd been able to since that night.

Something beyond strange had happened to her the night of her attack.

Something inexplicable.

The idea terrified her.

CHAPTER 6

After Avery unlocked the door and closed it behind Luys, his dark brows lifted as his gaze roamed over her body before settling on her face. "You look like you're feeling better than before. I'm glad." He smiled, flashing those incredible white teeth. He even had a too-sexy dimple on his left cheek.

She flushed, still reeling from the abnormality of her quick healing and strange and unsettling amplified hearing. "It's amazing what a shower will do."

"Well, food should make you feel even better." He lifted two bags of groceries. "Lead the way."

Luys followed her into the U-shaped kitchen, where he made himself comfortable, finding the necessary pots, pans, and silverware. She brushed her palms against her hips to warm her clammy hands. Over six feet, he filled the small room with his large frame. As he twisted to one side and grasped the handle of a cast-iron skillet, the cords of his forearm flexed, and the fabric of his t-shirt stretched across the broad width of his shoulders, hinting at his strength. His faded jeans hugged his hips and thighs. Avery couldn't deny he was sexy. Dimples, killer smile, dark sultry eyes, and thick mahogany hair any woman would love to run her hands through. From the moment she'd crossed paths with him, she'd considered him disconcertingly attractive, and now that he was in her too tiny kitchen, she found him even more so.

She scowled, not sure of herself and hating the feeling. Was she crazy to have let him inside? He could easily subdue her. Mayor had been a safety valve, but now it was just the two of them with thick walls that could muffle any cry of help from her.

She didn't know him. He could have been the person behind what had happened to her. What better way to get to know your victim than by pretending to be a friend or someone who cared?

Luys could be dangerous.

Her frown deepened as she watched him for several minutes move about in the kitchen and start the pasta. She wasn't always the best judge of character. She'd let other people into her life who not only disappointed but hurt her. Take her last boyfriend. When she'd confided in Blake, took a chance on him, he'd dumped her so fast she'd had whiplash.

She'd considered Luys rude and cold. He didn't look like either now. Could she have misjudged him completely? He didn't have to do what he was doing. He could have easily grabbed some fast food and dropped it off.

He was being kind. And he'd done everything right, not hesitating once to ensure her wellbeing.

That didn't sound like a man who would slice and dice a woman.

After he opened a drawer to grab a large spoon to stir the pasta and pulled a colander from a cabinet, he pivoted in her direction. "It looks like you have someone watching over you."

Avery frowned, for a minute wondering who he was talking about. "Oh, you mean Mayor."

"Are you good friends?"

She leaned against the fridge as he poured the water and pasta from the pot to the colander in the sink. "Not really. I met her a couple of months ago."

"I see," he murmured, dumping the contents of the colander into a frying pan and retrieving the spoon from the counter. A sudden stillness settled around him.

Or maybe it was her imagination…. She cocked her head to the side. No, there was something there in his face even though he tried to hide it. He knew Mayor. She waited for a bit, hoping he'd say more, but when he kept silent, she finally said, "Yeah, we're both coffee addicts. She lives not too far from here."

Metal hit the stove, then clattered to the floor. "Damnation!"

"Oh, here!" She hurried over and picked up the spoon from the floor he'd dropped. When she rose, she found herself between the counter and Luys' very large and very masculine body. He towered over her with what felt like a good foot.

The sudden look in his gaze sucked the breath from her lungs. Anger radiated from his dark brown eyes. She shifted backward, but the edge of the counter bit into her back. Unable to get a safe distance between them, she clutched at the large spoon and held it between them. Maybe she'd been stupid for judging Luys after all. He could easily snap any of her bones with a quick flick of his wrist.

He stepped back, giving her space while the sudden anger in his eyes just as quickly dissipated. He rubbed his thumb with his fingers and winced. "I apologize. I didn't mean to alarm you. I surprised myself. I am usually proficient in the kitchen and don't usually burn myself."

When he became emotional, his words thickened to where he rolled the vowels in such a way that the dialect didn't sound like anything from Spain or even Mexico, at least to her ears.

She didn't loosen her grip on the spoon. "Let me see. I'll get some anti-bacterial cream."

"No. No. It is nothing." Dropping his hand to his side, he smiled, and the darkness in his gaze shifted yet again and turned into warm, dark chocolate. He stepped further away until he rested against the opposite counter.

Her grasp on the spoon's handle eased. Maybe she'd read too much into his expression. She could have mistaken anger for pain.

"I'll need another cooking utensil to stir the shrimp and pasta."

"Yes, of course." After discarding the old spoon in the sink, she pulled out another from the drawer beside her and handed it to him, trying not to notice that his hand was almost double in size from her own.

The scent of butter and garlic drifted toward her as he mixed the noodles with the shrimp and peas. Hunger hit her stomach. "It smells delicious!"

"Almost done." He rummaged through her silver-ware drawer and pulled out a wine opener. "I did get some white wine. I didn't know if you liked dry or sweet, so I picked a semi-dry."

"No, that's perfect."

"How about you sit down. Relax a bit. I'll set the table."

"Oh, no. It's the least I can do with you cooking dinner."

With both plates and wine served, Luys joined her at the table. "So, what do you think?"

She took a bite, letting the butter, pasta, and shrimp linger on her tongue before swallowing. She moaned—she couldn't help it—and met his earnest gaze. "It's delicious. If I tried something like this, I'd probably cook the shrimp until they were hard rubber."

His teeth flashed. "I'm glad to hear it. I've had no complaints so far."

"Do you like to cook?"

"I love it..."

"But?"

He shrugged. "I have few people to cook for."

"Oh." She glanced down at his left hand. She'd already noticed long before he didn't wear a ring, but she didn't feel comfortable asking whether he was divorced.

He made a face. "I've been single longer than I like to admit. I do have family...a brother who lives out of state."

"And your parents?"

"Mine passed years ago. I remember very little of them, but what about you?" He searched her face with unmistakable interest. "Do you have a large family?"

"No. Just me." When he continued to stare back at her, she surprised herself by adding, "I never knew my parents. They died when I was a toddler, and it's just been me most of my life. I had a couple of foster families, but none of them really stuck until I was twelve, but that relationship ended abruptly. From then on, I stopped trying to compete with babies, toddlers, and little kids."

"That must have been hard on you."

Avery stared at her plate, her hand tightening on her fork. "Yes, well, life is never easy."

"I didn't intend to upset you, and—"

"No, you didn't. That was a long time ago." Avery shook her head quickly. "If nothing else, it's made me stronger. Far stronger than I even imagined." She forced a smile. She didn't want to go back there. She'd folded the past and put it away in a safe, dark closet.

During the rest of the meal, they talked about the weather, movies, nothing too personal, which was just as well. Becoming intimate with Luys, even as a friend, wasn't the best idea right now, not with her future. Among everything else, she had an attacker with a dark, obscene motive she couldn't understand. Anything happening with Luys would end up messy. Granted, she had an idea anything messy with Luys would be a good messy.

She shouldn't even be enjoying herself. She should be talking to someone at the police station again to see if there were any recent developments. Yeah, she'd already called them today and left a message, but that was this morning before Mayor had shown up at her door. Any number of things could have happened. They could have arrested someone during that time.

This morning, she'd also talked to the condo's homeowner's association and tried to get information as to any new residents. They'd given her the standard, "We can't divulge that information. It's against our privacy policies and the law to release anything."

So, she'd have to do some detective work on possible suspects. But she had no clue where to start.

Then she stared across the table at Luys. "You've lived in the complex for a while, right? Longer than I have, I think."

"A good six years."

She nodded, staring down at a pea as she moved it around her plate with her fork.

"Why?"

Oh, God. She had to tell him something. "Someone attacked me, and the police don't have any suspects yet, and I thought you might be aware of anyone new in the complex who might—"

"Hurt you or anyone else?" He placed his fork slowly on his plate.

"...yes." She hated this topic. It made her feel vulnerable, raw, exposed.

"I cannot think of anyone in the complex..."

"But...?"

He slid a thumb up and down the handle of his fork. "What about someone else? This Mayor? Where does she live?"

"Oh, she lives over on Gold Dust off of Scottsdale Road. One of the older houses." She shook her head. "There's no way she could have attacked me."

"Why is that?"

Definitely some antagonism between the two. She was tempted to ask why, but she didn't want to delve into something she didn't want to deal with now.

"You saw her. She might be taller than me, but there's no way she could overpower me. I work out with weights when I'm not running or using an elliptical machine."

"Hmm."

Then silence, awkward and thick. The mood was getting dark, and she'd had enough of dark to last the rest of her life. "Enough about me. What about you? Have you always lived in Scottsdale?"

He shifted. "No."

"Oh?"

"I've lived in too many places to mention, but now I consider Scottsdale my home. The heat is something I enjoy even in the summer."

"Even when it hits 115 or higher?" she teased.

"Even then." He chuckled. Then he rose and retrieved both plates. "I did buy a dessert."

Avery groaned. "You're going to be the death of my scale."

"How about a bit of molten chocolate cake?"

She loved chocolate and had little self-control when he placed the dessert in front of her. After eating every morsel, she groaned again and sat back in her chair. "You're going to have to roll me out of the kitchen. I ate way too much!"

"I'm sure a few extra calories will do you some good." Luys grinned back at her, his eyes crinkling at the sides.

Then when his brow dipped, she believed his thoughts had veered back to her attack. She jumped up and started picking up the dishes. "I'll clean up."

"No. I'm not having that." He took the salt and pepper shaker from her, his fingers brushing against hers.

"I'm feeling fine." Which was the truth but strange after being brutally assaulted.

The kitchen was small. Avery grew distinctly

conscious of his large frame, of how his arm would brush against hers, of the warmth of his body inches from her own as he moved around the kitchen and helped stack the dishes in the dishwasher. At one point, as she edged to one side and pressed her back up against the counter, she looked up and met his gaze as he reached over her to put a plate away. He paused, and her body stilled at the way his eyes seemed to darken with some emotion. Passion? Hunger?

She held her breath as her pulse stuttered and lust roiled through her body to pool low in her belly. Slowly, he placed the plate on top of another in the cabinet and dropped his hand to her shoulder. The heat of his palm burned into the thin fabric of her shirt as they stared at each other.

Impulse moved her hand upward. She grazed her knuckles along the side of his neck, then slipped her fingers into the fringe of his hair by his ear, relishing the silken texture.

His head dipped. Their lips touched. Their breath mingled.

An ache in her belly escalated to the point that she gasped at its intensity. She hadn't had a man in her bed for what seemed forever and hadn't realized she'd been starving herself until now. She clutched his arm with her other hand as he edged closer until his chest flattened the rise and fall of her breasts.

The kiss deepened. His lips tasted of wine and chocolate. Someone groaned; she wasn't sure who. She then slipped her fingers into the thick, luscious waves of his hair above his nape and arched into his body, gasping against his mouth as the heat of his arousal pressed into her belly. Knowing he was equally hungry made her want him that much more.

If she wasn't careful, she was going to lose complete control…if she hadn't already.

Then he stiffened and stepped away, forcing Avery to drop her hands back down to her side. She felt strangely bereft. Only a kiss, but it had hit her like a two-by-four. It made her wonder what it would be like if Luys hadn't stopped. Would she have let desire cloud her sanity, make her do and say things she would have regretted hours later?

No. She wasn't that impulsive. At least she never had been before.

The kiss had been more innocent than most, hadn't it? No open mouths or tongues involved. Just bodies touching, hands not going anywhere inappropriate. Then she remembered the ridge of his erection against her body. No, he'd been equally aroused and, like her, hadn't been thinking innocent thoughts.

"I better go." He stepped away, giving her needed air. A distinct flush darkened his cheekbones.

She nodded, not about to argue. Having him here was dangerous and tempting at the same time. "Of course."

"I'll check on you tomorrow."

"You don't need to," she forestalled as she followed him to the door.

With a hand on the metal knob, he looked down at her and slipped several strands of her hair over one ear. "But I want to, and make sure you lock up behind me. Your safety…"

He stumbled over the last words before he kissed

her on her brow, and her breath caught in her throat at the unexpected but tender caress. Then he quickly opened the door and disappeared outside.

Her toes curled into the carpet as she closed the door after him. Sighing, she leaned her back against its frame and pressed a fist against her chest to calm her heartbeat.

This evening, she'd never been so conflicted in her life. One minute she wanted to have him sweep her into his arms, and then the next, she wanted him gone. She'd received as many mixed signals as possible from Luys.

She locked the door and the deadbolt.

A sound broke through her thoughts. The wail of a siren. The noise strengthened. She stood against the door as the cry in the night reached a crescendo but then dimmed. The police or an ambulance, she couldn't tell. But someone needed help.

In less than a second, sudden panic exploded inside her chest, shattering the warmth of Luys' visit as she double-checked both locks with a trembling hand. She stepped away from the door. Had her attacker struck again? Had they cut up their next victim and left them to die alone this time?

She tried to shrug off the fear, the loneliness, but it was impossible tonight. For years, she'd told herself she was alone but not lonely, but she couldn't lie to herself this evening, not with the way her anxiety amplified her sense of isolation.

She was tired, tired of fighting life on her own, of being strong when she felt anything but.

Was it so wrong to want to find a man who knew not only her body but her mind intimately? To share a moment or two with someone else other than herself? Was she asking too much? Were her expectations too high?

She wanted to be selfish. Moments lasted only so long. She wanted more than a day, a month, a year with someone.

But would it be fair to let someone into her life with what she knew about herself?

Thursday, August 21ˢᵗ – 7:28 pm

Avery stopped by the grocery store on her way home, grabbing some salad and frozen dinners. If Luys showed up at her door, at least he would find she had more than orange juice and eggs in her fridge. As she drove down the main road leading into her condo community, she glanced in the rearview mirror. A vehicle was bearing down on her at a ridiculous speed. In ten seconds, it would hit her back end if she didn't do something, and fast. Then she realized it was a police car. She veered to the right and hugged the side of the road, all the while gripping the steering wheel with rigid fingers as she slowed.

One, then two cars raced past.

No sirens, no lights. Strangely silent. Unlike last night, where she couldn't get rid of the sound of the police or ambulance's wail from inside her head, to the point she'd given up on sleep and gotten up to recheck the locks on the windows and doors.

For some reason, the silence felt worse than if the police cruisers had their lights flashing and sirens blaring, signaling their approach. Both vehicles turned into her condo complex. Her heart rate kicked up. For a moment, she thought of Luys, then of her friend Cristina. Life could change so in a moment. One second, sure and stable, and then the next careening into chaos.

She pulled back onto the road and turned left into the complex and in the same direction as the police. Probably not the best idea to follow them. She rolled to a stop halfway through the north parking section. Two squad cars blocked the section leading to her reserved spot, forcing her to park in a visitor parking slot. The barricade wasn't a good sign.

Behind the wheel, she sat in indecision. Leaving her groceries behind and grabbing her purse, she slipped from the car. Did she dare go out amid whatever was going on? A wave of hot air blasted her from all sides and sucked the oxygen from her lungs. She blinked against the sun's glare as one of the squad cars backed up to let an ambulance through. The vehicle passed without its lights. Another silent emergency vehicle, another bad sign.

She frowned, surprised at how easily she could hear static and the officer's PA system from half a block away.

"Hey, Avery!"

She turned to find Cristina rushing down the sidewalk toward her from the opposite direction. The gleam of sweat clung to her friend's face. She must have been outside watching the drama unfold for some time. "What's going on?"

"Someone was murdered."

CHAPTER 7

Thursday, August 21ˢᵗ – 7:35 pm

"Are you serious?" Avery asked Cristina, grabbing the strap of her purse and pressing it against her side. "In our complex? When? Just now?"

Cristina pulled at the front of her shirt's collar and waved it up and down against her skin. "Yeah. The police aren't saying a word, but I started talking to the neighbors. I'm getting that it happened sometime last night. It was a guy—not the killer, the victim. Not sure you know him. I don't. His name's Noah—Noah Harris. I was talking to his neighbor. She said his sister found him."

"I've never heard of him." That didn't mean she hadn't met him around the complex. Tension cut a swath down her back, and she clutched the strap of her purse harder. "Do you know what happened? Or how?" She didn't want the answer, but not knowing was worse.

Avery thought of her stitches, of her attack, and how she'd missed over twenty-four hours of her memory she'd never get back. A memory that could hold a multitude of sins. But did she want to remember? Then again, her imagination could conjure worse horrors than the actual truth.

But she had no truth, no justice.

Who had attacked her could be anyone. They could be the same person who had killed this Noah. It was too much of a coincidence. Crime in the area consisted of petty burglaries, drug deals. Not murder. Or physical assault.

And now two violent acts within a week and miles of each other. There was the other murder in north Scottsdale. A woman too. The papers had said she'd been stabbed.

Coincidence? It might be...

"All I know was there was a lot of blood. Something about his heart or chest and some type of sharp object."

Oh, God. She'd been right. His death was somehow related to her. Her stomach roiled. She fought back nausea rising to the back of her throat. Blinking back tears, Avery looked down and rummaged inside her purse for nothing in particular. She didn't want Cristina to see how upset she was as she managed, "Are you sure?"

"Not a hundred percent. You know how rumors go. I overheard two other people mention it." Cristina sighed. "Hey." She grabbed Avery's elbow. "I'm sorry this is freaking you out."

She gave up looking inside her purse and met Cristina's gaze. "Well, yeah. Of course it is. Anyone would be upset at a neighbor getting murdered."

"You're acting like you knew the person."

Avery laughed, which threatened to grow out of control, so she sucked in a breath and almost choked on it. *Get control, damn it.* "No. I have no idea who this Noah is."

"Okay, if you say so." Cristina shrugged. "I don't

know all the details yet, but I do know the police want us all to stay inside our condos, but at least there's no helicopter." She glanced up and made a face. "So I guess that's something. In the place we stayed before, we'd get several in the neighborhood every week. I always got nervous when I heard those things humming in the sky at night when they ran those beams into our windows and made it feel like they were right in your face and someone was going to break through the glass and tackle you."

Stephen jogged up from around the corner of one of the buildings. "I tried finding out more, but no such luck. The cops got angry at me for nosing around and getting in the way of doing their job. Avery, they got your building surrounded by yellow tape."

"The murder was that close?" A bead of sweat trickled down her temple, and Avery impatiently wiped it away. The heat wasn't helping her state of mind.

"Yeah, his condo number was 156." Stephen jerked his head to one side to toss his long hair over a shoulder before wrinkling his nose at Avery. "His front door is on the opposite side of the building from you, but you shared his back wall with him. The police will probably want to talk to you eventually. You didn't hear anything, did you?"

"No." Why hadn't she heard anything? My God, she'd been awake most of the night. She should have heard *something*! Especially when her hearing had been spot on for days now.

Cristina wrapped both arms around her middle. "Great. Since hanging around here isn't an option—I'm about to expire from the heat, and the police are going to start breaking up the loitering—what are we supposed to do then? I don't want to stay in my condo. I'm way too hyped up."

"Have a drink over at *The Thing*?" Stephen suggested.

Cristina wrinkled her nose.

"It's better than waiting around to find out more while sweating to death!" Stephen argued.

Avery thought of her frozen dinners in the back of her car. In this heat, it wouldn't take much for them to spoil, but the idea of ducking under the police tape and going inside her condo alone with only her thoughts didn't appeal in the least. She was as unnerved as Cristina.

A car rolled up beside them and into a parking slot that had been recently vacated.

When she recognized Luys behind the wheel, thoughts of the murder disintegrated, and her pulse broke into a gallop as if she'd been injected with adrenaline. Ugh. Such a strong reaction at just recognizing the man wasn't good. Not good at all.

Luys rounded the hood of his car and strode toward them, his gait smooth, his long legs quickly demolishing the distance between his car and their group. The setting sun turned his dark hair to burnished gold in places. "Is everyone okay?"

"Yeah, we are, but someone else isn't so okay," Stephen was quick to comment. "They've got Avery's building cordoned off right now."

Luys frowned. "Why? What happened?"

Stephen explained about the murder, not adding anything that Cristina hadn't told her.

Luys' frown deepened. "Are you sure it wasn't something other than murder? What about suicide?"

"I've never heard of anyone being able to stab themselves in the chest to end it."

Luys cocked his head to one side. "No gun? Are you sure? That's pretty unusual."

"Well, it sounds like some type of sharp object from the rumors we've heard so far," Cristina argued, wrinkling her nose. "Plus, I would think someone would have heard a gunshot and reported it."

"Not necessarily," Avery argued.

"Ahh, yes. Apathy seems to be the new normal." Cristina's lip curled. "Better to just lock your door and ignore it and pretend you hear fireworks."

Avery searched Luys' face. "Did you know Noah?"

"No, not at all. I know very few people by name in the complex."

"A cop is heading this way, and he doesn't look like he wants to chat." Cristina elbowed Avery in the arm. "How about we take this to *The Thing* after all?"

Luys backed up a step. "I don't know. It's been a long day."

"Oh, come on. It's down the street. What else do you have going on tonight?" Stephen asked.

"A drink might do us all some good," Cristina added. "Hell, I'm pretty sure I'm going to need something to get some sleep tonight."

Luys met Avery's gaze. Some type of emotion, serious and dark and intense, flickered in his eyes. Finally, he shrugged and relented. "You're right."

Avery let out a silent breath, not realizing how much she'd wanted him to come until he'd agreed. He was becoming far too important in far too short of a time. They'd only had dinner together and an innocent kiss.

But he'd also helped her, brought her to the hospital, stayed, and waited when no one else had. Someone with that kind of compassion didn't cut another person and leave them to fend for themselves.

All four of them moved in the opposite direction of the officer coming their way and crossed the parking lot to the street leading to *The Thing*. Glancing over her shoulder, Avery realized the officer was moving toward a squad car and not them. They weren't the target of his interest, after all.

Luys and Avery dropped behind the other couple as they walked across the parking lot toward the sidewalk that led to the restaurant. Other residents dispersed in their cars or behind closed doors. "I swear," Avery murmured while rubbing a damp hand against her hip, "I've never seen so many people venture outside their homes and talk to each other like tonight."

"Talking. Sad that a crisis brings people together. All too often, people hide inside their homes and avoid the rest of the world."

"Including yourself?" Avery teased.

He smiled, revealing the slight dimple on his left cheek. It made him look more approachable. "I'm sure I'm as guilty as everyone else. It's less complicated to avoid people. Getting involved with anyone—friendships, lovers, family—complicates your life, increases your chance of some entanglement, and risks the pain of a damaged heart when that person leaves, which inevitably happens with a breakup or death. It's easier to become an island and live without disappointment. But on the other side, being self-sufficient, having walls all around you, and not letting anyone else in your life makes you focus on your disappointments and how truly alone you are."

Avery nodded, finding his words deep and too intimate. They also held too much truth. She wanted to keep the conversation superficial, but then she realized a murder tended to keep things sober.

"You know," Avery said as the silence between them lengthened and started to feel awkward. She didn't want to delve into more intimate topics. "You never told me what you do."

"Something very boring."

"Okay, that just made it more interesting by you brushing it aside. So what could be so very boring?"

"I work for a medical research facility. I head one of their departments."

"Does that mean you're a doctor? That's far from routine." Her step faltered. A doctor. Someone who knew how to cut a person open and stitch them back up. A wave of fear slithered across her flesh and pebbled her skin.

"Yes, but not in the way you would think. I'm not a medical doctor. I don't have patients."

Still, she didn't relax. She forced herself to nod, to keep her expression neutral. She would be stupid to fully trust Luys, and to her, trust came after having some type of history.

They stepped into the restaurant and followed Cristina and Stephen, who bypassed the diners and veered right past the bar to the outside terrace. Along the edge of the roof's veranda, a sprinkler system misted and cooled the area, while bright pink bougainvillea flowers wound up several trellises and edged across the balcony.

Avery sat beside Luys and across from the other couple. She crossed a leg, her foot accidentally brushing against his calf, and then shifted away. Carefully, she folded her hands in her lap, conscious of him as a man, and maybe a dangerous one at that. After a few minutes, the waitress took their order and returned with their drinks. Talk was limited as the music from a guitarist inside the bar filtered through several speakers.

Luys lifted his beer to his lips. He'd been nursing his drink compared to Stephen and Cristina. So far, his one to their three. Avery sipped her one glass of wine. She needed her wits.

She stared at his hand around his mug of beer. Large, strong. Capable of butchering someone like herself? Or snuffing the life out of someone else?

Jaw tightening, Avery brushed the thought aside. At least for the moment. The night was unpleasant enough. Then she glanced across the table at Stephen, who placed a possessive hand on the back of Cristina's chair. She didn't understand their relationship. From what she'd seen so far, he liked to control her friend, making a point of never letting Cristina alone for any length of time. She wondered if he chose her friends, decided who she talked to, where she worked.

Could Stephen be more than an abuser? Could he be Noah Harris' killer? But what type of motive would he have? Avery couldn't think of one. A wife-beater was far different than a serial killer. She was letting paranoia control her thoughts and being ridiculous. Cristina was a strong woman, opinionated, and had her own mind, didn't she? She worked as an accountant, while Stephen had some type of sales job. Still... she eyed how he played absently with the strands of Cristina's hair with his fingers.

Maybe Avery was jealous of their relationship? Could that be why she didn't like him? She was alone while they had a marriage that seemed to work.

"So..." Stephen began, his laugh like chalk against Avery's senses. "We're all wondering, even though no one is saying a word, who do you think the killer is?"

Cristina looked up from her phone. She'd been staring at it off and on since they'd sat down.

Luys covered the top of his beer with one hand. "I don't know if right now is the best time—"

"I think the victim knew the killer," Cristina interrupted. "I'm not sure if the killer lives in the complex, but I'm pretty sure it was personal."

"You can't know that," Avery argued.

"Actually, I do." She tapped a finger on the screen of her phone. "I just got a text. According to Houston, the victim was stabbed to death."

"Who's Houston?" Avery asked.

"He's a neighbor that's completely infatuated with Cristina," Stephen replied.

With her gaze still on her phone, Cristina mused aloud, "No, he isn't." She shook her head. "And usually, stabbings are personal."

"So, you're an expert now?" Stephen joked.

Cristina glanced over at her husband and rolled her eyes. "Of course not." She looked back down at her phone. "The police aren't commenting on any of the details of the crime right now. But..." Cristina paused and frowned at whatever she was reading.

"But what?" Avery leaned forward, hating herself for being so morbidly interested.

Cristina wrinkled her nose. "A witness—"

"There was a witness?" Luys interrupted.

"No, not in that way. The sister saw the victim after the slaying." Cristina used a thumb to scroll through a message. "Houston texted the killing was gruesome, unusual, and brutal. The chest was cut open…" She scowled. "This is freaking sick. He's saying a body part was missing. Eww!" She looked up and glanced at Avery and then Luys. "The sister thinks it's the heart."

Avery glanced over at Luys, his face blank of emotion, and downed the rest of her wine. To hell with her wits, but the alcohol didn't ease the constant twisting of her stomach. Then her grip on her glass tightened, and before she broke it and did something stupid like cutting herself, she set it on the table with a shaky hand.

The evening seemed to get hotter, even suffocating. She fisted a hand against her chest, feeling the erratic beat of her heart. Why hadn't her attacker killed her? Why hadn't the person taken her heart like the neighbor?

Stephen and Cristina weren't aware of her assault. Luys knew, though, but he didn't have the entire truth, and what he knew, he wouldn't mention that to the others, would he? He must have sensed her glance because he turned, met her gaze, and reached over to squeeze her hand briefly in reassurance, almost as if reading her thoughts.

She needed to call the police department first thing in the morning and get answers. Or maybe show up at the precinct so the operator couldn't forward her to some answering machine.

Cristina swiped her phone with a finger, then set her phone face down on her thigh and covered her yawn with a palm. "Well, this has been an interesting night. I've had enough. The alcohol is finally kicking in, and I think I'll be able to get some sleep. At least I'm hoping."

"I'm hoping for something more than sleep." Stephen sent his wife a wicked smile.

Cristina laughed. "I bet you are. Let's go home." She eyed Luys and Avery across the table. "Are you about ready to go?"

Avery scraped her chair back from the table. "Let me go to the restroom first."

But when she returned, she found only Luys sitting at the table.

CHAPTER 8

"Where are Stephen and Cristina?"

"They decided not to wait and headed back." Luys shrugged one shoulder. "Something about some show Cristina wanted to watch."

Avery's lips firmed, but she didn't say anything. She didn't know if Cristina was trying to fix them up or not, but she did know she didn't want to go home alone with Luys. She didn't feel entirely safe with him but walking back to her place by herself in the dark didn't sound much better.

She must have revealed her trepidation—not for the correct reason—because he rose and said, "I'll make sure you're completely safe."

"Black belt?" she teased, trying to shrug off her uncertainty. Why get her to the doctor if Luys wanted to hurt her? It was too much of a contradiction, and her paranoia was seeing suspects when there weren't any.

"No," he returned, his face serious, his gaze solemn, "but I can defend myself."

She nodded sharply at his calm confidence. His thick biceps, broad shoulders, and athletic body backed up his words. She suspected he'd be the victor in hand-to-hand combat involving any wicked-looking knives as she led the way out of the bar and then into the restaurant. The night air clung to her body in a hot blanket.

Even with the setting of the sun, the temp didn't feel cooler.

During the walk back, he matched his much larger stride to hers. If nothing else, he was considerate, even sensitive to her needs. Nothing annoyed her more than having someone walk ahead of her. The last boyfriend... Well, that was a good two years ago, and he wasn't much to remember... A three-month stint, and she'd had enough. Better alone than having to deal with an inflated ego and self-centered view on everything.

When they reached the complex, the police cruisers had disappeared, but when they walked down the sidewalk toward the north wall of the building and the front of her condo, she glanced down the pathway that led to the opposite side of her property and caught sight of yellow tape draped across one of the doorways.

She winced. "I feel bad that I don't feel anything for him."

"You didn't know him."

"True. But still, I feel like I should."

"It's a lot to take in." Luys followed her to her door. "Just be careful."

"I can handle myself."

"I'm sure you can..." He stood over her, a good six inches over the top of her head. "You've got my number in case you need help. I'm minutes away."

She'd never thought of herself as tiny, but somehow he made her feel dainty, which was crazy. She looked up. Shadows clung below his eyebrows, effectively obscuring his thoughts, but she sensed his concern, his tension.

Her heart twisted. It had been a long time since anyone had shown genuine concern for her without wanting sex or a favor of some type in return, but with Luys, she hadn't yet been able to figure out what his motivation was other than kindness.

To have someone care...

She shivered, mentally shaking off feelings of wanting him to be more than her neighbor.

He hesitated by her door, and she stood for a moment looking up into his face, and before either of them did something stupid, Avery backed up and started to turn but stopped when she caught sight of a man standing twenty yards away and beneath a lamppost. As the man shifted, the light from above thrust him into view. The police detective from the hospital. It had to be.

But why was he still hanging around when everyone else had left the crime scene?

For a moment, they stared at each other across the gravel yard. Then his heel scraped against a rock as he turned and disappeared around an adjacent building.

Luys turned to where she had been looking, but the detective had already disappeared.

Before he had time to question her, Avery said in a whisper, "Goodnight."

Then she stepped inside her condo, determined not to look over her shoulder at his reaction, and firmly locked the door.

I hate this need to stand in line for food. I feel like a cow herded in one direction toward a feeding trough. But I need nourishment. My head is pounding from lack of water and food. I have been too preoccupied with other matters.

In front of me, a man and child wait in line to check out their food. They have the same dark hair, the same warm skin tone. Father and daughter. The girl, no more than three stone, with wavy brown hair past the shoulders, carries a sack of potatoes. She shifts, struggling with holding the heavy weight in her arms as it inches downward. The bag thuds to the ground.

"Pick it up!"

She looks up at the man, her eyes large, her gaze uneasy.

"I said pick it up," he snarls.

My lip curls at one side. He is but a predator feeding on the weak.

Hunching over, she picks up the potatoes, hugs the bag to her chest, and shifts beneath the burden.

"Be more careful," the man rebukes, slapping his hand against the back of the girl's head, sending wisps of chocolate hair flying into the air.

My eyes narrow as anger bubbles through my insides. A tyrant belittling smaller fragile children. I have seen too many not to recognize the type. The hardness in their eyes, the arrogance in their swagger.

The female cashier checking the man and girl out seems agitated at the man's behavior, but she says nothing. Her silence condones his behavior. I am no better by staying silent.

Once through the line, the father picks up a grocery bag filled with items and makes the girl carry the potatoes.

With the girl in the lead, the duo moves toward the glass door exit, and in a harsh voice, the man growls, "Move faster."

Still struggling with the weight of the potatoes, she quickens her pace. Two more steps, she stumbles but rights herself, but she is not fast enough.

The father shoves a knee to her back, forcing her forward. She lands on all fours, the potatoes landing to her side. "Damn stupid girl! You can't even walk right."

He grabs the bag and exits the store, not looking to see if the girl follows. Scrambling to her feet, she races through the doors and after her father. Then they disappear around the side of the building.

I follow them to their home. They don't know they are being watched because I am careful. I am always careful.

I expect a rundown apartment on the worst side of the city, where addicts litter the ground like dead leaves. I find instead a one-story house comprising manicured hedges, trimmed bougainvillea, and a yard and driveway without a hint of a weed. My lips curl into a sneer. He takes care of the house more than he does his child.

A woman appears from the front door. The mother. Her hair has the same texture and color as the girl's. They both have the same fragile frame. From where I stand, I can see the bruising below her eye, the marks on her arms. Another victim of his wrath. But it's not these signs that give away her true trauma. It is the look in her expression, the emptiness in her eyes.

She looks like you. She's given up.

I have not given up!

You lie to yourself.

No.

I try to shake off the voice. It's seductive, knowing.

I force myself to focus on the woman and how she shuffles across the yard, so similar to how the girl walked in the food store. But would the woman look like this if he were no longer there terrorizing her? And the child? What of her? She is powerless, nothing more than a vessel to his perversion.

I think of my daughter, and fury roils through me. I have always welcomed the rage. It blocks out the pain, the hurt, the loneliness.

Kill him. Kill him now. He deserves it.

I press my hands to my ears. I take in deep breaths. No. Now is not the time to cave into the voices.

Do it. He is worthless. Just as worthless as you.

Are you too afraid? I thought you were powerful. I thought you were smarter than everyone.

No one will find out.

No.

The urge to kill overwhelms me. I back away before I act on the need. There are witnesses. I cannot terrorize the child with a bloodbath.

Now is not the time.

I leave but come back later that evening, then again, and again. I wait, I watch, biding my time for an opportunity. Because there is always an opportunity.

Friday, August 22nd – 8:12 am

The next morning, another day without work—her boss firmly rebuked any mention of her working for the week and insisted she start fresh on Monday—Avery called the precinct with the number on the card Detective Hatcher had given her. When the receptionist answered then transferred her call to his desk, Avery left another message.

Grunting, she hung up. By lunch, with the television having lost all her interest and the four walls closing in on her, she decided to go out, shop, see a movie, do anything but stay inside her four walls. She needed to get OUT, no matter how short. After a quick shower, while avoiding any mirrors in the bathroom and bedroom, she dressed in shorts, a tank top, and slide-on sandals before slipping outside. The last time she'd looked at her reflection, she'd seen the same two scars, both appearing as if she'd had surgery as a child, not days ago. She also didn't like how they resembled a cross in the middle of her chest.

She'd canceled her follow-up appointment with her doctor for two reasons: she didn't need her wounds checked because they'd clearly healed, and she didn't want to deal with questions she couldn't answer.

Once outside and seeing no one liable to jump her, she let her pent-up tension ease fractionally. She hadn't been able to relax for what seemed like forever. The sun had shifted to the west, limiting shadows, and the heat was at its most oppressive as she hurried to her car. Every night she'd listen to sounds by her windows and the front door. A can of pepper spray by her bed was her only form of protection. A knife was out of the question. The way her luck was, an attacker would more likely use it on her rather than the other way around. While a gun... she'd probably shoot herself with no training.

"Hey, Avery!"

She stiffened and turned to find a man striding toward her. She stuck her hand in her purse for her pepper spray but eased her grip and slipped her hand back out when she recognized the younger detective from the hospital and the one she'd seen only last night. He didn't have his work clothes on today but wore a pair of workout shorts and a muscle shirt.

"Hey, sorry." He stopped a couple of feet in front of her on the sidewalk. "I didn't mean to alarm you."

"That's okay." She wondered what he was doing here dressed as he was. "Did you need to ask me any more questions...? Sorry, I don't know your full name."

"It's Ben, Ben Atkins. And I'm not here for an official visit." He cocked his head to the side and nodded in the area behind him. "I live two buildings behind you."

The idea of a police detective nearby made her feel somewhat safer. "Actually, I'm glad we bumped into each other. Maybe you can help. I left a message at the station. No one's called me back. Is there a reason?" She searched his face. The lines fanning out from his eyes, the few strands of gray at his temples she hadn't noticed until now. She'd thought him younger. Maybe the drugs she'd had at the hospital had left her brain foggy, but today she realized he was edging near forty rather than topping his twenties. She hadn't gotten his looks wrong. He was an attractive man with a sensual mouth, a smooth, angular nose, white, even teeth, and a smile that lit his brown eyes with flecks of gold. His close-cropped hair added to his masculinity.

His mouth dipped as he fanned the top of an oleander bush beside the walkway with his palm, scattering loose pink petals to the ground before he dropped his hand to his side. "No, other than we've been swamped. I apologize for us not getting back to you."

Her lips firmed. It had been over 48 hours since she'd left her first message with Hatcher. A simple call would have been nice even if they'd told her they didn't have any news.

"This recent murder has us working long hours."

At his words, Avery felt a little ashamed of herself for not thinking of the victim. At least she'd survived her attack. Her neighbor hadn't been so lucky.

She then noticed dark half-moons beneath his eyes. "Have you found the killer or any suspects? I heard the person was stabbed in the chest, and someone told me they were missing some type of body part. Is it in any way related to me? I think I deserve some answers."

"We haven't made any arrests, and I can't divulge more than that, I'm afraid."

"Are you sure? It would be nice to know what's going on, especially because of what happened to me. There must be a tie you're unwilling to tell me about." It was impossible to keep the frustration from her voice, and frankly, she didn't care if he heard it.

"Like I said, I can't get into the details."

"Okay, I understand you don't want to cross any lines when it comes to ethics." But secretly and selfishly, she kind of didn't. Answers, even small, would be better than not knowing a thing. She thought it only right that the people in the complex should have more answers than the general public. After all, they didn't know if the murder was a random act or something more personal.

"Sorry. But all I can say is to be always aware of your surroundings and the people around you." He opened his mouth, frowned, and then closed it as he hooked a thumb over his jeans belt loop.

"What?" She waited. It was clear he wanted to say something.

After a long pause, he finally said, "I saw you talking last night with one of the neighbors."

"That's right. And...?"

He rocked back on his heels. "Are the two of you close?"

She didn't know what he was getting at and didn't like how he avoided her question with one of his own, and she also didn't know if he was asking questions because it was personal or job-related. She decided to be honest, though. "No. He's helped me out a couple of times. As you know, he's the one who drove me to the hospital after my attack."

"Yeah, I'm aware of that." The detective's lip twisted into a sneer. "I'd steer clear of him."

"What do you mean by that?"

"Just that."

"Come on. You've got to give me a reason."

"He's like everyone else here at the complex. A suspect."

Avery lifted her chin and searched his face again. She couldn't read beyond the kindness in his eyes.

"Are you saying he's a suspect?"

"I'm not at liberty to discuss that."

"But?"

"Don't trust him, okay?" Rubbing the back of his neck, he sighed and admitted, "I know things about him that aren't good."

"Well, he's never given me any sign of being dangerous," Avery felt compelled to argue since Luys wasn't here to defend himself.

"Most criminals don't appear dangerous." He tossed a set of keys in the air and caught them. "And call me by my name. It's Ben."

"Okay, Ben." She rolled back on her heels.

"If you're ever worried or feel you need help, I'm in the next building. Condo 298." The lines by his eyes crinkled into a smile.

The warmth of a flush rose up her neck and into her face. There was definite interest in his brown eyes.

"I'll see you around. And I'll talk to Hatcher. He's

the one in charge of the investigation. I'll make sure he calls you back. He's awful when it comes to dealing with the public. But still, that's no excuse to ignore you."

"That would be nice. Thanks."

He smiled. "I'll check on you in a couple of days, if that's okay?"

"Ahh, sure."

She watched him leave before walking to her car. From behind the wheel, she stared through the windshield and beyond the palo verde trees to the buildings across the street. Slowly, she put the key in the ignition but didn't turn on the engine.

I'd steer clear of him.

I know things about him that aren't good…

It was all too mysterious.

Any interest in a movie or shopping evaporated. Never one to ignore a puzzle, Avery jumped out of her car and hurried back to her condo, eying Luys' front door before slipping inside her place.

She grabbed her tablet from the kitchen table and turned it on. Once she found a pen and paper, she dropped into a chair at the table and started searching for Luys Martinez. The Martinez part would have been a nightmare if she had to search by his surname alone. But the name Luys—now Luys had some meat to it.

Ugh.

After five minutes, she didn't pull up anything on the internet, which was strange. Then she went to various social media sites. Nothing. Okay, so maybe he didn't like social media. Many people didn't. But still... It was odd not to be able to find anything on him. Even peculiar.

That didn't mean nothing existed...

Tapping her fingers on the kitchen table, she stared at the tablet as if it would give her an answer. She scrolled through several pages. Okay. This had to be easier. Those detective shows made it seem so simple.

Think.

Okay, she had his telephone number, his address. That should lead to something. Scrolling through the county database of recent arrests didn't pull up anything. The entire website was confusing. Maybe she hadn't gone far back enough...

There had to be something. Why else would Ben Atkins have warned her? It couldn't have anything to do with him wanting to date her. That would be ridiculous.

There had to be something. She knew she sounded like a broken record, but a person couldn't completely be invisible. Not today, with social media added to the mix.

Unless he intentionally scrubbed his name from the net. That would probably involve hiring a professional company. That in itself sounded ominous.

Or he was lying about his name...

Maybe Luys Martinez was someone completely different and was living under an alias. But no. That couldn't be the case because Ben seemed to imply he knew something about Luys. She was sure he'd had Luys investigated, and if he'd found any outstanding warrants, Ben would have had him arrested.

Someone knocked on the front door.

Avery jumped. She thumped her fist against her chest to quiet the sudden gallop of her heart. Muttering several choice words under her breath, she slipped from the chair and snatched the pepper spray from the end table by the sofa. She'd purchased two on her last outing. On that, she felt like she wasn't paranoid. Not after what she'd experienced.

Clutching the tube in one hand, she looked through the door's peephole. For a moment, she didn't see anyone. She wasn't going to be stupid enough to open it if she couldn't make them out.

Then Mayor's white-blond hair and elegant features moved into view, and Avery's fingers eased around the pepper spray. Sighing in relief, she hid the spray in a drawer by the foyer table before opening the front door and squinting against the glare. Even as the sun's rays beat down on her face and body, she shivered for some reason.

Mayor smiled. "I thought I'd drop by and chat."

Avery didn't move from the doorway. Undeterred, Mayor brushed past and closed the door.

CHAPTER 9

After Mayor walked further into the condo, Avery noticed the other woman holding two cups. Mayor smiled and offered her one. "I was bored and thought I'd drop by with a pick-me-up. Herbal tea with no caffeine. I hear it is a fan favorite at the coffee shop. I thought I would try something different."

Avery glanced over at the large Roman numeral clock on the wall. Twenty after three. "Thanks. I usually need something around now."

Mayor's smile widened. "I am glad I came by then. I saw your car in the parking lot earlier today and was surprised it was still there."

She wasn't going to explain why she was home and not working, though she did back up a step and offer, "Did you want to sit down for a bit?"

"Oh, no. I would not want to intrude." Mayor tossed her blonde locks over one shoulder and nodded to the front door. "I did see the yellow tape on my way here. You must find it unsettling every time you walk by, yes?"

Avery was about to shrug, then decided not to make light of the situation. "Yeah. The murder happened in the same building. The awful part is I share the same wall and didn't hear a thing. If I had, I might have been able to call the police. I feel terrible. If his murder was random, it could have easily happened to me. I might have been the one—"

"But you're not." She held her cup of coffee close to her chest with both hands. "Don't worry. You're safe."

Avery took a sip of tea, but its heat didn't warm her insides. Mayor didn't know about her attack, and she wasn't about to tell her. Their relationship hadn't progressed to that point, and she didn't know if she'd let it. She'd never been good at close relationships.

"No. I'm not safe. No one is. Not until they find and arrest this killer."

"The police are estúpidos. They know nothing."

"You don't know that."

"I know."

She met Mayor's solemn expression and grew uneasy.

"You worry too much." She lifted her cup toward Avery. "You don't need to. The killer did not pick you. As I said before, you're safe. I am sure he or she had a reason to spare your life instead of this other person."

Avery scowled. "There's no way you can know that."

"Oh, but I do."

"Why do you say that? Are you psychic or something?"

"What if I was?" Mayor shrugged a shoulder, her expression bland. "You will believe what you believe."

Avery's frown deepened as she stared at the lid of her tea. Until this afternoon, she'd felt comfortable in the other woman's company. "Well, I'm pretty sure the police may have suspects, but clearly they don't have enough evidence to arrest someone. Otherwise, it would be all over the news."

"What do you know of this neighbor of yours? Did he have enemies? Someone who disliked him?"

"I don't know."

"Did you see him with anyone you did not recognize days or weeks before?"

"Not that I can think of. I wasn't paying attention. I rarely do when it comes to my neighbors. I'm sure I'm not the only one who's like that. My day consists of home, car, work, and back again. I'm only friends with one person and her husband in the complex."

Mayor tapped a thumb on her cup. "And who is that? Maybe I know her?"

Tensing, Avery rubbed a hand along the side of her cup's lid. "Why all the questions?"

"I am only curious. This person, after all, was murdered in the neighborhood. All of us who live nearby are concerned."

"Well, I'm as equally concerned, but, so far, the police haven't given me any answers. They've avoided my calls. I'd feel safer if I had some more information from them."

"I am sure you can find answers to some of your questions." Mayor sank down on the edge of a living room chair with fluid ease. The slit in her long flowing skirt gaped open as she crossed a long and lean leg over the other. She adjusted the hem with a flick of the wrist, sending several gold bracelets clicking against each other.

"I wouldn't know where to start."

"Why not start with the condominium where the person was killed?"

"All I have on the victim is his address, name, and an internet search didn't pull up anything unusual. The detective in the complex wasn't of any help either."

"I don't think I was clear. I am not talking about him. I mean his place." Avery must have still looked confused because Mayor gave a pained sigh, rested an elbow over her crossed knee, and leaned forward with her cup dangling from one hand. "If you think knowledge will make you feel safer, why not search his home for your answers?"

"His home?" Eyes widening, she stared back at Mayor. "Are you serious?"

"What else could I mean? I am sure you might find something inside this place, yes?" Mayor smiled. "At the very least, you would be able to learn more about who this man is. If you learn you have no similarities or background ties other than living in the complex, that will surely ease your mind. What do you have to lose?"

At Mayor's last question, Avery paused. There seemed to be something hidden in her words, but that didn't make sense. She brushed the thought aside and instead focused on the outlandishness of her suggestion. "I can't go in there. The place is locked."

"No." Another smile, this one far more mischievous than the last. "I checked. The door is unlocked."

Avery dropped down in a living room chair, unable to take her gaze from the other woman. "That's crazy. Why wouldn't they have locked it? That's completely irresponsible on their part." She rolled her cup between both hands. "And why would you even think of checking to see if it was locked? Did you go inside?"

Mayor shrugged. "It is of no real interest to me."

"Then why did—"

"No more talk," Mayor insisted. "I will show you. We can look together. The police are incompetent with their narrow minds."

"I—no."

"But you want answers."

"Yes, but I don't want to break the law."

"You are not breaking the law if you accidentally walk inside."

"Accidentally?" Mayor was serious. "It's called trespass."

"You're playing with words. If the police discover you, the most they can do is reprimand you."

"I don't think I'd get a slap on the wrist. Anyway, it's dangerous. The killer could come back."

"Pah. The killer is unlikely to do that unless they are a fool." Mayor shrugged a shoulder, but a distinct sparkle flashed in her light blue eyes. "What is a little danger, yes?" When Avery didn't immediately reply, she asked, "Do you not want to know what is inside the living space? Are you not a little curious?"

"Of course I'm curious."

Mayor arched a brow. "But yet, you will not feed that curiosity."

Avery's lips firmed. She didn't like being pushed into situations.

Mayor waved a hand in the air and swiftly rose to her feet. "Fine. You're a modern woman who makes her own decisions." Mayor searched her face, and she nodded as if she'd come to some decision. "It is getting late. I have things I must do. But you only have so much time to decide to find out what is inside this place. I am sure the authorities will soon discover their mistake."

Avery closed and locked the door behind Mayor and stood in the middle of the room in indecision. She glanced at the living room wall. The same wall as the victim's condo. It would be stupid to check the place out. Knowing her luck, the minute she stepped past the threshold, Ben would probably catch her in the act. Plus, they'd probably searched the premises and removed all clues or evidence.

But she wanted to find answers to whether or not the killing was related somehow to her attack. The police department was like talking to a brick wall, and they weren't likely to reveal anything about the murder. Not on her timeline. She'd probably get more information from the news than them.

Sighing, she looked away from the wall and over to the main window. A mesquite tree nearby offered the only shade across the landscaped rock. What would a quick look do? Folding her arms, she paced the confines of her living room, thinking of the pros and cons. She couldn't believe she was contemplating the idea of walking into a crime scene.

Now wasn't the time unless... It was too light outside. Someone could easily see her and just as easily report her.

She turned on the television and learned nothing new about the murder. Sighing in frustration, she watched a sitcom or two, but no amount of comedy could pull her from her morbid thoughts. After another hour of debating with herself, Avery gave up. Damn the woman for telling her about the unlocked condo. Ugh, her curiosity was too intense. The need to know what was inside the victim's condo was driving her nuts.

When evening turned to night, Avery dressed in a pair of black jeans and a t-shirt, grabbed her keys, pepper spray, slipped outside, and locked the door behind her. The evening rush of people from after work had dissipated hours before. The sidewalks were clear of residents. The leaves rustled above, and the scent of rain clung to the air. Earlier, a monsoon had swept through, coating the ground and clearing the air of dust and pollution.

She walked around her building and hovered on the sidewalk where it split into two directions. She took the one that veered toward the back of her condo. Yellow tape still clung to the doorway of the victim's home, making her wonder when they were going to get rid of it. Every time she walked by, it seemed to scream back at her, and vivid images of waking up naked in her bed with her chest cut and stitched back together bombarded her.

This was ridiculous.

Still, she didn't turn back around. Instead, she glanced around, found no one about, ducked under the tape, and strode to the door, where it faced away from the complex's security lights and stood in deep shadow. Standing in those shadows, she eyed the doorknob.

Curiosity. Was she willing to walk over the threshold because of it?

Answers. She might not find any, but by going inside, she wouldn't wonder looking back if she'd made the mistake of not trying to find those answers or proof as to whether or not there was a tie between Harris and herself. And if there was, she might find the reason behind her attack.

With a distinct tremor in her hand, she pulled up

the bottom of her shirt and wrapped the hem around the metal.

Maybe Mayor had lied. And why had she gone to the victim's condo and checked the door in the first place? What type of person did that? The same type of person as Avery?

A woman who needed answers?

She moved her hand to the right. The knob turned in the same direction.

Avery sucked in a breath, slid inside, and closed the door behind her.

CHAPTER 10

Friday, August 22nd – 8:34 pm

Inside St. Paul Apostle Catholic Church, Luys sat in a few pews back from the altar and stared up at the wood cross with the sculpture of Jesus. The silence in the room sounded loud yet eerie and hollow. He had several minutes of solitude before he had to leave, and they locked the doors behind him for the night.

He had stayed at work long after everyone had left for home and decided to stop here to clear his head. When it came to his job, being the last one to leave had become a habit. He didn't dare do any research on a side pet project until he was alone, knowing he would likely get fired if word got out he was delving into areas that were unrelated to the medical facility's research programs.

Hours before, staring at his computer screen, he had not believed the results. He had researched bacterial and protozoal infections, also autoimmune diseases. He had gone down the virus route years before with nothing to show for it, but then a couple of years ago, he'd decided to retrace his steps and focus on a different hypothesis: an unidentified virus, one yet to be discovered, ran through his blood system. He had then researched various modern viruses and turned his focus on the West Nile virus.

He toggled to another screen, replaying the formation of new cells. He had been working with the new protein RBBTS for some time, hoping one small deviation might be the trick to create a new and distinct virus. He was banking on a new virus that would fight and eradicate the cells inside his body. Finally, it looked like he might not be running down another rabbit hole.

Luys should be ecstatic. He was closer to finding a way to normalize not only his blood cells but the people he loved.

But what was normal? He did not know anymore. And if he did become *normal*, what would a cure solve? His death and that of his family?

He was asking those questions all over again as he wrapped both hands around the top of the pew in front of him. Raised a devout Catholic, but having lost faith long ago, he still found himself gravitating to a place of worship during times when he needed answers or a sense of balance. Even knowing he would be excommunicated from the Catholic church in today's modern times, never mind decades or centuries before, it was the energy within the walls that soothed his soul if he even had one. Faith. Hope. Conviction of something bigger than this earth. Those beliefs seemed ingrained in the brick, the wood, the plaster, the paint.

And if he died, did he go to hell or heaven or somewhere else? Was he damned as the church insisted?

The idea of dying terrified him. He'd thought he wanted a cure, but now over the years, the closer he came to the possibility, dread would mount and erode the urge for answers.

Soon he would have to start testing. A hypothesis

only worked so far. He would have to experiment on himself. He couldn't ask Gabriel, not when he'd finally found some token of happiness with Amanda.

His hands tightened around the top of the pew.

Enough.

It could wait until tomorrow.

He'd been searching for a cure for decades, if not longer.

The fall of a footstep startled him. For a moment, he'd forgotten he wasn't the only one here searching for solace. He glanced over his shoulder.

A woman moved her hand into the sign of the cross before slipping into a pew on the opposite side of the aisle, sinking down on a padded kneeler and bowing her head. Her cap of red hair gleamed beneath the electric sconces on the walls and reminded him of Avery.

He turned back to the altar. He shouldn't think of Avery other than as a woman he needed to protect. He found her beautiful. The sheet of auburn hair that flowed past her shoulders, the gentle curve of her cheeks, the long slope of her neck, the intelligence, even fierceness in her eyes. Her femininity, vulnerability, and strength called to him. There was something about her that touched him as no one had for years.

Which wasn't good. He needed to keep his heart out of it.

But how could he when it was already starting to crack from an emotion he'd long thought he'd lost?

His lips thinned. He needed to remember what happened the last time he had let a woman into his life and his heart.

He almost lost his freedom because of it.

Bowing his head, he prayed for strength, wisdom, and a path forward when it came to dealing with Mayor. He had searched for the house Avery had mentioned over by Scottsdale Road and Gold Dust but had no luck, even with his brother's help. Mayor probably had created a new identity.

Luys looked up at the marble figure of Christ on the cross, arms outstretched, hands open. Streetlights from outside beamed through the stained glass over the dome above the altar, creating a kaleidoscope of colors and turning the sculpture's skin strangely to gold.

Feeling calmed, somewhat centered, he slipped from the pew and moved quietly down the aisle, passing one or two others in prayer. As the double door closed from behind him and he took the shallow stairs to the sidewalk, his phone rang. Frowning, he almost did not answer it, assuming it was a junk call, but then he thought of Avery.

"Yes."

"Am I speaking to Luys Martinez?"

"Yes. Why?"

"This is Detective Hatcher. I'd like you to come in voluntarily for further questioning."

Luys grabbed the arm rail. The temptation to hang up overwhelmed him, but he didn't disconnect. Why did they want to talk to him? Thoughts veered to the murder in the complex. "This is about Avery, right?"

"That, and I had a couple of other questions. I'm sure you're aware of the murder in your building, correct?"

"Of course. Everyone in the area is familiar with it."

"So, can you come in?"

Did they think he was the killer? Savagely murdering another person? But then he thought of his last conversation with Detective Hatcher. The suspicion... *Guilty before proven innocent.* "When?"

"Monday morning. Say eight."

"I have to work."

A sigh filtered through the connection. "We all have to work. How is your lunch hour?"

Luys stopped midway down the steps. "I'll have to call you back. I'll need to find representation before I speak with anyone."

"I don't think you'll need it. We only have a few questions."

Luys hesitated. What were a few questions? Then he thought of another time when he had been questioned. The suspicion in both officers' eyes. Their glib words. The feeling of being guilty before he had even said a word. He would be a fool to think this was not any different.

Guilty before proven innocent.

"You can leave by your own free will at any time," Hatcher encouraged.

Luys was not a fool. At least, he liked to think so, sensing an ominous quality beneath Hatcher's words as he took the last couple of steps and turned down the sidewalk to the parking lot. Nerves curled around his stomach. They must think he was a suspect. Why else have him come to the precinct?

"I'll come by during my lunch hour."

"You do that," Hatcher clipped out.

Disconnecting, he realized he'd almost walked

past the parking lot to his car. On the drive home, he tried to keep his thoughts from scattering into various scenarios. He did not dare let panic form his thoughts and actions.

By the time Luys parked and got out of his car, exhaustion wove through his muscles. He rubbed at the back of his neck but could not remove the knots beneath his skin as he strode to the complex's mail center. After he had retrieved several pieces of junk mail, he turned toward his condo. A flash of blonde hair caught against his peripheral vision.

Mayor.

The mail crumpled beneath his rigid grasp. He rushed down the sidewalk, past his and Avery's front door, and rounded the corner of the building. Another flash of blonde hair. He broke into a run.

After turning another corner, he stumbled to a stop. Mayor had disappeared. He swore savagely. Realizing Mayor was playing one of her sick games, he pivoted and rushed back the way he'd come, horrified she might do something to Avery.

He banged on Avery's door. If Mayor so much as touched Avery, he'd kill her. Slowly. With pleasure.

Avery didn't answer.

"Avery! Are you in there? Are you okay? Answer me!"

Still no answer.

"Avery! Tell me you're okay!"

When he didn't get a response, he shoved at the door with the entire weight of his body. The door buckled, metal broke, and the door flew open, hitting the wall with a loud bang.

"God's teeth. You have to be fine. I'd never be able to live with myself if anything happened to you."

He stumbled to a halt in the living room. No sign of her. The lights were on; voices rumbled from the television. Alarmed, he hurried through the bedroom and adjoining bathroom, not finding any sign of her. Back in the living room, he stared at the front door leading to the outside. Laughter erupted from the television. The sound scratched across his senses. While the silence from outside screamed louder at him.

She'd been attacked before. Mayor was hanging around her with some sick cat and mouse game in mind. She couldn't have been the one who'd assaulted Avery, could she?

That wasn't like Mayor. She liked mind games, violent games, but Mayor always lost interest quickly. If she'd been fixated on only Avery, Mayor would have killed her long before now.

Plus, she'd never touched a woman before. Ever. All her victims had been male before...

Avery stood unmoving for a good thirty seconds as her eyes adjusted to the darkness. Streetlamps from outside the complex stabbed through the living room window blinds, throwing knife-like lines across the flooring.

A staleness clung to the air, and some distinct scent permeated the place. Death? No. She was too fanciful. Dust or disuse?

She edged farther into the room and listened,

breathing in and out slowly to calm her sensitized nerves. Noise, at first soft and indistinct, grew and formed into meaning. Loud, then louder. The hum of the fridge, voices—a couple—from another condo. The footsteps of someone else not far away.

Impossible. They were too far away for a normal person to hear.

Stop. Stop it!

She shook her head, and the noise shattered into stunning silence.

Taking in a deep fortifying breath, she moved deeper into the condo and slipped into the bedroom. Drawers were half-open while others lay upended on the floor. Jeez. Didn't the police have any respect for the dead? What must his family think?

She'd be furious if the police went through the belongings of someone she loved with such disregard, never mind dead or alive. Then she realized maybe this was how the police had found Harris' place, and the murderer had been the one who'd rampaged through his possessions.

After stepping over to the dresser, she swiped her phone for the flashlight and shined the beam's light into one of the drawers. Rumpled clothing spilled from the inside. She touched a sweater, the material cool to the fingers. It felt stranger than strange nosing around in a dead person's dresser drawers. This man had worn the garment. He had parents, brothers, and sisters, didn't he? Most people did.

She moved the sweater aside, delving deeper, searching between the other garments. Not finding anything other than clothing, she folded the sweaters back in order and moved on to the other drawers. After finding nothing unusual in the dresser, she crept across the floor to search the rest of the room.

She stumbled to a stop. Until now, she hadn't noticed the stains on the carpet. Dark, like spilled red wine, but alcohol had nothing to do with it.

Blood. It had to be.

She'd been right when she'd stepped into the condo. She'd caught the scent of death after all.

Avoiding the side of the bed with the bloodstains, she moved in the other direction. The drum of her pulse pounded in her ears. She checked under the bed, between the mattress and box spring, the adjoining bathroom, determined not to miss any spot, no matter how unlikely—even the medicine cabinet.

Not finding anything in the bedroom—she probably wouldn't know if she saw something pertinent, but she needed to try—she crept down the hallway to the central part of the condo. A sound whispered from behind her. She jerked around and threw the flashlight's beam toward the noise as she hurriedly backed away, ramming her calf against a piece of furniture. Not seeing anything in the hall, she swung the light back around and illuminated the corner of a gray sectional where she'd banged her leg. Great. She was now hearing things. Still, even with no one out to get her, her heart continued to drum wildly as she edged around the sofa and stepped toward the kitchen. On seeing a desk in the dining area, she paused. Computer cables snaked across its surface and down the sides to disappear into the shadows. Nothing else rested across the tabletop. The police or detectives must have removed his computer. She almost walked away, believing any evidence they might have found was probably on the computer and already taken or destroyed. But that damn curiosity and need to know made her walk over to the desk and search for other possible, though dated evidence.

She opened the top two drawers. Only some sticky notes and a couple of pens. The very bottom drawer, much deeper than the others, stuck, and she closed and opened it several times, only managing to pry it by two inches. Something was wrong with it. Muttering to herself, she gave it one strong tug. It jerked open, the corner of it hitting her knee.

"Damn stupid thing!"

Swearing a couple more choice words, she rubbed her thigh and peered inside.

Empty.

Well, of course. What should she expect? She was running around inside a murder victim's condo, looking into things that she shouldn't be looking into. The police had come and gone days before, and they were professionals and knew what they were looking for when it came to evidence or clues.

She could be arrested for breaking and entering. But she needed answers. There had to be a tie between her and the victim. There was too much of a coincidence. The police knew it too, even though they'd been closed-lipped. Trying to get answers from them was ridiculous. They might think of her as some type of number, but she was a person deserving of the truth. Yeah, there was Ben Atkins and his warning about Luys. But he'd left her with no reason why she needed to back away from him.

Was she supposed to have blind faith because of a police officer's badge?

Shaking off her growing discontent, she searched the drawer, thinking there might be a false bottom. Nothing. Absolutely nothing. But what was she expecting? Evidence of his death jumping out at her saying, 'Here I am!'

Muttering under her breath, she turned to the kitchen next. The room took longer than the others. Too many pots, pans, and utensils. Several cupboards later, with zero proof of anything unusual, Avery moved across the floor on her knees to the cabinets beneath the sink. Probably the least likely place to look.

After moving a multitude of different cleaners and discovering zilch, she thought of searching inside the boxes but decided against it. The chances of him hiding something there were minuscule. Still, stubbornness, and nothing more, made her slide her fingers across the interior above the doors.

Frowning, she ran an index finger over some type of protrusion. She stilled. It didn't feel right. Hunching lower on her knees, she angled the flashlight into the cabinet and upward. Still unable to see, she used her fingers to feel around inside. Something was taped inside and several inches above the cabinet opening. A rectangular shape. Using a fingernail, she pried the object loose and sat back on her heels.

A thumb drive.

Okay. That's weird.

But smart. If someone was trying to hide anything of value, no one would think to look there.

She palmed the thumb drive before slipping it into

her pocket, then snapped off the light from her phone and moved through the rest of the condo, using her flashlight sparingly. Her remaining search felt anticlimactic. She didn't find anything significant in the living room.

A muffled bang carried through the room. Avery stilled, cocking her head to one side. The noise sounded as if it was from her own condo. For the last two days, she'd tried to ignore her heightened sense of hearing, making herself pretend it was all her imagination and that her life hadn't changed at all. She couldn't ignore her hearing any longer. She'd known something was seriously wrong before. She'd brushed it aside, but that had been a disservice to herself.

Frowning, she closed her eyes and focused, this time wanting the array of noise and distinct sounds to bombard her. She flinched as a multitude of sounds hit her from every area. Struggling against the onslaught, she focused on where the bang came from.

Then Luys' voice slammed into her head.

"Avery! Are you in there? Are you okay? Answer me!"

She hurried across the living room, thankful for how the carpet muffled her footsteps.

Why was he in her condo? Had something else happened?

As she reached the door, a thin layer of light lined one side of the entrance. She stiffened. The door was ajar. Unease crawled across her skin. She'd closed the door. Pivoting, she faced the living room and snapped on the switch on the wall. Light flared. She blinked against the glare as she fumbled for the pepper spray in the back of her pocket.

No one was in the room with her.

A sigh wafted in the air behind her, a whisper of breath against her hair.

Sucking oxygen into her lungs, she turned back to the door, her thumb on the nozzle.

Again no one. But she couldn't dispel the sense of someone having been in the condo with her.

She reached over to turn off the entrance's light for fear of drawing attention but paused.

The doorjamb. She hadn't noticed it when she'd first entered Harris' home because she'd been in the dark. But now—now—

Jesus. Someone had jimmied the lock and broken into the place before she'd even stepped through the threshold.

She'd been wandering through all the rooms, and someone could have easily been inside with her, watching her every move.

And Mayor? Was she the one who'd broken into the victim's condo?

If so, then why? More importantly, why would she goad Avery into searching the victim's rooms if she'd already been inside the place? Unless she was hoping Avery might find something she might have missed?

Avery traced the outline of the thumb drive in her pocket with a finger. That would explain the way the place had felt ransacked. Maybe it hadn't been the police or the murderer but Mayor all this time. And if that was the cause, maybe she was the killer.

But again, why? Why would she kill Noah Harris? Could she have killed the neighbor because he'd been keeping something from her?

Luys' voice boomed through the wall and into her head.

"Avery! Tell me you're okay!"

Then, "God's teeth. You have to be fine. I'd never be able to live with myself if anything happened to you."

Something was wrong.

Forgetting the door and Mayor, she slipped from the condo, careful of keeping to the shadows until she was several yards away. From there, she rushed around the building to her own condo and stumbled to a halt.

The door to her home stood wide open. Light from inside reflected onto the sidewalk and desert landscaping.

She rushed to the threshold but paused. "What the hell?"

Luys stood in the middle of her living room.

"Luys, what's wrong? What's going on?"

CHAPTER 11

Friday, August 22nd – 10:53 pm

At the sound of his name, Luys turned.

The porch light illuminated Avery standing in front of the entrance to her condo. Several wisps of hair fluttered around her flushed face from an outside breeze.

He quickly searched her features, the black jeans and t-shirt, the gray athletic shoes. No bruises. No scratches. "Are you okay?"

"I'm the one that should be asking you that." She remained outside on the condo's welcome mat.

He then noticed the small canister fisted in her hand and suspected it was a personal defense spray or taser of some type. "I was concerned when I knocked and you didn't answer. I thought of the murder and—"

"Reacted?"

"Yes."

"I'm fine. And safe."

But she didn't look fine. She looked winded and alarmed.

"Has something happened?"

"No," she quickly retorted.

She was lying. She was not good at it, but he did not pry further. Maybe in time, she would trust him.

"The door." Eyes widening, she ran one hand across the side of the threshold. The metal strike plate rested drunkenly at an angle, wood frayed along one section of the jamb, and both screws protruded from the side of the door at odd angles. "You broke it?" Her gaze flashed to him and back to the door. "Why?"

He grimaced. "I was concerned..."

She worried her lip as she stepped inside and attempted to shut the door. After the fourth try, she gave up and let the door creep open, leaving an inch-wide gap.

"It won't close," he stated the obvious. By overreacting, he had placed her in a vulnerable spot. He had also ruined the door to the point that repairing the jamb would require more than a screwdriver and a few extra screws. "I'll call a maintenance company."

"No, I already have one on my phone." As she dialed the number, she paced back and forth. Then she sank down on a living room chair and stared at the door. After a moment, she left a message. "I don't know how long they'll be."

"They might not respond until tomorrow."

"That's not going to work. I can't sleep here with the door broken." She worried her lip again. "Not when someone was just murdered."

"No, you can't."

"I know, it's—"

"Dangerous," they said simultaneously.

"I dislike the idea of you waiting here even if a company gets here within a few hours. You must stay at my place for the night. You'll be safe there. It's the least I can do."

She looked everywhere but at him as she stuffed her phone in the back pocket of her jeans. "I don't know. I can always get a room at a nearby hotel. There should be a vacancy."

"And an added expense. I have an extra room." He rubbed at the back of his neck. "I will, of course, pay for whatever damages that are incurred."

He should not be trying to convince her to stay under the same roof. Having her sleeping in the next room would try his self-restraint. He thought of the flawless complexion of her skin, her light blue eyes with flecks of gray, and the way her lips curved to one side when she smiled. Then there was her independence and a vulnerability she failed to shield completely. If he were not careful, he would find himself addicted, vanquished, undone. Many years of celibacy magnified this growing need and longing.

He needed to be stronger. His background and history demanded more of him.

None of this would have happened if he had remained calm. He should have waited, been patient, checked back on her instead of rampaging into her home. This caring for her was not good for either of them. It was dangerous. It was even deadly.

"At least stay until they can fix the door. It's not safe to be alone without the protection of a locked door. Not after..."

She searched his face with intense eyes. Something in his expression must have reassured her because she nodded. "Okay. Give me a second. I'll get a change of clothes."

After disappearing into her room, she came out

and patted a large bag slung over one shoulder. "Just a few valuables in case someone decides to enter and steal some things." She made a face. "If they want to take my silverware, they're welcome to it. Pretty much everything in here is replaceable. Thank God for insurance."

When she brushed past him into his condo, her scent wrapped around him while her proximity threw him off balance. He was not used to sharing his quarters with anyone, never mind a person of the opposite sex. No one had stepped over the threshold in this home other than an occasional home repair company. With Avery feet away, the rooms seemed far smaller than a few hours ago.

As she stepped deeper into his home, a glass case on a table against the wall caught her attention. She paused and peered inside. Luys stepped up beside her and remained silent as she stared down at the large silver cross on top of a deep red velvet cloth with a thick chain wrapped to one side. In its center rested a large, roughly faceted ruby about the size of a thumbprint. The design around the stone was well worn, but a person could distinguish several vines twining from a primitive face and down the cross' four arms. He suspected she found the face grotesque with the ruby protruding from its open mouth.

She glanced over to him. "This is really unusual."

"It has been in the family for a very long time."

"It's beautiful in an ugly sort of way."

"Thank you, I think." He smiled.

Avery chuckled. "Just being honest."

She leaned over the medallion. She probably found it strange that he had it under glass and a focal point in the room, but there had been no time to move it to a private part of the condo.

She turned and faced him. "Do you know how old it is?"

"No," he lied, deciding the truth would generate more questions from her and lies from him.

"Well, it looks like something you'd find in a museum. It has to be older than a good century. If I had to guess, I'd say the medieval period, but it could just as easily be a good replica of an artifact since I'm no historian. I'm sure it has a great deal of history if you have it protected under glass. Do you know much of its history?"

"No. I'm sure it is of little consequence," he lied again. "Our ancestors were a religious lot but not very adventurous."

As she continued to stare at the medallion, he took in her bowed head. Her auburn hair glowed like warm cinnamon against the light of a nearby lamp as it curved over her shoulder and flowed like liquid halfway down her back. Her t-shirt clung to her breasts and abdomen, while her black jeans, torn at one knee, clung lovingly to her thighs and hips. Her figure was curvy but athletic and a perfect fit in his arms.

He thought back to their kiss and its brevity. He wanted to kiss her again, but this time not light and fleeting, but rather filled with lust and need.

Her scent wrapped around him again. Sunlight, flowers, and a hint of something earthy. He stopped himself from moving closer, and the spell collapsed as she stepped into the center of the living room.

Avery dropped her bag by the sofa. "Oh, I forgot you had a kitten!"

Eyes softening and teeth flashing a smile, she scooped the long-haired tortoiseshell in her arms and rubbed the kitten's chin with an index finger. Then she paused, her hand hovering over the cat's bandaged tail as she glanced his way. "What's wrong with her?"

"She's fine now. They had to dock her tail at the vet."

"Why?"

"I found her on the side of the road on my way to Flagstaff. The vet seems to think someone threw her out of a moving car with the injuries she sustained. Clover will be fine, though. It turned out her tail was the only major damage that needed to be fixed."

A look of utter disgust washed across her delicate features. "Seriously. Who does that?"

"Not someone I would consider knowing." He sighed and shrugged. "There's much darkness and hate out there, all wrapped up in fear. I find the idea of doing such a thing unfathomable."

"And why the name Clover?"

"I like to think she found a four-leaf clover when I found her. Or maybe it's the other way around." With a self-deprecating smile, he shrugged again. But in truth, he'd always had a fondness for animals. They were honest and rarely killed their own.

She gently stroked Clover's head. The cat's purr rumbled from her tiny chest. "If you ever need someone to cat sit, I'd be more than happy."

"I might take you up on that," he replied, unable to take his gaze off the way she stroked the kitten. "Sometimes I have to travel for work. And I need to visit my brother one day soon. I have a fake rock in the gravel by the door with a key. You can let yourself in, and I'm sure Clover would want the company."

"Ahh, giving away secrets. You trust me not to steal anything in your place?" she teased with a smile.

His gaze lingered on the way she fondled Clover. "I have a good idea I can trust you. Cats are an excellent judge of character."

Her smile dimmed. "I used to have a dog."

He waited, hoping she'd reveal a bit about herself. He sensed she didn't open up to many people and was pleased when she expanded.

"His name was Dozer. A golden." She smiled fondly down at the cat. "We were the best of buddies for the longest time. Then the vet diagnosed him with congenital heart failure, and I eventually had to have him euthanized."

"I'm sorry. Pets become part of the family." He walked over and rubbed the kitten's ear with a finger and thumb. "And no interest in another?"

Her brow creased. "No. I got far too attached to him. I don't want to go through that pain again. I know he was only a dog but having another wouldn't be fair."

"Fair? Why?"

She flushed, looking disconcerted. "I don't have time for one. I'm always at work. A dog deserves to go out for walks. He deserves more—"

She abruptly stopped, shook her head, then stared up at him with an earnest expression and another emotion he couldn't read. Disappointment? Regret? He wasn't sure. Then something changed in their depths, and her hand stilled on the kitten.

His pulse broke into a full-blown gallop, and his

groin tightened. The auburn waves with cinnamon undertones framed a face both beautiful and vulnerable. Their fingers brushed as he took Clover from her hands and placed the kitten on the ground. When he rose, the distance between them somehow seemed to have diminished. Inches separated them, not feet.

She did not step away when he skimmed an index finger along several strands of hair by the long sweep of her neck. When he edged closer and brushed a thumb over her full bottom lip, she still didn't retreat. He noticed her hitch of breath, her shiver, and the almost indiscernible lift of her chin.

Desire, thick, palpable, and unmistakable, radiated from her eyes.

He dipped his head and caught her mouth in a slow, exploratory kiss—a glide of skin back and forth as their breath mingled.

Her fingers clutched his upper arm as she leaned into him, her breasts pressing against his chest before her hips molded to his. With her other hand, she grasped his nape and slid her fingers into his hair, urging his head lower.

"I've waited for so long..." he murmured against her lips.

"How long?" she breathed against his mouth.

"From the moment I saw you."

"Why didn't you do something—say something?"

"Because...because the timing was all wrong."

"Why do—"

He cut off her words with a deep kiss. He didn't want to talk, and he especially didn't want to think. He wanted to ignore his thoughts—the smart and ethical notion of walking away, of turning his back, of keeping away from Avery.

But...

He groaned and urged her closer. With a shaking hand, he ran a palm over her spine, down the dip at the small of her back, and still lower until he palmed her ass. He couldn't get enough of her.

She moaned, lifting her other hand to anchor his head as she met his kiss with equal fever, fitting her hips perfectly against his.

Before he lost it, he drew back, dragged in a ragged breath, and muttered against her temple. "This isn't a good idea."

"To hell with good ideas."

At her words and the heat in her eyes, his chest expanded, his erection thickened, and intense hunger swept through his insides, painful and exciting at the same time. At the way her fingers massaged his scalp, curled through his hair, she'd turned him into a junky and complete addict for her touch, for her kiss.

She tugged his head down again to meet his lips in a hot, mind-altering kiss. He did not fight her, did not push her away. He did what he promised he would not do.

He caved to his body's needs, to the longing of being with Avery, of feeling connected to another human, no matter how brief.

She pulled back. "Your bedroom?"

He didn't reply. Instead, he tugged Avery toward the hallway, down the hall, and into his bedroom. He did not bother with lights. The moonlight would be sufficient.

He then gently draped her onto the bed, where her

hair fanned across the comforter. The mattress dipped as he settled over her body and kissed her again.

She groaned into his mouth and arched her hips against his. His whole body shook with need as he caught the hem of her shirt. She lifted her arms to help him tug it free. The garment fell to the side. Her bra came next. Moonlight, though faint, caressed her body in silver-blue light and illuminated the beauty of her breasts, their fullness, their taut peaks.

More clothes followed. Then there was skin. Blessed beautiful skin. Silken legs against his rougher thighs and calves. Arms, stomach, hips, everywhere gorgeous, impossibly erotic, silky skin. Nothing compared to a woman's body, a woman's passion, or a woman's touch. A woman like Avery.

He caressed the sweep of her hips, the sharp angles of her knees, elbows, shoulders, and the softer curves that molded over his hard body. Every move and touch from him dragged a groan, a sigh, a gasp of pleasure from her lips. She made him feel like an expert when he was a fraud and an amateur.

Cradled between Avery's legs, resting the bulk of his weight on his elbows, he stared down at her lips, parted enough to show the edge of her teeth and tongue. They were perfect. Swollen. Kissable... *God's teeth*. Jaw clenched, slowly, carefully he entered her. As his gaze drifted to her eyes, he eased deeper into her body. She was tight, fitting around him in such a way that it tore the breath from his lungs. He was so close to coming, and he had done nothing, not really.

Eyes widening, Avery gasped, then stilled.

He bunched the sheets within a fist. "Am I hurting you?"

"No... no..." Avery breathed, shocked he would think that. "It's just that—It's just that you feel so good!" she admitted in a whisper as she adjusted to his thickness and felt like she was going to explode with pleasure.

He touched his brow to hers, the act surprisingly intimate and tender, before kissing her temple, the corner of her lips, then nibbling an erotic path along her jawline to the pulse below her ear for a moment. Then he returned to her mouth, sliding his tongue inside, wet, hot, urgent, and breathtaking.

When he adjusted his hips again, she sucked in a breath and arched again into him, loving how he filled her, moved inside her.

Then matching each beat of her heart, his pace quickened. She grabbed his shoulders, dug her fingers into his skin, and wrapped both legs around his hips, gasping at how the movement pulled him deeper into her body.

Slowly, he moved, each thrust and retreat measured and expert in dragging out her body's response. She wanted to climb inside him. Desire clutched at her insides, stoked a mind-numbing need. She cried out, clawing at his shoulders, his hair, his back, tightening her legs around him as a climax roared through her, sending waves ricocheting through her limbs and tightening her body until she thought she'd explode from the pleasure.

Seconds later, he clutched her hips, his fingers almost painful as he gasped and shuddered, his back slick with sweat bowing beneath her palms.

Her pounding heart calmed, the blinding hot passion moments before eased, then abruptly cooled. Luys twisted to the side and pulled her along with him to where her head rested against his shoulder. Being in his embrace felt too good, too intimate, and wrong. Avery eased away from his body and stared up at the ceiling. The enormity of what she had done smacked her hard. There was no alcohol, no traumatic event, or moment that gave her an excuse...

CHAPTER 12

Avery didn't want to hurt him. She honestly didn't. She'd sensed from the beginning Luys wasn't a person who slept with someone lightly. He seemed old-fashioned. It wasn't the formal way he spoke, but something deeper.

"What's wrong?"

She turned and found Luys on his side and propped up by an elbow. She smiled, then realized it didn't look convincing and tried to make it reach her eyes. "Nothing at all."

Shifting to her side so she could fully face him, she skimmed a hand over his waist and hip. "Thank you."

His brows arched. "I don't think anyone's ever thanked me before."

She chuckled. "Then you've been meeting the wrong women." She tapped his chin, wanting to keep things light, safe. "You were perfect. I couldn't have asked for a better partner."

"Well, I thank you too." His teeth flashed.

"Seriously." She inched far enough away so she could get a good look at him. "I needed to feel alive, at least for a little while. You made that happen for me."

Moonlight from the window deepened the angles of his face but caught against the light of his eyes. Something shifted in their depths and added a new intensity as he rubbed a thumb back and forth along the slope of her shoulder. Her breath caught in her throat. He was truly a beautiful man and not because the lighting in the room masked his imperfections. She'd seen him beneath Arizona's harsh rays. The prominent cheekbones, square chin, and long lashes added to a face she found breathtaking, particularly now when he was naked and mere inches away. A bit more frazzled than she liked to admit, she glanced away from those amazing eyes but took in the hard line of his jaw, the protrusion of his Adam's apple and collarbone. Every nuance of muscle beneath his golden skin drew her eye until her gaze landed on the disfigurement on his chest.

Suddenly she stilled. A vertical scar ran several inches down the middle of his chest, and another intersected it below his collarbone and above his nipples.

Images flashed inside her head. The dark and angry incisions between her breasts, her naked image in the bathroom mirror. Scars strangely healed as if they happened years and not days ago.

With her scars came her strange, amplified hearing that was beyond what was normal, and with it, no plausible explanation as to why. Those same scars looked exactly like Luys'.

Impossible, but his disfigurement glared back at her.

She scrambled into a sitting position and pulled the sheet up to cover her breasts. "What happened to you?"

"What do you mean?"

"Your chest."

Still resting on an elbow, he lifted his free hand and briefly ran a thumb across the jagged marks. "It happened a long time ago."

"When you were a child?"

"No. It was a time when I was naïve and had a very different vision of my future."

"What do you mean by that?" *What type of crazy answer was that?*

He shifted to where shadows clung beneath his brows and shielded his expression. "It's not important."

"No. No, I think it is. I have the same type of scars." This discussion was feeling surreal and far different from moments before. Any trust she'd held for Luys was quickly dissolving into moondust.

Luys pushed himself up until his back rested against the headboard. He dragged the sheet up over his waist. "That's impossible."

"Impossible? I don't think so." With the sheet bunched in her fist and up against her breasts, she reached over and turned on a bedside lamp with her other hand. She swiveled back around and dropped the sheet, making sure the light hit her chest. She fought back the temptation to cover herself, feeling shockingly exposed as if she'd landed naked in the middle of a university lecture hall. "I've got scars that look like yours. They might not be as faded, but that's not the insane part of the whole story. This happened over a week ago. Some crazy person operated on me. The worse part of all this is that there's no plausible reason to cut me open and stitch me back up. The doctors couldn't find anything wrong with me or why someone would do anything like this. There may be things wrong with me, but I know my heart's perfectly fine. I had a battery of tests to make sure."

She didn't mention her amplified hearing. It was too strange for even her to say it aloud.

A muscle pulsed on the side of his jaw. "It doesn't make sense."

"What? That someone did this to me or that we have the same scarring?"

"Both." He drew back, shadows now fully obscuring his face.

Avery's brow dipped. "Of course it doesn't make sense. None of it does. Maybe it's not one person but some sick cult."

"You don't know that."

"Of course, I don't!" She glanced down at her chest, and the marks on her skin blurred from the tears she couldn't keep at bay. "I don't understand any of it. Who or why? We have nothing in common that I can think of other than being neighbors. You said your scars happened a long time ago, right?"

"Yes—"

"What happened to you? I've looked at current and past heart surgeries on the internet. Our marks don't look like anything I've seen in pictures or videos."

"I haven't talked to anyone about it."

"Why?"

His mouth tightened. Then he finally admitted, "It's painful, and I've never trusted anyone with the truth."

When he didn't elaborate, she asked, "That's all you're going to say?"

He opened his mouth but then snapped it shut and looked away.

She scrambled to the edge of the bed, dragging the sheet with her and covering her body up to her neck. "Did you do this to me?"

"No!"

He jerked his head back in her direction. He honestly looked horrified. She didn't think he could be that big of an actor. "Can you prove it?"

"Prove it? I don't have proof. But I would never hurt another human or living being. Not intentionally. I was raised to value all life."

"Anyone can say that."

He looked up at the ceiling for a long moment. Then he met and held her gaze. He opened his mouth, closed it, and then rolled his shoulders as if deliberating about what he was going to say next. The silence lengthened between them until he admitted, "I was once a priest."

She stared at him in disbelief. "A priest?"

Clover jumped on the bed, trotted over, and rubbed against his thigh. Luys scooped up the kitten in one large hand. His touch was gentle as he caressed the animal behind her ears and cupped her against his chest. "Yes. For several years I was an ordained Catholic priest. Other than family, you're the only one else I've admitted this to."

Reading the uncertainty in his gaze, she could tell the admission was difficult for him. Maybe he expected her to judge him. Maybe he'd been judged before and found wanting? The idea of him as a priest was both shocking and made sense at the same time.

The way he'd made love to her had been different from any other man in her past. As if the act was more than sex. She couldn't forget how he'd held her, how he'd trembled, or how the expression in his eyes had revealed absolute wonder. Never had she experienced such reverence. A man wouldn't act that way if they were a deadly psychopath, would they?

She thought of the cross beneath the glass case in the other room. Instinct told her that a man like Luys would never succumb to such dark violence. But he could be protecting a killer, someone far more dangerous than himself. Still, the situation and him didn't feel right. "You know something more. Something about the murder and what happened to me. Also, there's a tie between the both of us you're not willing to tell me about."

"I didn't say that."

A shutter seemed to fall across his gaze. He was hiding something.

"What do you know? I deserve answers!"

He finally admitted, "If I tell you anything, I might be putting you in even more danger."

She gaped at him, shocked he admitted to her being in danger. She was equally stunned at his unwillingness to explain himself or give her some—any—information. Obviously, she'd read more into his feelings.

She scrambled off the bed. Her clothes. Where the hell had she thrown them? She searched wildly on the floor for her underwear. After finding them tossed over in the corner, she got her bra and shirt on within seconds.

Luys set the kitten to one side, jumped from the bed, and hurried around the bed toward her. "I'm sorry you're upset. I—"

"Upset? Seriously? I can't believe you said that." She backed away from his large and very naked body as she glared at him. "Don't come near me."

Yeah, he looked concerned, shaken even, but she wanted nothing to do with him. More importantly, she didn't know what he was hiding.

"I want to protect you, but being with me endangers your life at the same time."

"Great. You just admitted having sex with you can get me hurt." With fumbling hands, she scrambled into her jeans and shirt and let sarcasm drip from her words. "This has been absolutely wonderful."

Then she grabbed her socks and running shoes and rushed from the room while yelling over one shoulder, "And don't do me any favors! I don't want your *protection*."

"Avery!"

She ignored Luys as she fled down the hall and into the living room, but by the sound of his heavier steps, he was rapidly narrowing the distance between them.

She whirled around and jabbed a shoe at him. "Keep away from me."

He lifted both hands in the air and stopped advancing toward her. "Don't leave."

"Can you tell me who did this to me?"

When he didn't answer, she bit out, "Then there's no reason to stay."

She stuffed her shoes and socks into the overnight bag she'd left by the sofa. She grabbed the strap to swing it around her shoulder. It wasn't much of a weapon, but she'd use it on Luys or anyone else that got too close. When she reached the door, his next words made her hand pause on the doorknob.

"Stay away from Mayor."

She whirled around. "What? Mayor?"

"Yes."

"Why?"

"Don't trust her. She's dangerous."

"You can't be serious. That's ridiculous." She shook her head. "Why do you say that? Is she out to get me because she's a crazy ex-lover? Is she the one that made those marks on your chest?"

"She hasn't touched me, but she's hurt others I have loved."

He was saying half-truths and being deliberately ambiguous.

"Just how dangerous?" Avery made a noise of distress against the back of her throat. "She wouldn't have the strength to overpower a man twice her size."

Mayor couldn't be the one who'd attacked her. It would have been too much of a struggle and taken too long to drag Avery into the condo without someone seeing her. Then Avery thought about her last conversation with the other woman. Mayor's words, her whole crazy talk about being psychic and 'knowing' nothing would happen to Avery. She frowned. Maybe the woman was off her head and not eccentric as Avery had first thought? Maybe she was more than dangerous? Maybe she was a killer?

But why would an adult woman in her prime go after a man? Money? Revenge? It would have to be personal from what she'd heard about the killing. Avery had nothing in common with Mayor. What relationship they did have was a superficial friendship. Nothing deep or meaningful. Her hand tightened around the strap of her bag. That wasn't necessarily true. There was a tie between both women.

Luys.

All this time, she'd thought their meeting had been random and with a shared addiction to coffee. But what if Mayor intentionally followed her to the coffee shop day after day, and nothing about their meeting was coincidental? But that was months before she'd even talked to Luys. That didn't make any sense.

"Is it Mayor? Is she the one you're protecting?"

"I can't protect her anymore. She has gone too far."

"Who is she?" Her stomach roiled with unease. "Are you married to each other?" She really didn't want to know. If she walked out the door, she could pretend none of this conversation was happening. But did she dare do that? When not knowing could be dangerous, even deadly?

A muscle ticked along the edge of his jaw. "My sister."

Avery took an involuntary step back and found herself saying inanely, "You don't look anything alike."

"And we're nothing alike." Bitterness thickened his voice. "Maybe once a long time ago, but no longer. Each year we grow further apart to the point we have nothing in common other than the parents who sired us."

"Then why are you protecting her?"

"I don't know what you mean."

"I always thought I was a terrible liar, but you're just as bad or worse." She hugged her bag against her side and lifted a lip into a sneer. He wouldn't tell her the truth about anything she asked. It was pointless to even try. She'd been stupid to ignore Ben's warning to keep away from him. "I don't want to see you again. You come near me, and I'll call the police."

She could call the police, but then she realized she had nothing—no proof, no motive—not one shred of evidence when it came to Luys or his sister and any involvement with Noah Harris or her attack. All she had were words and suspicions.

She didn't wait around for a response but whipped around and slammed the door behind her.

CHAPTER 13

Two minutes after she stepped into her condo, a repair company showed up at her battered door. Thank God. An hour later, she was inside alone with the door safely locked. The jamb needed a good paint job, but the door worked fine.

Still, she couldn't calm the frantic beat of her heart. The distance between Luys and her place might be short, but it didn't stop her from thinking of Mayor, Luys, or someone else leaping out from the shadows or bushes to attack her. She wasn't paranoid. God knows she had enough cause to think someone was going to get her.

After dropping her bag on the sofa, she yanked off her dirty clothes and dug through her jeans pockets as she walked over to the washer and dryer in the hallway. Every pocket was empty.

No. Impossible. With shaking fingers, she rummaged through them again on the off chance she might have missed it. No, no, damn it! Nothing!

Where had the thumb drive gone? She couldn't have lost it! Not after all the trouble she'd gone through.

Muttering a few choice words, she put her clothes back on and retraced her steps to the front door. She had to go back. There was no other option. She wanted—no needed—to know what was on that thumb drive.

Maybe she should call him to have him look for it. No. She didn't want to alert him. Even though she suspected he'd respect her privacy, she wasn't willing to risk the chance that he might look into what was in the drive and start asking her questions.

Groaning inwardly, she rushed back to his condo, wiped her hands on her thighs, and lifted a hand to his doorbell. She didn't get a chance to hit it before the door jerked open, and Luys stood in the entryway naked, except for a pair of black athletic shorts clinging to his hips.

"What is it? Are you alright?" he asked in a deep, husky voice.

"Yes, I'm fine." She jerked her head up and down, trying to ignore the heat of embarrassment in her face. "I forgot something. It was in my pants pocket. I must have dropped it."

She glanced down, this time pausing on the scars across his chest. They were faded and paler than the rest of his skin but thicker and appeared more jagged than hers. Shivering, she forced herself to meet his gaze.

He stared back, his gaze dark, unreadable as a muscle in his jaw flexed. Then he said somewhat grudgingly, "What happened to my chest was so long ago that it feels like another life."

"What does that mean?"

His lips firmed. "You wouldn't understand."

"Try me."

Luys rubbed the heel of his hand against his temple, then shook his head.

Her gaze narrowed. Still, he wouldn't relent. She wanted to threaten him with going to the police but now wasn't the time. She needed to get the thumb drive and get out of his place safely and with all her body parts intact. She could have read him all wrong. He could be dangerous, deadly even, and she might be stupid for coming back. Information wasn't worth her death.

He stood back and let her in.

She stepped past him and into his condo and took a chance on that stupidity. Thank goodness it took seconds to locate the drive. She found it under an end table in the living room. She'd been so busy trying to chuck her pants with the help of Luys that she must have dropped it and kicked it aside without knowing. As she rushed back toward the front door, her gaze caught on the glass case with the medallion. A simple cross encased beneath glass. But she didn't think it was so simple. There was something more to it, and she didn't think her imagination was running wild. Something was off—something about the age, the cross's mysticism, and how it was tied to Luys. But what? Did she dare dig deeper? She was already pushing her luck with sneaking into condos of murder victims.

Could it all be tied together?

Shivering, she muttered a goodbye as she reached the threshold. Before she managed a full escape, Luys called out, "Avery!"

She turned around in the doorway, met his gaze, and waited.

He looked about to say something, then shook his head. "Never mind."

She snapped her chin into a nod and finally, truly escaped.

Once back home with the door locked and the thumb drive safely on her coffee table, she took a shower. She didn't need a drink or sleeping pill to get her through the night. She rested a hand against the tile wall and bowed her head as the hot water streamed over her head, neck, and shoulders. Exhaustion slammed through her body as steam rose around her. Sleep. She could use some. Her brain was foggy. Maybe two minutes max to rest her eyes, to clear her thoughts. To hell with thumb drives, killers, and things that went bump in the night. She needed a moment to escape.

Quickly, she dried off, flung herself on the bed, and let a cool silken sheet drape over her body. Sighing, she closed her eyes briefly. She then promptly woke up to light streaming into the bedroom and across her face.

Groaning, she flung a hand against her eyes, then turned away from the sun's glare and grabbed for her phone. Her thigh muscles protested with the movement. She didn't want to think of the reason why, or with whom.

5:54 a.m.

She was still exhausted but strangely alert. The conditioner kicked on, and cool air flowed into the room, ruffling the open drapes. She hadn't even thought to close the blinds. Voices from outside drifted into the room. One male, another female, both distinct.

"The last thing I want to deal with is my ass of a boss. The way he talks down to Josie and me is disgusting."

"Then look for another job."

"That's easy for you to say. You have a job you like. I might not be a realtor but working accounting in real estate is almost as bad. The market is crazy, with prices skyrocketing. But no one wants to sell their house right now."

They sounded like they were arguing right outside her window. Frowning, she dropped the phone on her nightstand and hurriedly put on a t-shirt and underwear. The couple needed to move their business behind closed doors. She edged toward the window, peered outside, but didn't see anyone.

"You're always complaining. For once, just once, find something nice to say."

"And you're a complete jerk, you know that?"

Avery swore they were talking inches from her window. Still unable to see anyone, she pressed closer to the glass and then noticed a couple down the walkway and standing by the next building. They were over 100 yards away at the very least.

Impossible. But it had to be them. She could see no one else anywhere near, and their words matched the movement of their lips. She opened the window, the scrape of metal against metal hitting her ears. The volume of their voices increased. She backed away. Suddenly, tires on asphalt joined their voices. Not from one car but many. A leaf blower added to the medley. The noise rose in intensity, screaming into her eardrums.

"Stop it!"

The sounds continued to pound against her head. She put her hand to her ears and squeezed, all the while shaking her head. When she thought she couldn't take it any longer, the sounds rolled to a crescendo and abruptly ended. For a wild moment, she thought she'd gone and completely lost her hearing from the deafening silence. Then she noticed the gentle hum of the air conditioner.

Something was terribly wrong. It wasn't humanly possible to pick up those sounds in such glaring detail. Did she dare talk to a doctor? No. She quickly nixed the idea. A medical professional would think she was nuts. But then she bounced back to thinking it might be a good idea. She didn't have to reveal the truth or real reason. Maybe do a different spin. Say she couldn't hear as well as usual? Maybe a professional could tell her if there was anything physically wrong.

She grabbed her phone from her bedside table and did a quick search, then realized it was Saturday and doctor's offices were closed. There was no way she could make an appointment now. She doubted anyone would consider hearing loss an emergency. Again, a roadblock.

Swearing several four-letter words under her breath, she tossed her phone on the bed, then grabbed a hair tie and scraped her hair back into a ponytail. She was beginning to realize the person behind her attack and the experiment on her—that was the only way she could think to describe it—could have altered her hearing. There was no other explanation. The coincidence was too much. But like everything else that had happened this week, it was all conjecture. No facts, no truths. She'd had a whole week of nothing.

Monday she'd go back to work, and she was no closer to the truth. The police were a dead end. At least for her. They weren't telling her a thing. But they knew something. They had to. They must have found something in the neighbor's condo. Then there was Luys—

The thumb drive!

There had to be something on it! Why else hide it?

From the bedroom, she rushed down the hall, grabbed the thumb drive, and strode into the guest bedroom, where she sat down in front of the small desk by the window. She clicked her laptop and impatiently waited for it to boot up. She slipped the drive into the side and waited for any virus warnings.

Nothing.

Four folders. She started with the one labeled pictures, not knowing what to expect. Several snapshots were of temples. She couldn't tell from what country. None of the images were labeled. She moved down the page, clicking each thumbnail to enlarge. Cocking her head to one side, she hadn't expected anything like this—ruins of old temples and primitive architectural structures. At the next image, her fingers tightened on her mouse, and she sucked in a breath—a cartoonish picture of a tribesman cutting into the chest of another, a heart in one hand. Three more, even though only colored drawings, were equally gruesome looking. All were depictions of human sacrifices. But at the same time, she got the impression they were historical depictions from the clothing on each figure.

What was Noah Harris doing hiding something like this? So far, it seemed pointless.

She didn't like where this was going with all the grotesque pictures, but that didn't stop her from moving to the next folder labeled 'info.' One document inside contained three pages of links. After clicking on one, a video popped up, and a camera filmed the interior of *Teotihuacan*, a temple on the outskirts of Mexico City.

The commentator described the building material, the obsidian tools discovered there, and the system of complex buildings. She went through each link and found more historical information about Aztec culture and everyday life and the more important deities of their religion: *Huitzilopochtli, Tlaloc, Tonatiuh, Tezcatlipoca, Chalchiuhtlicue*… She couldn't pronounce 99 percent of them. What did these gods have to do with anything?

And why all this research? What was he trying to learn?

There couldn't be a tie between her, Noah Harris, and the rituals performed by the Aztec centuries before. Any correlation was beyond ludicrous.

It had to be…

Because that would mean someone was out there reenacting some sick ceremony. But still…there were sadistic, crazy people out there, ones who had no sense of right or wrong.

The air conditioner kicked on again, brushing the back of her neck. A shiver raced down the length of her spine. She glanced up from the computer and looked out the window that overlooked the parking lot. A man wheeled a stack of boxes on a bright orange metal gurney toward a moving van parked out front. A company name and logo were embossed on his shirt. But was he really with a moving company? Maybe he was hiding behind a uniform to wander through the complex without raising anyone's interest.

Okay, she was acting super paranoid.

She forced herself from looking at the mover and wondering about his background and back to the computer and the thumb drive's contents.

Another few articles explained the motivation behind sacrificing other tribesmen and children. One went into great depth of several ceremonies and how it was likely that the Aztec practiced a form of ritual cannibalism and considered the heart as the most prized organ when it came to devouring their victims.

Avery's chest tightened, and her stomach did a little flip. She whispered, "This is freaking disgusting and terrifying."

Placing her palm against her chest and feeling the rapid beat of her heart, she took a couple of deep, slow breaths to calm herself down. No one had stolen her heart. Everything was functioning fine. Well, except for her hearing…

She frowned and wanted to turn off the computer and look away at the gruesome pictures, but the sad part was that she was as morbidly curious as drivers slowing down in search of the victims in a car accident.

The next three links took her to sites that were as gruesome as the last. This was making her feel like she'd have been better off watching a horror movie.

What she didn't get was why Noah was hiding this. It seemed kind of strange to be murdered for several links to websites. Anyone could pull up what was in this folder.

Unless there was something far more dangerous in the folders she hadn't yet seen… The idea made her click on the next folder.

Great. More articles…and probably just as morbid.

But after a few minutes, Avery realized, even though they were as morbid as the others, these new links were far different. All were from reputable newspapers on murders in this state and several others. Two hours of reading, and she'd found one correlation with all the deaths: they were all violent, bloody, and detailed some type of decapitation or removal of human organs. Other articles mentioned crosses found at several murder sites along with sharp knife-like objects. The Aztec weapons were usually made of obsidian and ranged from clubs with embedded blades to short-range weapons used by jaguar warriors and carved knives specifically for their sacrificial ceremonies.

So it would seem someone was out there traveling the country and carving up people for some sadistic purpose. But why crosses? The two didn't match. Christianity and Aztec beliefs at each scene?

The thought of crosses made her think of Luys and the medallion in his living room, and her stomach did another nosedive. He couldn't be tied to what Noah was looking into, could he? Then she thought of his warning about his sister.

What was Noah getting close to? Had he been murdered for it?

But WHY? Maybe he had learned the identity of the killer in the articles he'd compiled on his thumb drive?

Pain pounded against her skull. Wonderful. A full-blown headache, and it wasn't even close to lunchtime!

From what she could tell from the next folder, the numbered documents continued Noah Harris's research notes.

Frowning and rubbing at her temples with a thumb and finger, she glanced back out the window that overlooked the parking lot. The moving truck was still outside. This time two men rolled a sectional across the sidewalk toward the ramp. Recognizing the sofa, she sucked in a breath. Hands suddenly clammy, she wiped her palms across her bare legs. The sectional was from the murder victim's condo. They were moving his items out of the condo.

Hurriedly donning a pair of shorts and adding a bra under her t-shirt, she flung her feet into a pair of flip-flops and rushed from the condo. She needed to calm down. Right now, she probably looked a sight, with wild hair and equally wild eyes.

She veered down the walkway and around the building toward the condo. A door stood open, and another mover wheeled out a load of boxes on a dolly. A woman, petite, round, and with a shock of orange hair, trotted behind him as they walked toward her. Avery abruptly stopped and drew in a steadying breath and then another because the first didn't seem to ease the pounding of her heart, and she was afraid if she didn't rein it in, she'd come across as a psychopath to the woman.

Avery waved a hand and drew to a stop. "Excuse me?"

The woman's pencil-thin brows drew together as her eyes narrowed. She slowed and said in a hostile voice, "What? If you're here like everyone else for a story—" The tightness around her mouth eased, and she stopped in front of Avery. Though, her gaze still held a light of suspicion as she eyed Avery's flip-flops, shorts, and t-shirt. "You're not a reporter, are you?"

"No, just a neighbor." She rocked back on her heels. Now that she was here, she didn't know how to start, but then she decided to dive in. "Are you a relation to Noah?"

"Yes." The woman's lips firmed, and distinct moisture clung to her eyes. "He was my brother."

"I'm so sorry for your loss. I didn't know Noah, but I'm sure he'll be greatly missed. We share a wall, and I wish I'd heard something—anything—so I would have known to call the police." Avery shook her head, feeling herself grow emotional from the woman's evident grief and pain. "I can't imagine what you're going through…."

"Well, it sure hasn't been fun. Somehow reporters found my phone number, and they've been inundating me with call after call. They're like rabid dogs with a bone."

"I'm sorry." Even knowing she kept on repeating herself, Avery didn't know what else to say. "I'm sure they're exasperating the whole situation with your brother."

"Well, I should have expected it. After all, Noah was a reporter himself. But he wasn't like some of these yahoos trying to get a story from me or making up things about his past." The redhead blinked rapidly, but her eyes continued to water. "You might have read some of his articles in the local paper. He works for the *Arizona Daily News*, but he was investigating something on the side." The guarded look in the woman's eyes eased. "You weren't the only one. No one else heard anything. That's what the police are telling me. They haven't helped one bit."

Tell me about it. "They must know something."

The woman grunted. "I don't know! I'm feeling like a nag. I keep on calling them for any news, but nothing. It's like they're hiding something or don't give a shit."

"Do you know what or who he was investigating?"

The woman squeezed her eyes shut and blinked

rapidly to clear her eyes. "He never said. It was something that made him pretty agitated, though. He was all hyped up, saying that he had something that was going to blow everyone's minds and that he needed proof. Otherwise, no one would believe him."

"You don't—you don't think what he was looking into had anything to do with his death, do you?"

"Yes. I'm positive. I've told the police that. Noah told me he was getting pretty close to finding out the who and what."

Avery stiffened. She hadn't expected such conviction, particularly to a stranger, but there was no masking the bitterness in the twist of her lips or narrowed eyes.

When Avery opened her mouth to ask more, Noah's sister lifted a hand to forestall her. "No more. I can't handle this. It's rough enough as it is, but all these questions. I know you mean well, but enough."

"Yes—yes, of course." Avery backed away. "Sorry to bother you."

Shaking her head and wiping at her nose, the other woman pivoted and retreated into Noah's condo, leaving Avery to feel like a complete ass. She hadn't intended to make the woman cry.

Avery hurried back into her condo, unable to shake off the woman's grief. Life was too painful. She couldn't remember the last time she'd felt any joy or happiness. Did it even exist?

It had to. She'd witnessed the emotion in other people: the wonder in a child's face, the delight in an elderly woman's smile, and the pleasure in a couple's gaze. And if she was truthful to herself, she'd experienced it herself when she'd thought life held meaning.

Shaking off such thoughts, which would only make her feel worse, she turned her focus back to Noah Harris and returned to her computer, where she searched for anything to do with the reporter.

There. Several links to previous articles at the *Arizona Daily News*, all reputable and fact-based. She clicked through several pages and paused on one particular link. Paranormal phenomena. She frowned. She didn't like where this was going…

This article was also fact-based. According to Noah Harris, there were people out there who considered themselves modern-day vampires, but instead of draining their victims of blood, they depleted their victims psychically until a husk of a person remained. This was also according to the people Harris was researching.

Several pages later, she found another article on Aztec history and folklore of blood draining and rituals people believed would lengthen a human's life.

She again thought of Luys. He didn't seem like a psychopath and couldn't possibly be running around killing people, could he? She was already aware that sleeping with him was clouding her judgement. He didn't seem manipulative or controlling… And he'd had many an opportunity to kill her. Hell, she'd been naked, vulnerable, and under him. A person couldn't get more vulnerable than that. But then he'd warned her of his sister. Could Mayor be as dangerous as Luys was making out? Could Harris' research have pointed in Mayor's direction?

No, that didn't make sense. The person would have to have superior strength to overtake Harris. Mayor was a woman and looked more fragile than herself. Unless an illegal substance had been involved. A little date rape drug, like Special K or GHB, in his drink? Or maybe she'd attacked him while he'd been sleeping, slammed something into his head before he even had a chance to react?

The woman was odd at times. But to rip out his insides? All because of some Aztec ritual? Which led Avery to wonder what type of ritual or ceremony led someone to believe it could lengthen a person's life?

Obviously, someone crazy.

Avery shivered. This was getting too freaky.

"Okay, reel it in, Avery," she breathed into the room. "Maybe this Harris was off in the head." But she couldn't seem to slow the wild beat of her pulse. Too many horror movies from her childhood stoked a fear that she couldn't stuff under some bed or hide in a closet.

He'd been asking too many questions—questions that got him murdered.

Now she was starting to ask questions. Word could get out to the wrong person. The same person Noah must have contacted. But she hadn't seen any names in his notes. Was that because it might have been too dangerous?

The biggest question—was he the end of the killings, or could she be next?

CHAPTER 14

Sunday, August 24ᵗʰ – 4:32 pm

Luys hadn't locked the door to his condo. He hadn't thought there would be a need. He had been gone less than five minutes and fifty yards away to retrieve his phone from his car.

After he closed the front door behind him, he realized he wasn't alone. A woman moved toward him from the dining area. A woman he both loved and hated. There had never been any half-measures between them. She fisted a hand over the top of a cloth-backed chair beside the table.

"Mayor." His words were barely above a whisper. "I don't want to see you. I don't want anything to do with you."

His sister's fingers dug deeper into the maroon padding of the chair. She was just as coldly beautiful. The silken and deep brown dress flowed over her sleek body, caressed her curves and sharp angles, and floated several inches from the ground, where her black painted toes in flat sandals peeked from the hem. The garment emphasized the pale, smooth texture of her skin and silver-gold hair that flowed almost to her waist. He searched her face, the strong angles of her cheeks, jaw, and nose, the unlined brow, the lips, normally full and wide like his own, now drawn into a thin line of anger. It was then he realized the hardness to her face, the coldness to her eyes had intensified. Emotionally and spiritually, he understood the young girl he once knew had died long ago in Spain. Darkness, self-gratification, apathy, and the need to crush anyone in her path had turned her into a dangerous adversary.

"I think differently. I think it is about time we face each other." A flash of rage flared in her icy-blue eyes, darkening the silver into swirls of smoke and turning them into a strange incandescent purple, as she came to a stop.

With the distance of the living room between them, he waited, expecting the worst. When Mayor's temper flared, there was no controlling it. They'd tried once to stop her, but he and Gabriel had failed. He knew she was in Scottsdale to seek vengeance against him. His brother had been her previous target. Somehow, with the grace of God, she had left Spirit Lake without killing Gabriel and his wife. Because of a child—the love of an eleven-year-old girl. He once thought Mayor incapable of love until he had learned of her fascination with Gabriel's stepdaughter.

Even though she did not immediately attack, he did not relax. Given time, she would. She always did. "You have always been good at hiding in plain sight. One of your many talents." His lip curled. "But I knew you'd eventually show yourself. You have never been the most patient of the three of us."

"Don't give me that tone. You sound too much like Gabriel. I expected the worst from him, but not you. Luys, we were once close. How could you do what you did to me? It was Gabriel, yes? He turned you against me."

His hands balled into fists as he forced back the guilt. He would not feel remorseful, not with the horrors she had wreaked against the people around her. "He did no such thing. You gave neither one of us a choice. You were about to expose all of us because of your disgusting acts, but that was not the reason. Your rage, it is explosive, has darkened your soul into something unrecognizable. No one can reach you any longer. We had to stop you before you killed and mutilated another."

Her nostrils flared. "Again, you sound like Gabriel! But I do not believe you about his influence on you. I am sure he wanted me dead, yes?" Her eyes darkened further until they were rimmed with blood red. Her lip curled to one side into a semblance of a smile. "But he did not stop me. I am back now, more powerful than either of you." Mayor brushed platinum strands over her shoulder. She lifted her chin, her stance regal. "You and Gabriel always think I am the estúpida one of the three. I am far from estúpida. I am so much smarter than the two of you. How else can you explain that I am standing in front of you, yes? I can easily crush you."

Luys stepped toward Mayor. "Are you threatening me? Is that how bad it has become between us?"

"Bad?" Mayor snorted. "It was bad the moment Gabriel buried me in that cave and you went along with it!" She moved closer until two yards separated them.

He braced himself, expecting her to launch herself at him. When she didn't, he asked, "Did you touch the neighbor?"

"What neighbor?"

"Did you kill him? What in God's teeth did he do to you?"

"You're not making sense."

He should know not to believe her innocent act. "The man in the same building where I live. A few doors away. His chest cut open. He was treated less than dirt, worse than any animal, and he lived in the same building as I. You must be the one who murdered him. For what purpose did you have to kill an innocent, other than proving a point? And what of the other man several miles from here? What did either of them have against you? Why do you have this sick motivation of creating another like us?" His gaze narrowed. "But it's not just that. You love sick games. You kill indiscriminately and for the pleasure of it."

"Gabriel has always thought the worst of me. But you… You, I thought was different." Her gaze narrowed. "So what if I killed these two humans? What of it?"

He shook his head, stupidly thinking she might change one day. "I don't want to know you. To me, you died back in Spain. Too long we've watched you sink into your depravity, treating a person's life as excrement."

"Then why didn't you kill me?"

His breath left his body in one loud whoosh. "Because I loved you! Gabriel loved you. You were family, made of the same flesh and blood. We had a history, a shared and horrifying past. God's teeth, you were our sister! We couldn't."

"You disgust me." Her lip curled at the corner. "You didn't have the strength, the will to kill me. Both of you are weak little boys. You would have been kinder, more humane if you had killed me when you had the opportunity. Instead, you let your guilt leave me inside that cave, binding me to the ground with the family cross and poisonous silver for decades. I was alone with only my thoughts. I had no one! Do you know how hard that is? Do you? You think you're holier than me, but you are no better after making me suffer like an animal, frozen in time and on a dirt floor, unable to move, to escape my prison, unable to do anything when all I wanted to do was end my life.

"If it were not for two humans exploring deep within the mountain where you hid me, I would be still in that cave. It was their fatal mistake, but my second chance. If they had not taken off the cross chained from around my neck and the mercury within it, I would still be there. Their lifeblood nourished me and gave me back my life."

"Two more people you murdered. You think nothing of ending a person's life. You've crushed others in your thirst for turning them into one of us. That is why you gave us no choice."

"Choice?" She lifted her chin. "Everyone has choices. Why is it so wrong to want someone to love me? I have been alone for as long as I can remember. I deserve to be happy. And with Gabriel hiding Maria—"

"Maria is dead."

"No, she is not! She's alive again. I know it. They call her Nicole, but I know she is Maria. My daughter lives on inside of Nicole's body."

"Don't go down this route. You terrorized the poor girl and almost killed her mother." Luys hated Mayor's fascination with Gabriel's stepdaughter. Mayor believed Nicole was the reincarnation of her daughter Maria, but Mayor's thinking was fractured and deadly when it came to wanting Nicole to be her daughter and by her side. "And I can't understand how you think you *deserve* a daughter after all you've done. Not when you ruin other people, Mayor."

Her nostrils flared. "I have been too foolish. I thought you would apologize, beg for my forgiveness, and we could go back to what we once had." She closed her eyes as if in pain. "I was giving you a gift…Now, I think I will take it back. I was wrong to think you would appreciate it, that we might move forward. I had thought to forgive you." Her lip lifted at one corner. "Another stupid mistake on my part. You're like Gabriel. Someone who will betray me every time."

Luys tensed. "What do you mean by a gift?"

She ran her fingers through a thick chunk of hair draped over one shoulder. Luys wasn't fooled by the serene, even distracted way she twined the strands between her fingers. All her senses were sharp, tuned to his breath and the beat of his heart. She might have extraordinary hearing, but she couldn't read his thoughts. At least, he hoped she had not amassed more powers.

"I have been watching you for months now. Until recently, you never approached her. That did not mean you were not interested. I saw how you looked at her when the two of you were nearby. You want her for yourself, yes? But how can you when she will rot and die, and you will live on? Gabriel is estúpido to think his relationship with that woman will last. He will live on while that *bitch* will become the dirt she walks on."

"I have no clue who you're talking about," Luys replied, hoping in God's teeth that she was rambling about something meaningless, but he suspected this had everything to do with Avery. "I don't understand."

"By the blood of Christ. Of course you don't!" She looked to the ceiling for a moment before turning her icy blue eyes on him. "I wanted to offer you a gift in hopes we could maybe start afresh."

Dread burrowed into his gut. He didn't like where this conversation was going. "A gift? I find that hard to believe."

"Why is that? I did it as a peace offering. I do not want peace with Gabriel, but I wanted to salvage some type of relationship with you if you make amends."

"Amends? You can't be serious. You still expect me to apologize?!"

"Why is that too much to ask?" She rested a hand on her hip. "You and Gabriel have always been quick to judge and label me because I have changed, unlike the two of you. I do not see humans as worthy—"

"The only difference between them and us is that death does not come for us."

"You're wrong! Few, if any, humans are worthy. They're cruel, prejudiced, and self-centered. But that doesn't mean that a few can't become like us. There are exceptions. Avery is somewhat different than the others."

Luys glanced over at the medallion encased in glass. He should have given it to Avery the moment he suspected Mayor was around.

"The cross cannot save her. It is too late."

"What's too late?" He focused on his breathing, his heart rate. He needed to keep both normal. She could not know how much her words terrified him. She would use them against him.

"Nothing will protect her from me, other than her power."

"What did you do to her?" He dreaded the answer but already knew. The scars on Avery's chest, her attack, his interest in her he'd tried to fight off.

"What I've been trying to do for years, but both of you have stopped me at every turn." A look of triumph lit her eyes. "I have finally turned a human into one of us."

"That's impossible. The doctors would have said something to her when she was at the hospital."

"It doesn't work that way." Mayor gave him a condescending look. "It's genetic, not something that will show up in a simple blood test or scan."

Gut-wrenching sorrow roiled through him. He did not want that of Avery. Fighting back the urge to hit Mayor, he stepped back, lengthening the distance between them.

"Why did you do that to her? Why her and not someone else? She's innocent."

"Because of how you feel about her." Mayor snorted, but not in a humorous way. "I have been in your neighborhood for months, and you were so blind to anything but your thoughts and emotions. Such a typical man."

His control snapped. "You can't be serious! You have ruined Avery's life. Because of you, she'll always have this burden. You don't get it."

"But she wanted to live."

"She was living!" Luys wanted to wrap both hands around his sister's neck. Instead, he fisted both hands until he thought his knuckles would crack from the pressure.

"You changed her to one of us as a gift to me? How can you think that? Being what I am is a curse!" His voice rose higher as rage flooded him. He advanced toward her and stopped less than a foot away, still keeping his hands from striking her. He glared into the icy depths of her eyes. "You destroyed a woman. How can she live with others of her kind if she has to watch them die again and again!"

She shoved him away. The force sent him back several steps before he regained his balance. She lifted a hand and sliced the air. "You're melodramatic. And an idiot! You have no clue!"

"And why is that?"

Her lip curled at one corner, and she paused for dramatic effect. "She was dying."

CHAPTER 15

He sucked in a breath, unable to mask the shock of her words. "That's impossible." His eyes narrowed. "She looks perfectly fine and healthy."

"Appearances can deceive." She looked at the ceiling again and sighed. "The signs of her illness would have eventually shown themselves. The cancer would have eaten away at her body, metastasized to more organs, even her brain, eating at her life force."

His eyes narrowed. "You're lying."

"Believe what you will." She shrugged a shoulder. "But I know she had cancer."

"She told you that?" Luys found that hard to believe, but he did know one thing about Mayor. She might be vindictive, and vicious when cornered, but she rarely lied. Even when she became delusional.

Mayor rolled her eyes. "Unlike you, I could smell death on her, but I didn't know why. I went through her computer and the papers on her desk. There was correspondence from a hospital and clinic."

"You still had no right," he argued, his equilibrium off, his thoughts scattered at Mayor's words. "Cancer is not necessarily a death sentence. There are cures. She could have found a way to live without you interfering."

"Really, Luys? Always the optimist, even when the

outcome is hopeless. Stage 4 melanoma. She had tumors in her liver, kidneys, and lungs. Before I saved her, she had a year at best unless she found another clinical trial. And before you discount my words, I've examined many scholarly articles on the topic through this internet."

He blinked, and his throat tightened with emotion. Knowing she was dying and being unable to do anything about it must have traumatized Avery. And now she was again traumatized by his sister. He felt—no—he was responsible for Mayor attacking Avery.

"See?" She laughed without humor. "You do care deeply for the woman. You've been hiding this, but I know. You forget I'm your sister."

"Of course you pried into something that is of no business of yours. You've never valued another person's privacy."

"And you were never one to appreciate me as an equal because I was a woman."

"Back then society saw women as—"

"Please spare me."

He didn't bother to argue. What Mayor didn't realize was how much he had changed as a man. He had been trampled on, beaten, left for dead at one point. Being humbled always changed a person, made them look at life with different eyes. But that didn't relate to what Mayor had done.

"You say Avery is the first you turned. But how many others did you try to turn that Gabriel and I don't know about? A dozen, a score, or more?" His eyes narrowed. "You don't fool me. She was another test, another victim. Because you consider this a success— and God's teeth, who knows how Avery's body will react over the coming weeks—you will now focus on Nicole. But Gabriel will not stand for it. He will never let you step within a mile radius of Nicole in order for you to perform this demonic ritual on her."

"Again, you disappoint me. Always. You and Gabriel. I save someone you care about, and you don't thank me but reprimand me! I can never do right in the eyes of both of you!" She advanced toward him. "You are a fool. You're such a man, so fixated on your own needs and wants." The ice in her eyes swirled and darkened. "If you had focused on enhancing your powers through the Aztec gods, you would know her body was failing her and could do something about it. You would have easily been able to smell the death on her. You and Gabriel are fools to think that our old lives were precious. Like me, you both could be powerful, unmatched in this world! But no! Instead, you decide to throw me in a cave. Your cruelty is far worse than any of what I have done. I kill my victims swiftly. I don't leave them in cold, empty holes in the ground to rot with only their thoughts, with no way of escape, no way of ending their pain and loneliness."

He didn't step away from the fury radiating from her eyes or body. Yes, he had the advantage of height and weight, but she was far stronger physically. If he showed any form of weakness, she would latch onto it and push further and further until she crushed him and everyone around him. He had heard what she had done to Gabriel and his first wife. "Revenge Mayor? Yes, Gabriel and I did something awful to you, but you left us no choice. You had become a murderer and killed innocents."

"I have never killed an innocent!"

"Tell that to the dead!"

"Bastardo!"

Fingers outstretched like talons, she lunged, crashing her body into Luys. His back slammed against the wall with the force of her weight as her hands grabbed at his neck. He grasped at her wrists and struggled to get them from around his throat. Her strength. It was shocking, frightening. He'd forgotten the power she wielded. She did it with such ease.

Pivoting, he twisted at the waist and downward, then rammed a hip into her stomach. He broke free from her grasp. She pulled back her hand and thrust a fist toward his face. He ducked. She hit the wall instead. Flecks of paint and plaster sprayed his face. Before she attacked again, he swiveled and dove toward her, shoving a shoulder into her soft belly. An oomph flew from her mouth as they both tumbled toward the coffee table. The wood corner cut across his temple before he slammed into the floor.

His thoughts scattered, and sparks flared across his vision. He was half conscious of Mayor scrambling from under him.

A loud banging hit his skull on all sides. Then he realized someone was pounding on the door.

Luys clutched the floor beneath him and tried to rise. A swirl of movement flickered across his peripheral vision and from the front window of the living room. Glass shattered. The sound cut into his head. He tried to focus, tried to find his equilibrium, but a buzzing sound filled his ears, and a thick fog rolled through his thoughts. His arm gave from under him, and he crumbled to the floor.

He passed out.

Phone in hand, Avery hovered in the front of her place as she eyed Luys' condo. The door stood closed, and the reflective sheen of the screen windows hid what was going on inside. Sweat trickled down her spine and the hairline by her temples, and her blouse stuck to her back as the sun's rays beat against her. The silence—even the heat had stopped the birds from singing—was deceptive. There was nothing calm about it because something was going on. Something dangerous. Something inside Luys' home.

The words *I kill my victims swiftly* reverberated inside her head. Mayor had spoken them. She'd recognized that smooth, sultry voice minutes before. But she'd missed most of the earlier conversation—something about caves and death and killing.

When she'd heard raised voices, and with her newfound hearing, she'd been able to amplify the words and focus on the location. Finding out she was listening in on Luys' conversation had shocked her at first, but the mention of killing had shocked her far more.

She didn't know who was in trouble. Mayor, or Luys, or someone completely different. They could be killing someone now, or Mayor, as implausible as it sounded, could be doing something to Luys. Or—she absolutely hated the idea—Luys might be attacking someone while she stood outside of his condo in indecision.

She didn't dare get any other neighbors involved, but she was worried. She swore she'd heard choking, but the idea of confronting what was going on inside his condo terrified her. She valued her life, probably more than most people.

Did she dare call the police? Biting her lower lip, she stared at the phone and swiped it with a thumb. She couldn't *not* do anything!

"Hey, is something wrong?"

She looked up and found Ben, the detective from the hospital and her neighbor, walking toward her.

"I—" She frowned over at Luys' condo as the detective stopped by her side. Here was her chance. She'd wanted to call the cops, and one had just dropped from the sky for her.

A bang reverberated from inside the condo.

Her heart rate kicked up. "I think there's some type of fight going on inside."

"With Martinez?"

She shouldn't be surprised Ben Atkins knew who the owner of the condo was.

"Luys and his sister, I think."

Ben's gaze narrowed, and a look of distaste flashed in his eyes. He swore under his breath, and he strode to the front door. He hit the doorbell, waited all of two seconds, then rapped on the doorframe. To the right of him, the front window of the condo erupted. The screen flew off its moorings and catapulted across the yard. Glass shattered and sprayed, following the screen's trajectory. Ben jerked back and flattened against the front door.

Dropping down on a knee, Avery threw an arm up to shield her face. A few harmless shards peppered her body and the ground around her. As she dropped her hand back to her side, an object swirled from the window. Some type of thick mist or fog. She'd never seen anything like it. Within the twisting fog, Avery recognized the profile of a human figure.

What the…? Impossible. She blinked, wondering if her eyesight was off. But no, the shape of a person with little substance appeared inside the fog and was unmistakable.

Unease crawled across her skin, and she stumbled to her feet and stepped back from the apparition. Whatever it was didn't feel benevolent. It felt dark, dangerous. Suddenly, the churning mist exploded. She jerked back, expecting it to hit her, but the fog bypassed her and dissipated into the air as if it never existed.

Glass fragments lay scattered on the ground by the empty window. Maybe she'd imagined it…

Ben banged harder on the door, drawing her attention to Luys inside. No one opened the door, and no other sound filtered through the window to outside. She focused, closing her eyes and centering her hearing on the inside of the condo.

Nothing.

Not good. Not good at all.

Maybe this thing had killed Luys. Maybe he was dead. The idea sent a painful fist around her heart. She should have done something sooner.

Ben grabbed the doorknob and shoved open the door, making her realize Luys' place had been unlocked the entire time. Had Mayor or Luys fled the place? Maybe Avery had it all wrong, and the apparition had been some figment she'd conjured up? Could either of them have jumped through the window without her seeing them clearly? But if that was the case, then why jump through the window if the door was unlocked?

When Ben disappeared inside, Avery stood momentarily in indecision. The idea of Ben being more than capable as a cop made her pause, but the thought of Luys' safety and the need to know propelled her after the detective and into the condo. Probably stupid, but she'd never called herself a genius.

Ben stood in the middle of the living room. She didn't see Luys or anyone else until she followed Ben deeper into the room and peered around his shoulder. Luys lay sprawled across the floor on his side, wedged between the sofa and a coffee table, with a torn pant leg.

She moved around Ben and dropped down by Luys' shoulder. She touched his arm with tentative fingers. "Luys!"

He lay unresponsive. She looked up at Ben, who hadn't moved from his spot. "Do something!"

CHAPTER 16

Ben continued to stare at Luys' crumpled form with an inscrutable look stamped on his face. "He needs an ambulance," Avery insisted.

"We don't know that." Ben nudged him with a shoe.

"Hey, don't," she protested, repelled by his callousness before looking back down at Luys. She then noticed the blood on the carpet by his head. "He's hit his head. He could have a concussion or something worse. We need to call for an ambulance..."

Ben didn't say anything.

Luys groaned.

"He's probably drunk."

"Are you serious?"

"Well, look at him."

"I am! And he looks anything but." She leaned closer and swept her fingers across his temple, tangling her fingers in the silky strands of his hair. The warmth of his scalp was reassuring. "Luys, it's me. Avery."

Ben hunched down beside her and checked Luys' wrist. After a moment, he rose back to his feet. "His pulse is fine."

Luys stirred just then and groaned. He blinked and stared up at Avery with blank eyes. Then they cleared, and Luys struggled to sit up.

Ben sighed. "I'll call the police department and have someone come in and take your report."

"He first needs to see a doctor."

"No hospital," Luys argued. "I'll be fine."

"But you're hurt," Avery insisted. What was it with both men? Couldn't they see Luys was bleeding?

"I need a minute to clear my head." Jaw rigid, Luys moved from the floor to the sofa behind him, sinking into the cushion with a grunt. He stroked the side of his head and winced, dropping his hand down to his leg.

"So what happened with the window?" Ben asked.

"I'm not sure." Luys met Ben's gaze with an unfathomable expression.

Ben ambled across the room and peered into the kitchen. "So it exploded on its own?"

"I don't know what happened," Luys replied.

"But didn't either of you see the mist?" Avery asked.

They both turned and stared at her.

"Mist?" Ben asked.

"Yes, it came out of the window. I swear there was someone there. I couldn't tell if the person was male or female because of the fog…." Avery stumbled to a halt and realized how strange she sounded. It had to have been Mayor. Unless the woman was hiding somewhere in Luys' condo, which made her ask, "Is Mayor here?"

"No," Luys answered.

"Who's Mayor?"

Luys glared at him. "That's no business of yours."

"Luys, he's a cop and doing his job." But Avery wondered if Ben was trying to help. "Mayor's his sister."

Frowning, Ben pivoted and strode from the room. The sound of his steps receded as he disappeared down the hall and moved through both bedrooms. He finally appeared a couple of minutes later. "Well, it's obvious Mayor isn't here now."

"Why the concern? Do you think I did something to my sister?"

"Did you?" Ben raised both brows.

Luys' chin inched up a notch, but his features remained impassive.

At the sudden tension in the room, Avery frowned and glanced back and forth at both men. Ben implied that Luys had a prior history, and it wasn't for the first time. But for what? It couldn't be anything beyond a DUI or something equally minor. Still, the possibility of something more serious sent a wave of unease crawling across her flesh.

"So are you going to tell us what happened? We both find you on the floor with a busted front window." Ben quickly glanced around the room, his eyes narrowing against one wall. He walked up to the wall and fingered a crumpled section of drywall. "Looks like someone did some heavy damage to your wall. From what I can tell, it's pretty close to the size of a fist."

"Nothing happened."

All she had to do was look at the blood at his temple and remember finding him on the floor to know he was lying. Avery wanted to ask questions, but she knew he wouldn't say a word with Ben in the same room. But what was he hiding? Did she want to hang around and find out?

Turning his back on Luys, Ben gave Avery a tight-lipped smile. "If he doesn't want to file a burglary, assault, or property damage claim for insurance, my hands are tied. If you get him to change his mind, it will probably be tomorrow before anyone shows up. We're short-staffed, and crime hasn't exactly been disappearing."

"Thanks." Avery wrapped her arms around her middle.

Ben shrugged. "Of course." He glanced down at his phone. "I've got to go. I had an appointment I'm now late for."

When Ben stepped from Luys' place, Avery hesitated in the middle of the room, wondering if she should go after him. Ben's behavior had been off from the moment he'd shown up in front of Luys' place with her. Maybe he hadn't seen the mist. Maybe. Even so, he was holding back on what he knew about Luys.

She glanced over at Luys. Exhaustion seemed to etch brackets by his mouth and add lines between his brows. "I'll be right back." But she wasn't so sure about going anywhere near him, not with everything she'd learned these last couple of days. She rushed outside and found Ben walking toward the parking lot. "Ben!"

He paused and turned around. "Yes?"

She hurried over, unable to quell the pounding of her heart. "What is Luys guilty of? This is the second time you've implied something."

A flush inched up Ben's neck to his face.

"Please, I need to know."

"Why can't you keep away from him? That would solve everything."

"There's more involved."

Ben sighed heavily and looked up at the sky for a moment. "Fine, but you didn't hear it from me. Someone reported seeing him loitering by the victim's place the night of his murder. There's a witness. They found it suspicious that he kept walking by the victim's condo numerous times that night, and there was no reason for him to travel that footpath to get to the parking lot or his home."

Avery flinched. "There has to be another reason other than what you're implying."

He gave her a strange look. "I shouldn't have mentioned what I knew. I could lose my job over it."

"I won't say anything. I promise." She frowned. "But have you interviewed him? Or asked why he was around the man's condo? Maybe there's a logical explanation." She didn't want to believe that of Luys. That would mean she had sex with a murderer. At the thought, she felt her stomach sink and roil. "Does he have a prior?"

"No, but he's on a list of possible suspects."

"Oh."

"Be careful! Someone was brutally murdered, and we have no clue what the motive was. This was done by someone with rage. I've been around a while and know when it's personal, and this was definitely no random act." He backed up a step. "Just be very careful who you trust. Sorry, I really have got to get going."

"Yes, of course."

She sighed. When it came down to it, what did she know of Luys, other than that he was a doctor who did research, lived next door, knew his way around the kitchen, and…had a psychotic sister? His sister was not only quirky but scary, according to Luys, but maybe he was the scary one. No. She was fooling herself. They were both dangerous—dangerous by association.

Ben looked over her shoulder, his gaze narrowing. Then he pivoted and disappeared around the corner of the complex's building.

Wondering what had caught Ben's eye, she turned around and jumped. It took a lot for her not to slap a hand against her chest. Face inscrutable, Luys stood a mere three feet away. He'd wiped at the blood from his brow, leaving red streaks across his fingers and temple.

She stepped back, needing the space between them. "Did you hear what Ben said?"

"Not all of it, but I have a good idea what I missed isn't good."

"You're right." She edged further away from Luys. "Did you know Noah Harris?"

"No. I never knew he existed until we found out about his murder. Why? Is that what he said to you?"

"No." She didn't like how he took a step closer. "It seems someone witnessed you hanging around his condo the night of his murder. The police have you as a suspect."

"I don't know who could have seen me around Noah Harris' place. I stayed in that night." He cocked his head to the side. "Do you believe I can brutally murder a man I don't even know?"

"I—No," Avery found herself admitting. "Not from what I know of you."

"Once they gather all the evidence, it will prove that I was never in his condo and that I am completely innocent."

"But what about Mayor?" Luys seemed to think his sister was dangerous, but she'd never thought of Mayor physically capable of taking on a man and killing him. But if she was filled with overpowering rage and hatred, which Ben seemed to think the killer had, she could have taken Noah Harris by surprise, hit him until he was unconscious, or done something else to subdue him. From there, it would be easy to murder him. "You told me to keep away from Mayor. But how dangerous is she? Enough to murder someone else?" The more Avery thought about it, the more she considered Mayor a possibility. "Do you know if she knows the victim? But maybe you don't even know that. Maybe she's the one that told the police she saw you hanging around Noah's condo. You've also told me before that your relationship is not the best. It's possible, right?" She kept on with the questions even as Luys continually shook his head. She had a good idea he hadn't mentioned everything about his sister. "Were they dating or having an affair? Was she jealous? Maybe Noah called it quits, and she couldn't take the rejection."

Luys dragged in a breath and exhaled. "Right here isn't the place to talk."

"Really? Well, I'd like to argue with you on that point. Being inside closed doors with you would be stupid, especially when you're brushing off my questions."

Twisting his neck back and forth as if to crack it, he rubbed at his nape. "And talking out here for everyone to overhear is not smart either."

Avery balled her hands at her sides. "I know you helped me when I needed it. You were there to get me to the hospital, but now I wished you'd left me alone. I'm seriously regretting ever meeting you. And that goes for your sister. She's odd in a way I can't really explain."

Something unreadable flashed in his eyes.

"What? Is it true? Could your sister have murdered Noah?"

This time, there was no mistaking the sudden sadness that darkened his eyes. "She has a skewed way of doing things even when she thinks she's trying to help. Her methods aren't always right."

Being deliberately vague and the way his voice thickened and deepened to what sounded suspiciously like guilt boded ill. She didn't think—no, she knew—she wasn't going to like what he had to say. "What are you talking about? Does it have something to do with me?"

Luys shook his head. "This isn't the place. How about we go inside?"

When he nodded toward his condo, she quickly replied, "No, no, I don't think so. Whatever you have to say can be said right here."

He sighed loudly, opened his mouth, shut it. Then he said in a rush, "Mayor knew you were dying."

"What?!" The shock of his words sent tension slamming against her spine. "You're lying. How could she even think that!"

All this time she'd kept the secret, tucked it deep inside, even avoiding the truth to herself on too many occasions, never mind having the guts to reveal it to anyone else. Not one person knew other than her doctor and his medical staff. She'd been deliberate, careful at work, of anyone finding out. She couldn't handle their pitying looks, their awkward conversations if the truth came out. And now not only Luys knew, but his sister. There was no way Mayor could have found out unless she'd deliberately started following her and digging into her life.

Sorrow—she'd call it more pity than anything—darkened his gaze. "She knew. Sensed it. She has an uncanny way of recognizing sickness in others."

"There's no way she could know that." She slashed a hand through the air. "She has no business discussing anything about me, unless she's nuts? Why would she even think of saying things like that?" She fisted her hand and pressed it against her chest.

"She might have problems, but I've never known her to lie."

"Tell me, why does she care? Why say something so crazy to you? Obviously, because she's nuts." Avery dragged in a lungful of breath, but she couldn't get enough oxygen into her lungs. "This is my life. It's no one else's business other than mine!"

He ignored her outburst and asked gently, "How many months?"

Avery blinked back tears as she pressed her fist harder against her chest. He was being brutal. He wouldn't let it go, didn't believe her denials. She couldn't take it.

Stumbling back, she lifted a scornful lip and raised a palm to him. "I've had enough of you."

She turned around and headed back to her condo.

"Wait! There's something important." The sound of his steps followed her. "There's more you don't know. Mayor chose you. The day we met—I know what happened to you."

Whirling around, she gaped at him. "Wh-what are you talking about?"

"She's the one…" He cleared his throat. At his side, he opened his hand from a balled fist, closed it, opened it again, and then rubbed his palm against the side of his thigh. "She…"

"She what?"

"She's responsible for what happened."

"No." She didn't have to ask. She knew what he was implying. Even so, he made sure she understood.

"She's the one who cut you, the one responsible for putting you in the hospital." His eyes misted with guilt, remorse, or some other emotion.

She suddenly became lightheaded, dangerously dizzy, and the muscles in her legs trembled as they threatened to give beneath her weight. She tried to grab for something to hold her steady, keep her from collapsing, but she grasped at empty air. Noises from around her exploded: a car's engine backfiring, the chatter of televisions beyond the stucco and brick walls, music, and laughter from the neighboring pool, even the whisper of the breeze against the leaves. The sounds slammed into her head, worse than ever before, to the point she thought she was going to vomit.

He made to help her, but she backed away, smacking up against the wall before slumping against the stucco. "Why? Why would she do something like that to me? What did I ever do to her?"

"I'm sorry. I don't know what to tell you other than I can't apologize enough for her scarring you, for altering your life forever."

"Sorry doesn't do a damn thing. How about call the police? Put her in jail? She's a danger to society!"

"She performed an ancient ceremony on you. She removed the disease from your body." He stepped toward her and lifted a hand.

"Don't touch me!" She slapped at his hand as she slumped against the wall. Her heart felt like it was going to explode inside her chest. "You're both nuts!"

"Stop it." Quickly, he moved over to her and gently grasped her wrist. "You look like you're about to faint."

"I—I—" Tears burned the back of her eyes. Humiliation, painful in intensity, washed through her. The muscles in her legs weakened even more. She blinked against sudden dizziness. In two seconds, she was afraid she was going to pass out. Damn him. All because of him and his crazy sister. When he reached for her again, she slapped at his chest, his arms. Luys didn't give her the chance to crumble to the ground and swept her up in his arms.

She shoved at his chest and demanded in a hoarse voice, "Put me down!"

Oh, God. She was crying and couldn't stop, couldn't even find the ability to scream because of her uncontrollable sobbing. She didn't have the strength to fight as he carried her down the sidewalk and into his condo.

When he gently set her down on the sofa, he stepped back far enough to give her some needed space. "I'll get you some water."

Grabbing the sofa's armrest, she closed her eyes and sucked in several deep breaths. She needed to calm down, get her bearings. She was beyond hysterical. What was wrong with her? She'd never lost it like this. Not even when she'd received her diagnosis. But she'd never been attacked under the pretense of some sick ritual.

Slowly, she got her heart rate down. She opened her eyes and wearily stared back at Luys and the glass of water in his hands. He stood between her and the doorway and escape. He didn't look like a murderer.

Hah! What person ever did?

She searched his face and eventually met his gaze. Unless she was completely off at reading people, and he was adept at hiding his psychopathic tendencies, she recognized kindness in his expression. She frowned. Or was it more pity? Did he feel sorry for her because she was dying?

She sat up straighter. She sure as hell didn't want his pity.

What else did he know about her? What did it matter? He knew *this*. And he *knew* about Mayor attacking her.

"Why? For God's sake, why? You just sat there and let her do what she did to me?" She dug her nails into the sofa's seat cushion on either side of her thighs. "You did nothing!"

"At first, I didn't know what had happened to you when I took you to the hospital. And then when she showed up at your condo, I was terrified of what she planned next. I thought she intended to kill me or torture me."

"And still you never warned me!"

He sighed, rubbing the back of his neck. "She's never hurt a woman before, and I didn't want to frighten you more than you already were. I tried to keep a close watch on you to ensure your safety—"

"That's a new one. You decided sex would be a great way to protect me from her."

"No! I didn't plan that. Being intimate with you was something I fought against from the beginning. I was afraid my attraction would cloud my judgment and make things more complicated."

"So I'm now a complication?" She snorted and shook her head. "Excuses. They're all excuses. You lied about everything. When I outright asked you about your scar and mine and the similarities, you lied yet again!" She looked up and down his body and backed up again, making sure when she met his gaze, he could read the disgust on her face. "And to think you were a priest."

A flush rose into his face. "I deserved that." He cupped the glass of water against his stomach. "If I had told you the truth about Mayor, you would never have believed me."

"Another excuse."

"I swear I didn't know she turned you, not until today."

Avery stilled. She didn't like his wording. There were many things about Mayor and Luys she detested. There was too much mystery, too many unanswered questions. "What do you mean by 'turned'?"

Gaze darkening, Luys paused as if to search for the right words. He then frowned. "There is no way to make this sound rational. She made you like one of us."

"Us?" Oh, God. What the hell? That was crazy talk. She didn't like where this was going. Before, she'd considered everything about Mayor and Luys crazy, but now this sounded beyond nuts. "What does that mean?"

"You won't grow old. You'll continue being the same age as you are now. Death isn't something you will experience. It's elusive from what I understand." He lifted the glass of water in his hand. "You'll probably want something stronger than this."

"I don't want your water." There could be something in it, and she wasn't about to touch any alcohol. It could easily mask some poison or drug. She scrunched deeper into the sofa. "You're nuts. Both you and your sister."

Her heart rate kicked up. How far was Luys willing to go when it came to such an unbelievable story? Obviously, he and his sister lived in some make-believe world.

"I understand this all sounds incredible," Luys admitted. "It will take time to digest."

This time, she stopped herself from saying something nasty. She'd let her mouth take over her brain. The last thing she should want to do was antagonize him. She didn't know what he was capable of. Just because he'd always been kind to her, that didn't mean he couldn't flip out on her now. She eyed the front door. He hadn't moved from blocking her way out. He'd stop her in seconds. Take a couple of breaths and keep him talking. Wasn't that what they always said in the movies? Yeah, but this wasn't the movies.

"You think—you're like some type of god?"

"Of course not."

Well, what was she supposed to think with him rattling on about immortality? "Okay…"

"I was too quick to answer. We appear to be immortal. We don't age for some reason. In truth, I don't know what we are, but I understand we differ from the rest of humankind. One does not live past 300 years and not realize that, but my questions as to why or how we exist have never been answered. I suspect there are others like us, but I have yet to find anyone after all these years." He searched her face. "And your health now? Mayor mentioned you had melanoma."

"Melanoma." She rubbed her hand against her eyes.

The tears still came. Sniffing, she swept the back of her hand against her nose next. "The doctors have done everything. All treatments have failed. There's nothing more anyone can do. Right now, there are no clinical trials available to me. I have tumors in my liver, kidneys, and lungs."

He winced. "Have them do a PET or CT scan. I can promise you they'll find no evidence of disease."

"That's impossible."

"Avery, nothing is impossible." He paced back and forth in front of her. "Think. How are you feeling? Has your energy level changed? You must have had symptoms."

"I don't know what to think! This is all too insane!"

But she thought about his questions. The tiredness had eased. Even the pain, but she hadn't been paying attention because of everything else that had happened. She'd also been in denial. She'd thought if she willed herself, she'd get better.

Sighing, he placed the water on a table, two feet from where he'd been standing. Avery tensed. There was now a direct path between her and the door, but still, if she rushed forward, it would take seconds for him to block her way.

"The scans will prove that the ritual Mayor performed on you has healed your body." He rubbed the heel of his palm between his brows, then dropped his hand. "I am not explaining this well. My history is not something I discuss. I guess for you to understand and maybe realize I am not delusional or mentally imbalanced, I should ask instead whether or not you have noticed anything about yourself? Heightened senses or unusual strength since the day after Mayor attacked you?"

His words sent her heart pounding harder. Suddenly, she thought of her strange, amplified hearing. All this time, she'd wondered, even doubted herself, but she had a hard time with the idea of Mayor cutting her open and performing some type of ritual or ceremony on her body to make her immortal? The thought made her stomach roll, but she couldn't discount his sister might be the cause for her heightened hearing. She had no logical explanation.

She frowned. If she believed some ritual heightened her senses, she would have to believe what Luys was saying.

No. It was too far-fetched, too insane. Still… "There is something…" Her frown deepened as Avery shifted uncomfortably on the sofa. "I…"

"What is it?"

Finally, she admitted, "My hearing." She shifted again against the cushions. "I'll get a rush of sounds all at once to the point I think my head is going to explode. At other times, I can hear people inside their homes or far away—too far for any normal person. All impossible before."

"Anything else? What about the power in your hands? Have you detected any increase in strength and balance or quickening of reflexes?"

She lifted her hands from her lap and stared down at them, flexing her fingers and then turning her palms up and down. "I have no clue." She looked around the room. "And I wouldn't even know how to begin to test to see if I've changed in other ways."

Luys moved over to the kitchen table. "I guess the only way is to see what you're capable of."

She made a face at him. She was starting to believe him, which was probably not smart on her part. But that didn't mean she wasn't still furious at him or that she didn't fear him. Her level of disquiet had eased somewhat, though. At least for the moment.

She eyed the door once again. He was far enough away that she might get a hand on the doorknob, but the need to know more kept her rooted to the cushion.

The cry of a siren penetrated the condo's walls. Luys stilled and stared over at the front window, and she did the same. From the open and ruined window, heat radiated into the room.

Her body tensed as she stood up. She hated that sound more now than ever.

The volume increased until she thought her head would explode with the noise. More sounds swelled around her.

"Focus."

She glanced over at Luys, wanting to squeeze her hands over her ears.

"Focus on your breathing. That helps with controlling your hearing or any other heightened ability."

She tried to do what he suggested, caving in and squeezing her palms against her ears, but it didn't smother the sounds bombarding her from every direction. She pivoted and recoiled, hitting her elbow against a floor lamp.

Silence crashed in all around her. Even the sirens had stopped. All she could hear was her agitated breathing.

Luys started to pick up the lamp, but he paused, lifted it to one side, and frowned.

"Did I break it?"

His brow creased as he reached inside the lampshade. "No, but there's something above the switch."

He pulled out a small circular, electronic-type device. "Someone's been listening to us."

Palming the microphone, he strode over to the kitchen, dropped it in the sink, flipped on the garbage disposal, and then turned it off.

"Do you know who?"

"I have no idea. It could be the police, Mayor, anyone."

Avery looked back at Luys in horror. She couldn't remember what she'd said in this room. The idea of another device in the bedroom was mortifying. She'd revealed so many intimate details about herself in there; they'd had sex, talked about her cancer, and God only knew what else. Her mind couldn't wrap around the idea.

Maybe the police were outside right now to arrest Luys. He must have thought the same thing because he strode toward the front door and opened it. Pausing on the threshold, he grabbed the doorjamb with one hand as he looked both ways.

"What?"

Avery hurried to his side and ducked under his arm. Hot air immediately engulfed her as she walked over to where two sidewalks intersected: one from his condo and the other running the length of the building. She glanced toward the parking lot.

The beam of red, blue, and white rotated across the building's brick walls and crushed gravel yard. The police had parked. The distant sound of a police radio filtered into the night sky.

She wasn't safe outside either. "Oh, God."

"We don't know what the sirens are for," Luys murmured as he moved to her side. "There might be a car accident."

"But we don't know that for sure. There could just as easily be another murder."

Luys closed his mouth and didn't reply.

Glancing up, she searched his expression and realized he believed what she'd verbalized aloud. The police's arrival had nothing to do with arresting Luys, a family fight or car accident, and everything to do with a murder.

She stayed behind as Luys walked up the path to see more.

CHAPTER 17

Monday, August 24ᵗʰ – 12:34 pm

Luys paused on the sidewalk before he turned toward the entrance of the local police depart-ment. He dreaded the next hour and prayed to a God he didn't have much faith in anymore that he would leave the building without handcuffs.

He rolled his shoulders. They had nothing to point him to the murders.

He didn't think the bug he and Avery found in his living room was from the police. He didn't think it was from Mayor either. She'd never been into new advances in science. The question left him floundering for an answer.

He'd searched the rest of his condo and didn't find any other microphone, but that didn't mean there wasn't one still there. Maybe he should have left the listening device alone and fed the person on the other side misin-formation. It was too late to rehash his mistake and how he'd let his emotions get the better of him.

Sighing, he thought back to yesterday and how he'd investigated the reason for the sirens. When he hadn't been able to learn anything from the neighbors or the police, he'd retraced his steps to find Avery had fled. He'd then thought of following her back to her place to make sure she was okay but decided he'd pushed her too far already with finding the bug and everything he'd revealed. Later that day, though, he hadn't heard of another murder on the television or internet.

The relief that they hadn't wheeled out a body had been immense.

But he felt anything but relief as he took a deep breath, opened the thick glass doors, and stepped into the police lobby.

The main area was crowded. He had to wait in line to go through the security checkpoint, placing his keys in a plastic bowl. In the last century, many things had changed. Security cameras, policing, constant surveillance, phones tracking every movement, and still, always violence. Always violence. He had never been able to escape it.

After he'd hung up with Hatcher the evening he'd left the church, dread had filled his head until his meeting with the detective.

He sat down and waited in a metal chair against the wall. Minutes later, Hatcher appeared from a secured door, his expression unsmiling, as he nodded and said, "Glad to see you were able to make it."

Luys didn't reply. It wasn't like he had much of a choice unless he wanted to get legal representation, which would be a red flag to Hatcher.

Luys followed him through the same door and into a small windowless room with a table and a couple of chairs.

Luys didn't bother with any preliminary small talk.

"Couldn't we have done this over the phone?"

"I don't like phones." Hatcher shrugged. "Plus, I wanted to see you in person."

"Am I going to need a lawyer?"

"I'm not charging you with anything. I only wanted to chat."

Chat? Luys didn't believe it for a moment. He had thought of hiring an attorney but doing so would have revealed guilt. "About what?"

Hatcher sat back in his chair and eyed Luys. "I mentioned it over the phone earlier."

Luys couldn't remember any such thing.

"Okay." Hatcher straightened and clicked on a recording device by his elbow. "I won't keep you long."

"They are expecting me at work later today."

"Oh, we'll be done soon enough." He rested an elbow on the edge of the table. "Are you familiar with Noah Harris?"

"I don't know him, but I am aware he was murdered last week."

"Really, you didn't know him at all? He lived in the same building."

"Yes, I've seen him in the complex. I might have said hello, but we were not friendly enough to have a conversation."

"What about others in the neighborhood? Do you know of anyone who's familiar with Noah Harris and who might have known if he had any enemies?"

"No."

"Did you see anything unusual the night of his murder?"

"No."

"What about someone hanging around in the area? Someone you recognized or who looked out of place?"

"No."

"What about days before his death?"

"No."

Luys knew continually repeating himself made him sound belligerent, but he didn't have any information on that night or Noah Harris. Right now, he was honest, but if Hatcher started delving into Avery, he might not be so honest.

"Do you know of anyone who might have something against Harris? Did you overhear anyone discussing Harris after his death?"

"No."

Hatcher's lips firmed. He drummed his hands on the desk. "I had hoped you might give us some additional information on the case. Maybe there's something you might have missed. A neighbor or someone you didn't recognize hanging around or entering his home within the last 48 hours before his death?"

Luys shook his head.

"What about someone who might have confided in you that might be related to his death?"

"No. Has anyone said something?"

"I am not at liberty to discuss that with you."

Luys shouldn't be surprised that the detective was unwilling to give him any information. But it would be nice if Luys knew what the police had, specifically if they were suspicious of a blonde-haired woman loitering in the area. Someone must have seen Mayor. She wasn't invisible.

He shifted in his chair. The idea of discussing Mayor and revealing her identity rose to his throat, but he kept his lips shut. If he started talking, the detective would never believe him, and he would undoubtedly become their lead suspect. They would question his sanity. Who would believe such a story? A woman with a thirst for blood, with the ability to kill another with the twist of a wrist? A woman strong enough to overpower a man much larger than herself? Worse yet, a woman who had preternatural senses and the ability to vanish into mist? No, he would remain silent. Years before, Luys had revealed too much to someone he had trusted and escaped with barely his life. Superstitions still existed. He would be locked up and analyzed for years if they believed some truth to his abilities and history.

From across the table, Luys stared at Hatcher, taking in the other man's salt and pepper hair, the age lines fanning from his eyes, the hard creases bracketing his mouth, and the inscrutable expression. No doubt the detective was an expert at keeping his feelings hidden. Luys wished he could delve into the man's mind, but his abilities didn't have that great a scope.

Trying to hide his frustration, Luys asked, "Do you suspect who is responsible for the man's death?"

Hatcher stared at him without blinking. "Again, not something I can disclose."

Even though Avery believed he was a person of interest, Luys still had to ask. "Am I a suspect?"

"Why would you be? Unless you have a reason for killing Noah Harris?"

He had expected suspicion, prying questions. Still, the reality sucked the air from his lungs. "I told you, I don't know him."

"Glad to hear it," Hatcher murmured as he sat back in his chair and eyed Luys, "but a witness has come forward and revealed that they saw you by the victim's residence that evening."

"That's not unusual. He is—was a neighbor. He lived in the same building. Of course, I am going to be seen in the area." Luys frowned. "Who came forward?"

Hatcher looked at him with disbelief. "I can't disclose their identity. I would think you would know that."

"But what are they saying?" Luys straightened, this time unable to mask his own suspicion.

Hatcher stared back for a long moment before asking, "Tell me about Avery."

Luys stiffened. "What about her?"

"Just how well do you know Avery Fleming?"

"I've already told you she's a neighbor. Other than the one time I took her to the hospital that day, we only said hi here and there when we passed each other in the complex."

"I've heard differently. We have witnesses who have seen you pretty chummy since you dropped her at the hospital. Seems to me you might have been far closer to her than before her attack." Hatcher cocked his head to the side. "Where were you the night of the murder?"

"I already told you. I was home."

"Oh, yes, that's right, you were alone that night." A nasty tone entered his voice.

Tension cut into the muscles of Luys' back. Hatcher had switched tactics, growing deliberately antagonistic, but he would not let the other man provoke him.

Luys wondered how much Hatcher considered him a suspect. He hadn't arrested Luys. Of course he hadn't. Because there was no evidence. Luys hadn't touched

Noah Harris. The other man could be fishing, trying to rattle Luys in hopes of getting information from him.

Yes, he didn't have an alibi. He was alone, but Luys believed in the system, though flawed.

"Are Avery's assault and Noah's murder related?" Luys asked.

Hatcher's smile didn't reach his eyes. "Maybe you can tell me?"

"Okay, I think we're done. I don't appreciate being baited. If you want to arrest me, do it, but otherwise, I'm leaving."

The other man's eyes narrowed. "I know you know something. Either you killed Harris, or you know the person who did. I've been at this job too long now to ignore my instincts. I also think you know far more of what happened to Avery than you're willing to tell."

"This time, your instincts are wrong." Abruptly, Luys rose to his feet. "Are you done?"

"For now." Hatcher slowly rose to his feet. He then opened the door and nodded toward the hallway. "I'll be in touch."

Luys kept his mouth shut. Nothing he said would change the detective's opinion or suspicions.

Even when he left the building, stepped outside, and heat engulfed him from all sides, a chill still raced across his flesh. He needed to find Mayor, stop her. Only then would he feel comfortable enough to distance himself from Avery.

It was the only way.

I watch the father and daughter's house. I have yet to find an opportunity where he is home alone. Focusing on him keeps me from thinking of my other challenges. I close my eyes against the sudden fear, but it clings to me like sweat coated to every pore of my body.

I hate the emotion. It is a sign of weakness, a sign of vulnerability I have always told myself I would not experience again.

Someone wants you dead. They're watching you.

You don't know that.

You need to kill them before they kill you.

Enough!

I wipe my eyes with the back of my hand. Tears, no less. I bite down on a scream of frustration. Now is not the time to cave into the voices.

I try to center my thoughts. The voice inside my head never wants to behave.

I refocus on the house. The time has come. The mother and daughter leave their home and drive off in the car. He is alone. He thinks he is invulnerable, but he will learn.

Five minutes later, I slip into the house.

He is unaware. I walk on silent feet through the living room, through the kitchen, where I pause to pick up an eight-inch blade from the butcher's block on the shiny, white-tiled counter. In a moment, nothing around him will be shiny but his blood.

I find him going through a top drawer of his dresser in the bedroom. How convenient. I don't have to drag him here.

Something must have caught his eye because he looks over at me in the doorway. "What the fuck? What are you doing here?"

I smile, not moving from my spot in the doorway, but fury fills my pores, coats my skin, enters my lungs with each breath I take.

"You're fucking crazy. Are you deaf? I asked what you're doing here? You're nuts if you think I'm going to let you rob me."

"I don't want to steal your possessions."

"Then what do you want?"

"Retribution."

"For what?"

"You are to protect the child, not abuse her."

"What?"

I slash the air with the knife. His eyes widen, and fear creeps into their depths. Stumbling, he backs around the bed, but I lunge toward him, slashing the knife again and again. The tip slices through his shirt to the tender skin below.

Reality seems to finally hit him that I am no joke, that I am serious.

The look on his face makes me chuckle. Then my laugh deepens and grows uncontrollable, as does my rage.

His fear turns to horror. He deserves his horror. He is a parasite on this earth, and no amount of begging will change my mind about his fate.

He scrambles across the bed to get away from me, but I am quicker. I am even quicker with the knife. A minute of struggle, and he surrenders like a rabbit within the jaws of a coyote.

He will no longer hurt an innocent child.

CHAPTER 18

Monday, August 25th – 5:34 pm

When sirens had distracted Luys, Avery had found the perfect time to slip away back to her condo. Knowing she wouldn't be able to talk to the police with them already occupied with an urgent call and Luys nearby, she thought of calling them once she stepped inside her home and locked the door behind her. But she'd stopped herself from grabbing her phone and punching in their number. They would think she was nuts. Stories of rituals, immortality, preternatural hearing wouldn't convince the police of anything but her insanity.

No matter how much she told herself that Luys was crazy and his killer sister was even nuttier, there was still the matter of her hearing. And…the possibility of being cured… The thought of living without a ticking clock counting down her mortality kept her silent. But at the same time, for the first time in six months, hope flickered to life.

She hated to acknowledge that keeping silent was wrong and the last thing she should be doing. By withholding information from the police, she was subsequently condoning Mayor and Luys. For now, she would have to live with that and pray to God that she wouldn't regret it.

After escaping into her condo, she'd been emotionally drained, and the idea of Luys or Mayor couldn't stop her from falling into bed. She slept deeply, the alarm dragging her from the depths of sleep in the morning. God, it felt like she had a hangover, the way her head throbbed. In the shower, her mind shifted quickly to Luys and Mayor, and she quickly shut thoughts of them off in her head. She wasn't going to get herself into a panic attack. She needed to focus on one thing at a time and work needed to be her priority for several hours. People relied on her.

But after work and once pulling off the street and into the condo complex, her mind started racing again. She hadn't found Luys' car in the parking lot and suspected he was still working. She hadn't asked him much about his job.

He'd mentioned being a doctor, not a physician but something else. Research? She wasn't sure and the details had gotten lost in everything else. But could that research be somehow tied to Mayor?

Avery stepped from the alcove of the complex's mail station, looked through several pieces of junk mail, then glanced over to the parking lot for a sign of Luys pulling into the complex. Hot air followed her from the mailboxes and down the sidewalk as she veered toward her building. Heat rose from the ground and wrapped around her legs. She hoped she'd be around when fall finally hit. Too many times, she'd been told a dry heat was much better. Hah. Tell that to her skin on a leather car seat in the middle of summer. If she could get inside before she started dripping sweat, that would be an accomplishment.

Movement at the corner of her eye caught her attention. Cristina had turned down the sidewalk to her place and toward the next building and her condo. She hadn't heard from or seen her friend since their last meeting at *The Thing*.

"Hey, Cristina!"

With her back to Avery, she kept walking, seeming to move faster than before.

"Cristina!" After stuffing her mail into her purse and hugging the bag against her side, she jogged down the sidewalk and caught up to her. "I haven't heard from you in a while."

Cristina glanced over her shoulder at her but quickly turned back the other way, not slowing her pace.

"Hey, what's wrong?"

"Nothing."

"Something's wrong."

Cristina laughed. "In a hurry is all. I'm late. Stephen and I have a hot date, and I don't want to keep my big man waiting!"

Avery's gaze narrowed. Her laugh and voice sounded off, and her behavior was even worse. She grabbed the other woman's arm and tugged. "Cristina. Look at me."

Finally, Cristina stopped and turned toward her, the movement causing her hair to fall forward to obscure her face.

While still holding her arm, Avery lifted the strands from her friend's face with her other hand and brushed them over Cristina's shoulder. Avery sucked in her breath. "Your face."

Cristina's chin lifted into a defiant angle.

"What happened?"

"I dropped my phone, didn't realize the car door was open and whacked my face."

"Come on, do you think I'm going to believe that?"

A deep blue and purple bruise with shades of green at the outer edges cut a swath below Cristina's eye, into her temple, and disappeared into her hairline. Blood vessels had ruptured, staining the white of her left eye and circling around her iris in vivid red. She looked awful.

"Oh, stop staring at me like that," Cristina quickly urged in a harsh voice. "I knew you'd react that way. That's why I didn't want to stop and talk to you."

Avery had kept her opinion to herself when she'd seen the bruises on the other woman's arm in the bathroom the other day, but she wasn't going to keep quiet this time. Saying nothing would be as bad as condoning Stephen's sick behavior. Her thoughts veered briefly to Luys and Mayor and the irony of keeping silent about them and almost winced.

She'd never said she was perfect or any role model. She'd considered her life and herself somewhat of a mess, but she didn't want Cristina's situation escalating into a disaster she couldn't dig herself out of.

Hurt at her friend's cold voice, she let go of Cristina's arm, frustrated that her friend continued to let Stephen treat her like garbage. "Stephen's a complete bastard. He wasn't happy enough with what he did to you before. He had to use you as a punching bag again. We need to report him and have him arrested. Now. This can't go on.

"And what about his younger brother who's visiting right now? Why doesn't he stop Stephen? Or is it only when he's not around that Stephen decides to hit you?"

Cristina looked away. "Don't."

"Cristina. This has to stop. One of these days, you won't be able to walk away. He's going to put you in the hospital if he hasn't before." Her voice softened into a plea. She needed somehow to get through to her. "You know you can get local support. I'll help you. I can get you to a safe house. He won't find you."

"He didn't hurt me." Cristina stepped away and tossed her hair over a shoulder, the bruising to her face vibrant against the sun's rays.

"That's a lie, and you know it. You can't let—"

"Drop it, Avery! If you value our friendship, leave it. Got it?"

Avery opened her mouth to argue, then shut it. She'd never seen Cristina this angry before. It took a tremendous effort to nod. "Okay."

Cristina backed further away. Avery remained unmoving in the middle of the sidewalk. She didn't get it. Her friend knew what options she had and could go to her for any help. Granted, she didn't work with abusive relationships as a social worker, but she knew who to contact to get Cristina the needed help.

She knew herself well enough to realize she wouldn't be able to let it go and have her friend get pummeled by some sick man with control issues, but right now, she'd back off. Alienating Cristina wasn't going to help her friend's situation.

Sighing in frustration and feeling futile, Avery eventually said, "Well, you know where I'm at."

"Yep," Cristina muttered before pivoting sharply and walking away.

She stood in the middle of the sidewalk, frowning

at Cristina's retreating back. When Cristina disappeared around the corner of the building, Avery retreated inside her home. She didn't know how she would keep herself from calling the police the next time she saw Stephen. The creep deserved to be thrown into jail. The thought of punching him herself entered her mind but just as quickly left. Violence never got anyone anywhere but more trouble.

She took a couple of deep breaths to calm down as she closed and locked the front door behind her. She grabbed her mail and phone from her purse and then slipped her phone in the back pocket of her slacks to remind herself to pay the bills later tonight. Right now, she was too hyped up to do anything, never mind focusing on her finances or hospital bills. There were too many questions that ran inside her head, but the idea of confronting Luys kept her within the confines of her home.

She lifted her hands out in front of her, palms up. Sighing, she looked down at them. Could her body have changed in more ways than her hearing, and she hadn't known it? Luys had alluded that she might have heightened abilities.

Nibbling on her bottom lip, she looked around the living room, then focused on the wall and stared hard, willing herself to see into her bedroom. She slowed her breathing and wiped any thoughts from her mind but what was beyond the paint and drywall. After several minutes and with the beginnings of a headache, she gave up.

Nothing.

Well, obviously, her vision hadn't changed. But

other things might have. Taste—that didn't seem too important. But what if she'd gained strength? Maybe that had altered. The idea kicked up her pulse. She'd be able to take on Mayor, defend herself if she had heightened physical power.

She could even protect Cristina from that slime ball of a husband.

With both hands, she grabbed a pillow from the sofa and pulled at both ends, thinking if she tugged hard enough, the material would rip. She yanked until the muscles in her shoulders and arms screamed back in protest. The pillow remained intact.

"This is ridiculous," she muttered.

Maybe it was mind over matter. If she believed in the ability, considered it the truth, and was fervent enough, then maybe something would happen.

She hurried over to the front door, eyed it briefly, then took a breath, and before she changed her mind and backed down, she punched the door with her entire body behind it.

She cried out as pain slammed into her knuckles, up her wrist, and into her arm.

"Son of a bitch!" She cradled her arm and closed her eyes, failing miserably at keeping the pain at bay. She stumbled back as a wave of dizziness assaulted her.

Oh, God. Maybe she broke something, shattered bones. The hospital. She squeezed her eyes shut. The pain. It was mind-numbing. She took in ragged breaths, floundering for some semblance of calm.

The ER. She needed to get there somehow.

The floor disappeared beneath her, and she was falling, falling into nothing but black space. Wind, icy and bitter, swirled around her, whipping the hair against her neck, face, and into her eyes. Her body slammed into an invisible force, sucking the air from her lungs.

Shivering, she opened her eyes while cradling her arm against her stomach. For a full minute and longer, she stood frozen, unable to understand. Her living room had disappeared. She glanced around, taking the sliding double doors from behind her, the blue chrome and cushioned chairs, the walls in blue and white. And finally, her gaze landed on the large red emergency sign above a reception area. Everything was vaguely familiar.

She finally recognized the place. She'd been at this hospital before when Luys had dropped her off here.

But how…?

She blinked as the pain in her hand receded. She had to be hallucinating. There was no other explanation. Cautiously, she moved deeper into the building. She blinked again. A mist-like film swirled around her legs and ankles. Gradually, the wisps slowed and dissolved.

Impossible. Crazy. She was losing it. She had to be. She'd just been in her living room. But the pain throbbing from her fingers and joints told her she was experiencing something tangible. She frowned down at her body. Her black work slacks and white shirt, her heels were what she'd worn the entire day.

The memory flooded her thoughts of how Luys' living room window exploded outward, as if from an unseen power. Had Mayor escaped that day amidst the fog and mist?

Heart pounding, she walked forward, conscious of the floor beneath her feet. It seemed solid, not some figment of her imagination. She inhaled, feeling the oxygen flow into her lungs. The air felt real too. With her good hand, she reached over and ran her fingers across the wall. Cool and hard beneath her touch. The pain in her other hand eased further.

"Can I help you?"

She glanced over to a woman with black, short hair behind the receptionist counter, this person different from the employee from when she'd visited with Luys. At least she thought so. "I—maybe."

From behind the plastic partition, the woman frowned. "What do you mean? Do you need help or not? Or are you here for someone else?"

Something moved in her peripheral vision. She turned and found a man sitting in a chair in the corner watching her. An odd look flashed across his face. Fear? Had he seen her suddenly appear? The receptionist didn't seem to act as if she'd appeared out of nowhere.

Both of them were staring at her. They saw her; the woman had talked to her. That must mean they saw her as real. Yet... none of it made sense.

She couldn't be dreaming. Or if she was, she'd never experienced something so vivid, so tactile.

Then she realized the woman was still looking at her. She glanced down at her hand and realized the pain had dramatically subsided. The abrasions across her knuckles had vanished, and her fingers no longer looked red or swollen. "I—" she started to answer. She flexed her hand, shocked at how she could move her joints easily and fluidly. "Actually...I think I'm fine." She nodded to one of the chairs in the waiting room and lied, "I'm waiting for a friend."

Avery sat down and glanced over at the man, the

only other person in the room. Limp gray hair hung past his shoulders, and his jaw contained a good week's growth of beard. When their gazes met, he quickly looked away and hunched his shoulders. But she'd seen his eyes widen. Alarm? Maybe she'd read him correctly…

She moved over a couple more chairs closer to him, needing some sort of validation. "You saw what happened, didn't you? One minute I was suddenly there."

"Leave me alone," he muttered, eyeing her from head to toe as the scent of stale alcohol wafted toward her. "Nothing happened. I saw nothing." He glared at her before making a point at staring at the wall.

Avery eyed his clenched fists and backed off. She had a good idea if she pressed him further, he'd use one of them in her face. In frustration, she sat down in the chair she'd vacated. Cold air blasted her from an air-conditioning vent, sending goosebumps across her exposed skin. Rubbing her arms, she slumped deeper into her seat as she contemplated leaving the hospital. She was over 5 miles away. Walking home wasn't a good idea. She'd be risking dehydration with the temperature over a hundred and no water. She didn't have a wallet, money, or—

Her phone!

She dug it from her back pocket. She'd gotten in the habit of sticking her phone in her pocket for easy access. She pulled it out and peered at a blank screen. She tried swiping the screen with a finger and hitting the power button several times. Nothing. Still a black screen. Somehow the battery had died. From traveling? The idea made her stomach crawl. If moving through space and time killed a battery, what did that mean when it came to her body?

She mentally shook the thought away as she put her phone back in her pocket. But she couldn't shake off the dilemma of getting back home. She'd need a credit card if she called for an Uber for a ride home. There was a taxi, and…there was Luys.

Luys wasn't a good idea.

There was another option. Crazier than all of them. She could try to will herself back to her place. She'd managed it once.

In case it worked, and the chair beneath her disappeared from under her, she stood up. She ignored the glare from the man in the corner. The woman behind the receptionist's counter had disappeared somewhere.

From a spot against the wall, she closed her eyes and took in slow, measured breaths. Then she paused. This could be dangerous. She could get trapped between two physical locations, she could land somewhere far more dangerous than a hospital, like the middle of a busy intersection, in the ocean, or… Enough. She had to try.

She envisioned herself in her living room, the cream walls, the neutral colors of tan, baby blue, and ivory furnishings, the television against the wall with the large potted palm beside it.

She opened her eyes.

Nothing.

Maybe she wasn't willing herself enough. She curled her hands into fists at her side and imagined herself jumping into the room, leaping through time and space.

She reopened her eyes.

Still nothing.

Maybe this was a dream after all.

Maybe she had lost her sanity.

Her heart rate kicked up. Okay. She needed to calm down. She also needed answers. So many questions. If it happened once, could it happen at another time when she least expected it?

The only person who had answers was Luys. She needed to know what was going on inside of her and how dangerous it was to go from place to place with a random thought. There had to be a way to control it.

Inwardly groaning at the idea of contacting him, Avery knew she really didn't have any other options. Unless she hunted down Mayor. She might find her at the coffee shop. Avery quickly nixed the idea. Luys was the far less deadly of the two.

She moved across the waiting room and eyed the receptionist's desk. The woman was back.

"Do you have a phone I could use?" Avery asked from in front of the plexiglass.

"You don't have a cell phone?" The woman's gaze narrowed. She probably had her share of strange people show up in the emergency room—some dangerous, some kind, but probably all in pain.

A sarcastic comment rose to her lips, but she stuffed it down. She needed the use of the phone. The woman could easily tell her to go to hell. "No, sorry."

After a lengthy pause, the woman relented. "Fine but be quick about it."

After she called—thank God, her memory was great with numbers—she waited tensely. Maybe Luys wouldn't answer. The phone number was probably unknown to him, and she personally never answered hers if she didn't recognize the person's number.

Before the line kicked into voicemail, he answered, the dark rich texture of his voice a welcome. Something she'd never thought she'd feel after the other day.

"Hey, this is Avery. I'm without a car and was hoping you could pick me up."

His voice sharpened. "What's wrong? Are you hurt?"

She eyed the receptionist, who seemed interested in the screen on her computer, but she suspected the woman was listening with avid interest. "No, I'm fine." She glanced down at her hand. The abrasions to her skin had healed, and the pain had completely subsided. She suspected the rapid healing was a result of what Mayor had done to her. "I just need a ride. I don't have my car."

"Of course," he quickly responded, thankfully not asking any more questions. "Where are you?"

She tensed, knowing he was going to think the worst. "I'm at the hospital, the one you dropped me off at the other day."

He sucked in a breath. "I'm on my way."

"Thank you," she whispered with difficulty, embarrassed that she had to ask him for a favor when she'd wanted nothing to do with him.

She didn't have to wait long for Luys to pull up at the entrance. Once she slipped inside the passenger seat, Luys didn't drive off. Frowning, she turned and met his gaze across the short distance, sensing a growing tension filling the car's interior...

CHAPTER 19

Monday, August 25th – 7:05 pm

Luys' grip on the steering wheel tightened as he searched Avery's face, the arch of her neck, the incredibly long length of her legs encased in black slacks, those strong yet delicate hands, the smooth, unblemished skin of her exposed arms. Even though there seemed to be no signs of any injuries, that didn't mean she wasn't hurt in some other way. She could have internal damage or been terrorized. If his sister came within yards of Avery, she'd rue the day she had him as a brother.

Luys didn't realize he had spoken under his breath until Avery asked as she snapped on her seatbelt, "What?"

"Did Mayor touch you? She's unpredictable, and even after decades, I've yet been able to guess her next move." The idea of his sister getting within two feet of Avery terrified him.

Avery slumped against her backrest. "No. I haven't seen her, and I'm not about to go looking for her."

"You won't find her at her old house. She doesn't live in the area you mentioned by Scottsdale Road. I checked everywhere and had my brother call in a favor with someone from public records. She must have found a new place under a different name, but she'll show herself soon enough," Luys muttered, pulling out of the hospital's parking lot. "You had me deeply concerned when you called. Being at a hospital usually is never good under any circumstances. It wasn't because of your cancer?"

"Ahh, no."

"Have you made an appointment with your oncologist?" He didn't care that he was becoming too invested in her wellbeing. Her health and welfare were important to him. Having her in his life was making him realize how empty it had been. "When is your next CT scan or MRI?"

She frowned. "This Friday. I can't schedule them when I want. Scans are authorized through my doctor."

"You'll find your cancer gone."

"Hmm. We'll see what my oncologist says." She slumped deeper in her seat. "I'll admit, all your talk of special abilities makes me want to think of miracles. But me and miracles, or anything close to them, don't seem to get along, so I kind of expect the worst." She shrugged. "Even so, there's something to my amplified hearing. There's no logical explanation for me suddenly to have something like that, and I've never heard of any cases with someone who has it. But all that thinking had me doing something stupid to where I banged up my hand pretty bad." She lifted a palm in the air. "Oh, no damages. At least now, see? The fault's all mine."

"And why is that?" He looked over and met her sheepish expression before double-checking her hand. It looked fine.

"Well, I thought I'd test out these 'abilities' by slamming my hand into the door. I know, not very smart, but I wanted to give it a shot. I swore I had thought I'd broken something."

He winced. "But you didn't."

"No. My fingers must have healed. The pain's gone. The abrasions have disappeared."

His hands around the car's wheel relaxed. He twisted his neck back and forth, stretching the joints to release the tension in his muscles. His fear for Avery eased. She wasn't completely powerless against Mayor or anyone else now. Given time, she would hone her skills. As long as she didn't turn into someone like Mayor and find herself sucked into the power that slowly grew within her.

He stared hard at the road in front of him. Avery wasn't going to be like that. She couldn't, wouldn't be seduced. She was too strong, had a maturity many her age didn't have. She wouldn't be swayed…but power could mold, corrupt—

"You don't sound surprised."

He blinked, focusing back on the road. A quick glance her way confirmed he was thinking the worst. Avery wouldn't turn into another Mayor. "No, all three of us have a strength no human can match. We have trained ourselves to know how much pressure to apply or how little. We used to break things all the time in the beginning."

"You should have told me!"

He gave her a side glance. "When? We haven't talked since the other night. You didn't want to be anywhere near me—not that I'd blame you. Even if I tried to talk to you, I don't think you were in any frame of mind to listen to what I had to say."

"Hmm. Even so, if I'd known, I wouldn't have ended up in the hospital."

He frowned. "I don't understand."

Avery sighed as if he should know what she was talking about. "When I hurt my hand, the pain was excruciating. I thought for sure I had broken something. All of that made me think of the hospital. Then suddenly, I was there. Poof. I was in my living room one second and then in the lobby."

The tension was back, wrapping around his neck, shoulders, and twining around his spine. He didn't like where this conversation was going.

"What? Is that bad? You look upset."

"I'm surprised more than upset." Luys made a point of keeping his voice neutral. "It's something that I never expected."

"Well, you don't look surprised. Is this supposed to be something I should be alarmed about?"

"No," he quickly replied while searching for the right words. "Did anyone witness what happened?"

"Well… there was a man in the emergency lobby and then the receptionist. I don't think she saw anything but the guy…I'm pretty sure he saw me show up like on an episode of Star Trek."

"Did he notify the police or the staff?"

"No. Nothing like that. I think I scared the hell out of him more than anything. I tried talking to him, but he wanted nothing to do with me. Anyone asking him questions about me would probably think he was hallucinating because he reeked pretty badly from alcohol."

"Well, that's something, I guess."

"I guess."

She shifted to where he could feel the full force of her gaze. He said nothing, sure she would ask when she was ready. He didn't have to wait long.

"Can you?"

"Can I what?"

"Okay, now you're being deliberately obtuse."

Luys couldn't help but smile. "No, I can't. Gabriel and I have tried to travel across time and space for years, which isn't one of our most intellectual pursuits. It's dangerous. So much can go wrong. But…"

When he remained silent, she urged, "But what?"

"Mayor is the only one who can travel across time and space. What took Mayor decades to do, you've done in days."

"Oh."

"I had thought…"

"What?"

Did he dare? Then he realized he had to trust Avery. It was pointless now to hold back. "I had thought Mayor garnered her extraordinary powers from dark forces."

"Like ritualist killing?"

"Yes," he replied reluctantly, surprised at how quickly Avery had grasped what he was getting at. He pulled into the complex's parking lot and parked in his assigned slot.

"Well, it's the only thing I can think of why she would be stronger. Maybe it's not the most logical reasoning as to why she can do what she can do. I guess too many nights sitting at home alone and watching sick horror movies on my end."

"But I am stumped now and unable to explain how you can do what you managed within a week when it took Mayor decades. I thought her focus on darkness, greed, sin, despair was instrumental in her becoming a dangerous and lethal adversary. But because of what you've accomplished in days, it tells me all my thinking has been false conjecture. Maybe a placebo is involved or a chemical inside her brain that Gabriel and I are missing."

"Maybe something in my DNA that I share with Mayor?"

Her wrinkled nose and horrified expression told him she didn't much like that idea. He'd feel the same. "It's possible."

"Hmm." She unbuckled her seat belt and slipped from the car.

He got out on his side, hit the lock, and the car beeped in reply. "Do you know what you did to transport yourself to the hospital?"

"I'm clueless," Avery murmured. "I tried recreating my thoughts to see if I could do it again, and nothing."

"No. Don't do that," he urged, looking across the top of the car at her.

"Why?"

"Traveling can be dangerous."

"Well, I figured that out." She scowled. "Is there more than just traveling to a wrong or dangerous location? Can I lose parts of my DNA?"

"I don't know. Mayor's been lucky. She's always traveled to other areas of the world without incident, but after so many times, I know her luck can run out. It has to be risky. We know nothing about what it entails. There's a chance of damaging or somehow altering your DNA. And even if you lose part of your DNA through the time and space continuum, you won't know of it immediately. Your body would still work for a time, but your immune system would eventually collapse until..." He winced. "Then there is the matter of becoming detangled with other matter. Those theories have been explored again and again through horror and science fiction movies but not in real life, at least not with anything other than hypotheses. No one really knows of the ramifications if something were to go wrong. When it comes to quantum mechanics—or teleportation— today's science is only familiar with quantum computing, networks, and the possibility of a quantum internet."

"You're going to give me a panic attack. All I can think of are movies like *Looper*, *Dr. Strange*, and that gruesome horror flick, *The Fly*, which was beyond disgusting and makes me think twice about leaping from one place to the other." She led the way to their condos and said over her shoulder, "You know, I might look like I'm super excited about the possibilities of time travel, but I'm not the type of person to jump into something without thinking it through and looking at all my options. This is no exception."

"Good. Maybe it's best you focus on other possible abilities that you might have," Luys mused as they came to where the pathway separated and went toward their respective condos. "If you're able to teleport, there's a possibility that you might have psychokinesis."

"What's that?"

"Telekinesis is another word for it."

"You mean *move* things?" she asked in disbelief.

"Yes, the ability to move matter with your mind." He shook his head and looked down at her upturned face. The wonder in her eyes did something to his chest. He hadn't seen that look in a long while from anyone. To feel such an emotion had been even longer for him.

"My, God, seriously? I feel like I'm now living in an alternative universe and like my mind is going to explode." She shook her head, awe lingering in those beautiful eyes of hers. "That's all soooo crazy! My life's done a complete 180, and I don't know what to make of it all. The thought of being able to move something with my mind is beyond amazing!"

He arched a brow and wanted to laugh at such enthusiasm. The sparkle in her eyes, the glow to her cheeks, the way her hair glowed against the sun's rays. She was truly a beautiful woman, and he had an idea she was clueless as to how attractive she was. Maybe some good could come of Mayor's actions after all.

Her face turned serious. "Can you do that?"

"No." He moved closer and stared down at her upturned face. He didn't like the gleam of excitement in her eyes. He suspected she was running through all kinds of ideas inside her head. He frowned as thoughts of her accidentally harming herself entered his mind. Everything was too new for her. She could also hurt someone she cared deeply for. But at the same time, he didn't want to dampen her feelings of wonder. "None of your newfound capabilities are something to take lightly. It comes with responsibility and strength of character." He ran a hand along the length of her upper arm and clasped her shoulder to get his point across. "Mayor wields her power with little regard to anything or anyone but her own needs."

Her smile faltered, and he felt like an ass for being responsible for it.

"Is that why Mayor has changed? She didn't start out like she is now, right?"

"No, she didn't, but it's much more than that. There's a rage inside her she refuses to dampen and makes a point of stoking it until she loses control. She lost her daughter when we were captured by the Aztecs. She saw it all happen, the ritualistic killing, the horror in her child's face, how they tossed her lifeless body from the temple." Images of that day flashed inside his head. They would never dim. He'd tried too long to stuff them somewhere deep inside of his brain to no avail. They still swirled to the surface. The sun high in the sky, the taste of dirt in his mouth when his captors shoved him to the ground because he'd fought back to get to his niece.

"That's awful!"

At the unmistakable sympathy in her eyes, he quickly said, "Don't feel sorry for her. Not now, not after the horror she's caused others. Maybe back when the loss was fresh and raw."

"But her daughter…"

His throat tightened, and he found his words locked in his throat. He still missed her. Maria's innocence, her belief in possibilities, her childlike wonder.

Then her eyes widened. "Oh."

When she stepped away from him, it forced his hand to drop to his side. "What?"

Until now she hadn't connected everything. "It all makes sense. Noah Harris. His research into the Aztecs and ritualistic killings. His murder. You're one of them."

"What? What are you talking about?"

"You killed him. You wanted to shut him up. He was getting closer to what you and your sister were doing."

Her words were alarming him. He didn't know what she was talking about.

"Avery, you're not making sense." Too late, he realized that was the worst thing he could have said.

Her gaze narrowed. "Don't even bother to act like you don't know what I'm talking about. You and Mayor have some sick, twisted way to keep on living. You kill people, torture, and perform some type of sick ritual on your victims. You can't die. Neither one of you can. Because you kill others. I don't know how it's done. There's something in the Aztec lore and the Catholic Church. They're somehow tied together. I don't know how the two mix. But I do know you're perverted along with Mayor." She stumbled backward. "I feel so stupid! I had it right in front of my face and didn't see it all this time. Probably because I didn't want to. You were born at the time the Aztecs were a powerful race. You lived and breathed their culture."

"I'm not one of them. I hated what they did to us," he spat, appalled she thought such awful things about him. "They captured us. It's the other way around. They enslaved us, tortured us, caged us in zoos."

Her eyes widened, and she opened her mouth. He was afraid she was going to scream.

"Get your hands up! Touch her, and I'll shoot!"

He turned at the same time as Avery and found two officers, guns drawn and aiming both weapons at his chest and advancing toward them.

"Hands up! Now!"

He recognized one officer. The neighbor. He'd seen Avery talking to him. By his rigid stance, steady grip on his gun, and narrow-eyed glare, the cop meant it.

Luys shouldn't be shocked, but he was.

"Luys Martinez?" the other officer asked. He edged closer. Sweat stained the blue, too-tight uniform under his arms and dripped down the side of his neck.

Luys didn't recognize him.

"Yes."

"You're under arrest for the murder of Noah Harris."

CHAPTER 20

Monday, August 25th – 8:09 pm

Avery stumbled away as Ben Atkins slammed into Luys' shoulder and spun him around. Quick and efficient, he incapacitated Luys by wrenching his arm up against his back. Using his shoulder and his weight, Ben rammed him up against the building's wall with a thump. She winced as the side of Luys' face hit and scraped across the rough stucco.

With a knee against the back of Luys' thigh, Ben grabbed his other hand and cuffed him. Then he yanked him back around suddenly, and Avery found herself staring directly into Luys' eyes. She sucked in a breath. Shock. For a moment. It flared in his eyes before he shielded the expression.

Shoulders slumped, he turned away from her gaze. He looked defeated. But she knew he could easily break away from both police officers and escape. He could kill them both if he was anything like Mayor. That is if he'd been telling her the entire truth about his physical abilities. But he could have been lying to her the entire time.

She frowned. He hadn't thought he would get caught. But didn't all criminals and killers think that way? They lied too. He could have distorted the truth about what she could or couldn't do. Glancing down at her injured hand, she flexed her fingers. It was hard to believe she'd hurt it earlier.

Her stomach roiled as they pushed Luys down the walkway, and all three of them disappeared behind another building. His betrayal stung far more than she liked to admit. She'd slept with a man, found him fascinating, blinded herself to the idea that he couldn't be a killer. She'd focused on the sister so she wouldn't have to deal with her own demons. She'd wanted to believe in Luys, making excuses for him when any normal person would have run like hell.

In her adult life, she'd never let anyone hurt her like Luys. During her childhood, yes, there'd been others who'd filled her head with promises: parents who had assured her of a safe home, a place to feel that she belonged, a loving family with no conditions attached. Their promises had all turned empty, except for one— that family had turned out to be the most painful of them all. But she'd reached adulthood, though cautious and wary, with some semblance of normalcy. Luys, though, ripped open the old wounds of her childhood: all her self-doubts, insecurities, and vulnerabilities. And she'd let him, so she didn't have anyone to blame but herself. She'd been alone for so long, working full-time and going to college, with no time for a deep, meaningful relationship, and then dealing with her cancer with no one to confide in about her deepest fears. Maybe it was her own fault for not making time because of her own anxieties of being hurt.

She sighed. Blaming others or herself wasn't going to get her anywhere.

When she retreated into her condo, her entire body shook in reaction. She hit both locks on the front door and paced the room. She asked herself again, why hadn't he escaped? He could have easily overpowered both cops. Frowning, she hugged her chest and rubbed both arms. Maybe he'd been too much in shock. Or he could have a plan, couldn't he? Maybe he let them arrest him for a reason she could only guess at?

Her frown deepened. It didn't matter what he was feeling. Or, for that matter, what she was feeling. She should be thrilled that he wasn't coming back. He was dangerous, a man she should never have tangled with, and that included his sister. They'd murdered Noah Harris. They were probably planning on doing her next. And she'd slept with him. She couldn't get the thought out of her head.

He'd taken in a lost kitten, of all things. Who would think someone that caring would be a killer? Ugh. She had. The poor cat was alone in his place, probably needing food and a refill of fresh water. Earlier, Luys had told her about his key hidden under a fake rock in the gravel by his door. She couldn't ignore the animal. After retrieving the key, and within ten minutes, she entered Luys' condo, smuggled Clover, her food dish, and the litter box into her home.

Once back inside her condo, the kitten seemed excited at her new territory after wolfing down a healthy meal. After investigating each room with interest, Clover jumped onto Avery's lap. She caressed the animal's silky ears and chin, feeling some of the tension ease. The kitten soon settled down by curling into a ball by her head on the sofa. Avery didn't have Clover's interest in a nap. She still couldn't fully relax. A hot bath wouldn't work, alcohol might fix things for a bit, but it would lead to more feelings of depression. The gym in the complex was the only thing she could think of to calm down.

After changing quickly into a pair of leggings and a loose-fitting shirt, she grabbed a towel, her keys, and pepper spray and then locked the door, jiggling the handle to ensure no one could get in. Avery grunted. It probably wouldn't keep Mayor out if she wanted in.

Her stomach revolted at the scent of barbequing meat wafting from the pool area when she stepped outside. Her insides hadn't yet settled. Wrinkling her nose, she rushed down the sidewalk, making a point of checking every pathway before veering off into other parts of the complex. Even though Luys was gone, there was still Mayor. She slipped inside the gym after using the key, the air-conditioning slapping her with its frigid air, and was relieved to find only one other person in the building running on a treadmill.

She started on the weight machine. From there, she moved onto the stair stepper. A few neighbors trailed into the room, none of them familiar. Sixty minutes later, her limbs shaking from exhaustion forced her off the machine. She was still wired, but she didn't feel like an electrical charge was going through every vein or artery anymore. Rubbing the towel against the back of her neck, she left the building and stepped into a wave of heat even though the sun had since set. A breeze kicked up, urging her back to her condo as she hugged her towel against her stomach and wrapped her fingers around her keys and pepper spray.

After she veered onto the sidewalk to her building,

a sigh whispered from behind. She twisted and looked over her shoulder, thinking the worst. Still, she jerked in surprise at a shadow advancing toward her. A man, judging from his size and height, strode toward her. Shadows obscured his features. Panic. It swept through her body as she quickened her pace, fumbled for the pepper spray from beneath her towel, and fingered the cylinder until her finger found the button.

She couldn't stop her body's reaction, even knowing she needed to calm down. The police had taken Luys away. The person was a neighbor going about his business. But it didn't help when his step quickened, sounding as if he was advancing toward her.

Twisting around, hand on her spray, she peered across her shoulder again. Light from a nearby lamppost revealed his face for a moment before he moved closer. Stephen. His teeth flashed, a sharp contrast from the rest of his shadowed face.

Avery's breath whooshed out of her lungs in relief. She clutched the towel to her chest to hide the tremors in her hands and chuckled. Even to her ears, her laugh sounded winded and forced. He'd scared the crap out of her, and he was the last person she wanted to see.

"Stephen! You startled me. How's Cristina? I haven't seen her in a while."

She hoped to God he wasn't controlling where she went and who she talked to. Avery wanted to yell at him to keep his hands off her friend, but by doing that, she knew she'd jeopardize Cristina.

A mere two feet away, he halted in front of her, his breath smelling unfamiliar, metallic, and laced with something she couldn't identify. If he hit Cristina hard enough to make her bleed.… Anger welled up inside her and kept her from backing away. Something was off. The curl of his lip looked more like a sneer than a smile. "Is something wrong?"

"Yes, something's definitely wrong. Or should I say, someone."

"Cristina? Is she okay?" Oh, God. Did he finally put her in the hospital? Beat her bloody? "What have you done to her?"

"I haven't done anything to her. It's *you* who needs to stop. Enough with the prying, of putting your nose where it doesn't belong."

"How can I when it's obvious she's being abused by you!"

"You don't know the meaning of abuse. You have no clue. But I'll be happy to show you."

He lunged, grabbed both her arms, and shook her. She gasped. The shock and force of his attack sent her towel, keys, and pepper spray flying to the ground. She strained away from his hold, but his fingers dug deeper into her flesh.

"What is with you? Stop it! Have you lost your mind!"

Avery glanced around. The gym was on the outskirts of the complex and away from the main buildings. They were alone.

"You need to cut it out," he bit out.

"Why should I?" she recklessly asked, uncaring that she was egging him on, too caught up in the injustice of him hurting someone smaller than him. "It's obvious you have some sick power over her. She needs a friend, not some bully who likes to show who's in power."

"You have no clue what you're talking about!"

"Tell that to the bruises on her body."

She shoved at his chest. It was like hitting concrete, but that wasn't going to stop her. If he thought he could treat her like he did his wife, he was in for a surprise. She lifted a knee to ram him in the groin, but he twisted too quickly. He then shoved and jerked her to the side.

Gasping, Avery found herself somehow backed up into the shadows of a building. His breath was hot and rancid against her face, the peculiar scent wafting into her lungs. She fought back the urge to vomit and opened her mouth to scream. He cut it off with a hand over her mouth.

"Nice try. I'm not that stupid."

For a wild second, she thought he was going to rape her, even kill her. She should have kept her foolish mouth shut, not gotten herself worked up from pointless, self-righteous anger.

She closed her eyes and willed herself somewhere else. *Come on. Transport somewhere, anywhere but here.* The pressure of his hand on her mouth didn't ease or disappear. It wasn't working. But she'd done it once. She could do it again. She squeezed her eyes tighter. All she needed to do was center her thoughts harder.

Focusing on moving through space and time, she willed herself away from her spot and Stephen. Still nothing. The sour tang of his breath on her face told her she was wishing for something that wasn't going to happen. She couldn't miraculously vanish, couldn't pull herself from his vice-like grip, couldn't scream.

She was being a victim, and she couldn't do anything about it.

His hand on her mouth didn't smother the whimper that slipped past her lips.

"I'm only going to warn you once."

Her eyes snapped open as he leaned over her, pushing her backward until her head scraped the brick wall. Avery's fisted hands were trapped against his chest. Her eyes misted with impotence as she glared up at him. She wouldn't show fear.

His hand on her mouth shifted, and for a moment she thought it was enough to get her teeth into his palm, but the pressure didn't ease. The pain turned relentless as he grabbed the hair at the back of her neck and twisted until he forced her to look to the side. Oh, God. What was he planning? She hadn't seen a weapon on him.

Now was the time. She closed her eyes and wished herself somewhere else. Anywhere but here. She needed to go, go now. Please, God, teleport me from here. Seconds ticked by. All her wishing didn't do a thing. She opened her eyes. He still loomed over her.

He yanked her closer. She stiffened. Then he ran his tongue across the length of her cheek as if he was marking her. Shock rolled through her body.

She flinched, feeling the moist warmth of his saliva against her skin.

Then, suddenly, he shoved her. The force slammed her against the wall. Her head snapped back and struck the brick. She grabbed onto the building to keep herself from falling. When she got air back in her lungs, she glanced around.

He'd disappeared.

CHAPTER 21

Avery sat in the waiting room of the police station. Glancing at her phone told her she'd been here a good 30 minutes. If she had to wait any longer, she'd have to leave. Her doctor's appointment was later in the morning. It was something she couldn't miss. She had a CT scan with contrast and blood work. It had been three months since the last scan. The scan would reveal how far her cancer had progressed. Last time, the images had been devastating, revealing several tumors forming throughout her body. If these scans showed progression, she suspected the doctor would admit he had no other options available.

The crazy part was that she wasn't feeling any symptoms of tumor growth or enlarged lymph nodes. The targeted therapy she'd been on months before had wiped her out, caused temperature spikes, elevated liver enzymes, fatigue, and extreme itching in the worst places to where the symptoms were so severe, they'd forced her to stop treatment.

The idea of what the doctor would find twisted her gut into knots. It shouldn't, though. She'd known her time was running out. Unless…what Luys had told her was the truth and that Mayor had cured her cancer. It could be a complete fabrication. Still, she didn't know why he would lie about something like that. Or he truly believed he was telling the truth.

The sigh of the door opening drew her thoughts back to the police station. Ben Atkins stepped into the waiting room. At seeing his familiar face, she found herself filled with a mix of emotions. She knew Ben cared about his job and would treat her with the respect that he probably did with everyone, but still, it would be nice to be completely anonymous. She'd have to face Ben later around the complex, and he would also continually remind her of her previous assault and now Stephen's threats.

She'd thought of calling the police and reporting Stephen's attack last night after she'd stumbled into her condo, but thoughts of Cristina kept her from reaching for her cell phone. She considered Cristina a friend, and she knew the other woman would feel betrayed if Avery contacted the police. But the thought of not doing anything felt like she was condoning Stephen's behavior, not just at what he did to her but also Cristina. She'd gone back and forth on what to do during the night, but she hadn't gotten a minute of rest. The idea of Stephen coming after her in the future sure didn't help. He was a bully, and she realized by morning that he needed to be stopped, even if it meant losing Cristina's friendship.

"Avery. Sorry I kept you waiting." He nodded to the door. "If you'll follow me."

"Of course."

When they entered a small cubicle of a room, he waved an arm at a metal chair across from a desk. He sank down in a matching chair across from her. "So why are you here? You wanted to file a report on someone?" He frowned. "It's not about Luys Martinez, is it?"

"No, no." When she realized she was fiddling with her phone, she slipped it into the back of her jeans pocket.

"I've never filed a report before." She frowned, searching for the right words. "A man. The husband of a friend of mine, well…"

He waited, his expression unreadable.

"He threatened me, grabbed me by the arms, and shoved me against the wall of a building by the fitness center."

"Did he hit you?"

"No. But I have bruises where his hands were." She shrugged out of a light summer jacket to reveal several blue and green marks on her upper arms. "From the way he was acting, I thought he might do more than hit me." She shifted uncomfortably and wrinkled her nose. "He also licked me."

Both of Ben's brows shot skyward. "How so?"

"Like I said, he had me against the wall of a building near the gym. I couldn't go anywhere. He was too strong. He must have thought in some sick way licking me was a form of a threat. He ran his tongue up my cheek. Maybe he has some type of communicable disease, and he wanted to use it to get back at me." Her skin crawled at the thought. She could be running around right now with some sickness that she wasn't aware of.

"I wouldn't be able to guess the reason. God knows what runs through some people's heads." It was his turn to frown. "And why would he want to get back at you?"

She sighed, hating to explain. "His wife, Cristina,

has her own bruises. She had a terrible one on her face. Not to mention the ones I've seen on her arms."

"Because of him?"

"It's the only logical reason I can think of."

"And has she reported it?"

"No."

"And why is that?"

"I'm not sure." She slipped her jacket back on. "Well, anyway. He must have found out that I was talking to her and trying to convince her to get help or leave him. It ticked him off because I was putting my 'nose' into their business."

"What else did he do other than lick you?"

"He threatened me that if I didn't keep out of Cristina's and his business, he'd be happy to show me what abuse really was. From there, that's when he licked me and shoved me against the wall." She touched the back of her head. The area still stung. "I have a pretty good-sized lump to my head where I hit the wall."

"Anything else, other than the bruising and bump to your head?"

"No."

"Did you go to your doctor's office or the hospital? Would they happen to have a report?"

"No..." She frowned, not liking what he was implying with the question. "The doctor's office has regular hours, and the hospital seemed a bit much for the injuries I had."

"I see." He leaned back in his chair and folded his arms. "And why did you wait until now to file a report?"

"I was worried about Cristina finding out and being hurt by me going to the police because of her husband.

I was also afraid to lose her friendship." She straightened in her chair. It felt like she was the one being questioned instead of Stephen. "I would think there was something you could do. I see all these stupid shows where the women always end up as victims, and no one does anything, but this isn't television."

"No, it isn't television. It's far more complex than a movie. I'm sorry, Avery. You can file an assault report causing injury, but it's pretty much he said, she said, and there's nothing we can do on our side. Filing a restraining order isn't possible with what you've given me. I need proof."

"But…" She slapped her palm against the table. She was feeling foolish and naïve. God, she wanted to scream.

He reached over and patted her hand. "You can be proactive by making sure you keep a log of anything he does here on out."

She pulled her hand away. She found his touch condescending even though there was unmistakable sympathy in his eyes. Still, she was frustrated with him, her, and the whole situation. And what if Stephen did a number on her to where she ended up in the hospital or worse? A stupid log wasn't going to help her then. "That's just great. It feels like I wasted my time by coming here."

"I'm sorry you feel that way. I wish I could do more," Ben admitted. "But by filing a report, you at least have a record if he does anything else. Remember, we need proof. Have your phone's camera running if he shows up near you."

Like she'd have time to get the app working and filming to capture Stephen before he attacked her. Pretty sad to think she had no options in defending herself. She'd thought going to the police this morning was her only recourse to protect herself. It would seem she had it all wrong. If only she could travel through time and space at will. Maybe she'd be able to figure it out soon. But she couldn't wait until then. She was going to have to protect herself the normal way. A gun she couldn't do, but a mace or taser. Now that she could do with confidence.

She could imagine Cristina's reaction once she found out that Avery had gone to the police about her husband. Forget any friendship. That was now down the toilet. They hadn't been that close, though.

After filing the report with the help from Ben, she left the station feeling like she'd wasted most of her morning. But on the way to the hospital, her irritation quickly dissolved into unease. Her morning wasn't done yet and could get far worse.

First on the list was a CT scan on the second floor of the hospital. The contrast injection into her vein always burned like someone had poured acid into her bloodstream. Feeling like she deserved a treat after her scan, she grabbed a chocolate chip scone and water at the cafeteria before walking into the oncology department on the third floor. After checking in, she sat down in the waiting room and couldn't help but notice a guy and a girl around her age. It was sad enough to see older people late in life having to deal with cancer but seeing someone as young as herself sucked even more. While the idea of children, well, she didn't even want to think of their pain. It broke her heart.

She washed down her scone with water. It tasted

not nearly as good as she thought it would. She'd barely brushed off the crumbs from her lips or had time to get more nervous than she already was when a nurse from the doorway called out, "Avery F."

She jumped up and strode over, muttering trivial greetings with the nurse as she followed her into the lab. After the nurse performed a blood test, another one quickly replaced her and led her to a private room.

Once alone, Avery found the silence inside the four walls suffocating. Tension crawled up her back and along her shoulders. She felt fine, but that didn't mean anything. Any minute the doctor would come in with the scan results. She swore she was about to heave up the chocolate chip scone she'd scarfed down earlier.

Luys' words kept on reverberating inside her head about being completely healed. She wanted to believe. She was scared to believe. She was flat-out crazy to trust such nonsense from him, especially since he was just arrested for murder.

The door opened, and Dr. Melwarren stepped through the threshold. Wisps of black hair like the down of a baby chick covered the sides of his head and circled his bald head. He settled down into a chair by the monitor and clicked on the computer. "Well…"

When he drifted off into silence, she nudged with, "And…?"

"I'm completely baffled." He turned away from the computer and stared at her. The silence between them lengthened.

Her chest tightened. "About what?"

"Your scan. It shows no evidence of disease."

"What does that mean?"

"You're in remission. There is no sign of cancer in your body."

Her heart leaped in her chest, and excitement thrummed through her body.

He shook his head. "I've never seen a recovery like yours. The change is dramatic." He glanced over at the screen and blinked. "Yes, targeted therapy, even during such a short time span, turned your case around. I can sincerely say I've never seen the likes of it before. If miracles do happen, I would call it that." He returned his gaze back to her. "I'll want to see you in three months and do another scan, just in case. But from there, if the results show the same thing, then we'll do six-month scans and then yearly from there."

"That's wonderful," she breathed.

The doctor grinned back, his blue eyes sparkling, looking as excited as she felt. "You, young lady, have managed to get to remission. It's a huge step. How does that make you feel?"

"Like I've got a new life."

So, it was true. She didn't have less than a year. No more infusions, no more pills, needles, injections, and no more infections. "Wow."

"I'll second that."

Avery let him believe it was a miracle cure because of the targeted therapy, but she'd been barely on the drugs. He wouldn't believe something more than science had healed her if she started ranting about her body's sudden super immunity.

She thought of the others in the waiting room and wished a better fate for all of them.

She left the hospital and walked toward her car

in a daze, feeling like she'd entered an alternative universe.

All this time Luys had been telling her the truth. No sign of cancer in her body. No tumor cells growing anywhere! She had more time to live, to breathe, to share her life with that someone special.

Then she thought of Luys. He'd kind of ruined the idea of finding her other half. One night with him, and she suspected it would take a good year to get over him and what he'd done to her. She wished he hadn't been so damn good in bed to where memories of his body and touch still curled her toes. Thank God it hadn't been more than the once. She would have been ruined then.

Okay, enough of Luys. She needed to focus on the good stuff. She'd received a miracle. She should be ecstatic, beyond happy. So why, when looking ahead at the coming years, did she feel like her life was dull, meaningless, and without value?

There was also one big headache still in her life. Nothing good would come of her life if that problem didn't disappear.

Mayor.

She suspected Luys' sister wasn't going anywhere anytime soon.

CHAPTER 22

I tried to get here sooner, but it was impossible until after your arraignment," Gabriel murmured into the speaker embedded in a partition between the visitation stations.

Luys stared at his brother sitting across from him in a metal chair through the polycarbonate glass separating them. Gabriel's visit flooded him with a mix of contradictory emotions. There was relief, of course, at seeing a familiar face, of having support, but there was also frustration at himself and the situation.

"Thank you, but you shouldn't have come. It's not safe. If Mayor discovers you're in the city, she'll follow you back. She has an unhealthy fascination with Nicole. I can't understand that she believes she's the reincarnate of Maria and—"

"I know, and I'll take precautions. There's no way I'll let Mayor anywhere near Nicole."

Luys frowned. "Don't underestimate her."

"Don't worry. I'll not make the same mistake. The woman I love and her daughter almost died because I didn't take Mayor's powers seriously enough. That won't happen again. Too many lives are in jeopardy."

"I need you to check on a cat in my condo. No one's been there for several days."

"A cat? I dropped by yesterday to make sure everything was okay. There was no cat. Or any sign of a food dish or water."

"Hmm. Avery must have taken her then. That's the only explanation I have."

"I would have come across an animal. I was thorough checking for signs that Mayor might have been inside." Gabriel's gaze darkened as he searched his face. "Why, Luys?"

He didn't have to ask what his brother meant. "I didn't murder Noah Harris."

"I know that." Gabriel's brow dipped. "There's obviously some mistake."

Luys gave himself a self-deprecating smile. "Of the three of us, I never thought I would be the one behind bars."

His brother didn't smile back. "Why did they arrest you? They must have something on you."

"No one's told me anything." The public defender didn't have any discovery yet." He drummed his fingers on his side of the counter. "All I can think of is somehow someone planted DNA or my fingerprints in his condo."

"Do you know who?"

"Other than Mayor? No. It seems she left you to find me. She expected an apology for binding her with mercury and keeping her trapped all these years. She also thought I would excuse her behavior. Unless that's a ruse, and she's seeking revenge against me."

Gabriel shook his head. "But why go to such lengths? If she'd wanted to, she could have slowly tortured and killed you."

"I don't know what to think. I do know she considers

me the favorite between the two of us." Luys grunted. "You know she loves her games."

"But she has never gone after you, not as she has with me."

"There's always a first time. From the moment she arrived, she's been nothing but trouble." He shifted and glanced over his shoulder. Two uniformed guards stood against the wall behind him and bracketed him on both sides. Neither was looking his way, but that didn't mean they weren't listening. He knew the phone line was being monitored by someone in another room. "The woman from the hospital…"

"Yes?"

"Mayor found a way to turn her. Unlike all the others, she succeeded this time."

Gabriel sucked in a breath. "Are you sure?" He looked over Luys' shoulder at the guards before returning his gaze to him. "And the woman? Has she recovered?"

Luys tried to phrase his words so only Gabriel could understand. "Yes. She's different. Her hearing…"

"Has she changed in other ways? She hasn't become seduced by what Mayor is?"

"God's teeth, no. She can't stand Mayor…or me for that matter."

"This woman could be the beginning of something worse. Maybe that's why Mayor has you here." Gabriel rubbed at his jaw. "I wish we knew what she planned."

"Me too. At least the public defender assigned to me seems smart and experienced."

Gabriel snorted. "I'm sure he or she is, but I retained a reputable attorney who will fight for you. Money's always a great motivator. And as for leaving you to this battle on your own, that's not an option."

Luys' lips firmed. "I think you're making a mistake. You should leave before she finds out you're here."

"I'll leave soon enough. I wanted to ensure you were okay with my own eyes and in capable hands. Jeff Peters' office will contact you later today if he doesn't himself. If you're unable to contact me, go through him. He has my number but little else."

"Things will work out," Luys insisted. "I have to believe I'll be found innocent."

"Don't sound too confident. I'm not getting a good feeling." Gabriel's expression darkened. "Holy Mother. Why did you let them take you? There must have been an opportunity...." Gabriel swore under his breath.

Luys sighed deeply and shook his head. "And start over again? I'm tired of moving."

"Staying for any length of time isn't an option."

Luys looked on either side of him and the other inmates in orange. He'd become caged, as he had been when he first landed on the continent. He couldn't help but find the irony of how life seemed to have come full circle.

"Luys, you know eventually you'll have to uproot. People will wonder...your age, how young you look—"

"You don't have to tell me something I don't already know." Luys warned, "This isn't the place."

"Yes, of course. But I suspect you being here has nothing to do with hating the idea of moving again but everything to do with the woman. The one Mayor—"

"No! She has nothing to do with me being here." His brother didn't need to know about his non-existent relationship with Avery. Any feelings she had for him had turned to ash. She thought him a killer.

"You protest too strongly." This time it was Gabriel who sighed. "I'm not one to talk. Love. It comes into one's life when it's the least convenient." He drummed his fingers against the counter. "I hope this woman will not betray you like the last."

"I'm the one who betrayed her," Luys argued, hating being reminded of another time, another woman he'd made the mistake of trusting and falling for. Had it been only ten years ago? Silvia, blue eyes, chestnut hair, and a mischievous smile. He'd let himself get caught up in how she floated through life, believing how things always worked out in the end. Her optimism had captivated him, and he'd found himself trusting her to his detriment. When she'd learned of his powers and lifespan, she'd turned against him, completely disgusted with everything about him. Her fear of him had cut deeply. He had been lucky then that she hadn't revealed his secret or tried to prove to others what and who he really was.

He thanked God he had his brother whom he could trust, but the idea of anyone thinking him guilty made his stomach knot. "I'm not a murderer. I didn't do it."

Gabriel laughed. "Of course you didn't. Anyone who knows you and thinks that is a fool." His expression turned grave. "We will get you out. Hopefully through the court system."

But through other means, if necessary, was his brother's implication. Luys smiled without humor. "We shall see."

"I'll keep in touch." His brother slapped the counter. "You're in expert hands with Peters."

Gabriel stepped from the booth, and_one of the guards on the other side of the polycarbonate glass led Gabriel through the door and away from the visitation room. A door that led to freedom. A freedom Luys wondered if he'd ever find again.

Was that what Mayor had intended all this time? Have him locked up in prison with no hope of escape? Like he and Gabriel had locked her in that cave decades before? Maybe she lied to him about wanting an apology and to start anew. She always shocked him at her uncanny ability to maneuver and manipulate people with her sick games.

Mayor had struck her first move. He hoped it wasn't checkmate.

He guessed time would settle it, one way or another.

Luys rose and followed one of the guards back to his cell.

CHAPTER 23

The front door flew open, crashing against the wall. With the television program forgotten, Avery scrambled from the sofa and stood gaping at the open door. Five minutes before, she'd gotten back from the gym and had collapsed onto the sofa. She hadn't yet taken her shoes off or bothered showering and changing out of her leggings and t-shirt. Dust and wind flew into the living room. She thought it was a haboob until smoke thickened and swirled amid the dust. A form materialized.

Holy crap. Shit, shit, shit.

Mayor.

The woman stepped toward her. She wore another one of those flowy-type dresses with a hem that swirled around her ankles, but this one was in white-gold and black. Her white-blonde hair, thick and disheveled, flowed past her shoulders and down her back. Eyes blazing shards of blue ice, she strode into the room and pointed her finger at Avery.

Looking for any type of barrier to keep the woman away, Avery skirted around the sofa until she was behind it. Not the greatest move. Nothing would keep Mayor away if she wanted her hands on Avery.

"Where is he?"

"Who?" Avery stalled.

Mayor's gaze narrowed. "What have you done to him?"

Avery backed away, pulse thundering in her ears. She found herself against the living room wall.

Mayor pointed a finger at her. "I would never have done what I did if I had known you were going to ruin his life."

The woman was crazy. Like Avery had anything to do with Luys killing someone and getting himself arrested. "I thought you hated Luys."

"You don't know a thing, do you understand?" She slashed a hand through the air. "He is family. People get angry with their families, yes?"

Avery huffed. "Well, I got the distinct feeling you wanted him dead."

"Do not speak to me in that tone!" Her gaze inched slowly up and down Avery's body. "And to think I thought you could do good for Luys. Hah! Estúpida. I should never have given you to him as a gift!"

"A gift?" Avery pushed off the wall and grabbed the back of the sofa. "What do you mean by 'a gift?'"

"Do you think I randomly chose you of all people? You really are an idiot." Her gaze narrowed. "I saw how he looked at you over the months. I have watched him. I know him. No one else would be able to see that he was pining for you. You didn't even know it!"

Avery shook her head, having a hard time following. "So let me get this straight. You cut me open, performed some ceremony to make me what I am now all as a gift for Luys?"

"Yes, fool that I am. He is lonely. Given time, lone-liness would have him search for a human, and he would have to endure the pain of his lover dying. Humans die too quickly. He may hide his unhappiness well, but he is my brother. I feel the same. That is why I know."

"You did this to me because he was lonely? Seriously? Who does that?" Avery's fingers dug deeper into the back of the sofa. "You never once considered my feelings, or what you did would have ramifications to my life!"

"Spare me. You would have been dead by the end of the year if I had not done what I did."

Mayor's words strangled the breath momentarily from her lungs. "How…how could you know about my illness? I've never told anyone. Luys didn't know—"

"All I had to do was smell you. You reeked of death." She arched a brow. "Don't look so shocked. Animals sense it. Humans have lost that ability. For too long, mortals have focused on modern needs society has created and dictated to them. They drown in greed and are completely blind to their inner instincts."

"Get out. I want you out of my house."

Her brow dipped, and her jaw flexed. "I'm not going anywhere. What did you do with Luys?"

"Nothing. I don't want anything to do with him." Her fingers dug deeper into the fabric of the sofa. "They took him away. That's what they do with murderers."

"Who? Tell me!"

"The police. They arrested him. Luys killed Noah Harris. All the evidence must point to him."

"Psssh. Luys would not know how to kill a mouse, never mind a human. I have no compunction of killing anyone if they are a threat to my family." Mayor took a couple of threatening steps toward her. "I dislike how you take me for a fool. You did something to him. There's no other explanation. I've smelled your scent in his home. He must have trusted you, and you betrayed that trust. You lie about the police. If you have harmed him, I will rip the air from your lungs."

A red flush rose up Mayor's neck to stain her face. The woman was rattling on about nonsense. But her fixation on Luys' innocence made Avery doubt Luys' involvement. If she was so adamant about Luys being unable to murder anyone, then who had killed Noah Harris? Avery swallowed. That was a stupid question. Who else but Mayor? She had the strength, the rage. Maybe Mayor realized what Noah was digging into about ritualistic killings and was about to have evidence point to her? Mayor could have ransacked Noah's home, not found anything, and had hoped Avery would uncover something she might have missed.

Still, there had to be something more when it came to Luys' arrest. "He has to be the one who killed my neighbor," Avery insisted. "The police don't work that way. They wouldn't have arrested him. There had to be some type of evidence against him."

"You lie!"

Avery tensed. She could literally feel the rage radiating from Mayor. "No. I was there." Why wouldn't the woman believe her? "They must have proof! I've told you, they wouldn't arrest him otherwise."

"You are an idiot! I should know better, yes? You people don't live long enough. Your brains are feeble."

"Feeble?" She was sick of Mayor's insults. "We're not as sick as you, cutting up people for their brothers!"

"By the blood of Christ!" Mayor sprang, launching herself over the sofa and slamming into Avery. She would have fallen if Mayor hadn't grabbed her by the shoulders and lifted her into the air. She shook Avery with such force her skull hurt.

The woman paused her shaking long enough to ask, "Who took him?"

Avery's answer died in her throat as Mayor shook her even harder, lifting her higher until her toes dangled in the air. Vision blurring, she struggled to focus and get her tongue to form a reply. The woman's strength was shocking. She could swat Avery and kill her as easily as a gnat.

"Their names!"

"I—I can't—t—talk!"

The shaking stopped. With a vise-like grip still around one shoulder, Mayor used her other hand to cup Avery's neck and rub a thumb against the pulse point throbbing on the side of her neck. "It would not take much," Mayor whispered. "I could break your breastbone with ease, grab your heart and squeeze my fingers…."

Avery finally wrapped her tongue around several words. "There was our neighbor. He's a cop. He warned me about Luys, but I didn't listen."

She was afraid to give out his name for fear Mayor would murder him. She couldn't handle it if someone died because of her.

"And you're not listening now!"

She tapped two fingers against Avery's upper chest before sliding them to the scarring between her breasts.

Oh God, she was going to kill her. Avery closed her eyes. The idea of dying filled her with terror. She'd always known the time would come soon enough because of her cancer, but not like this, never like this. If she'd never known Luys or Mayor, she wouldn't be in such a dire predicament. She might have died of cancer, but she wouldn't be threatened or throttled before her life ended.

She wanted to feel safe, carefree again. That's all she wanted. She squeezed her eyes tighter. A place to hide, to lick her wounds, to feel like there was hope again. Please, she just wanted to be free. Free from the woman, free of the terror, of the pain, of being in this room. Somewhere safe where the crazy woman wouldn't find her. That's all!

She gulped in oxygen. The pressure on her shoulder and chest stopped abruptly, and she was suddenly free of the death-like grip on her shoulder. Her eyes snapped open as she stumbled backward into space. Clouds swirled around her, thick, moist, cold.

Oh, God. She was falling… Blackness engulfed her on all sides. Then lights, almost strobe-like, flashed past on all sides of her. A feeling of weightlessness swept through her body as if she no longer had a physical form.

CHAPTER 24

Friday, August 31ˢᵗ – 9:58 pm

Avery's feet hit the floor, the act jarring her entire body. She stumbled backward. Arms flying out, she caught her balance before falling on her ass. Blinking, she tried to focus on what was around her. She sucked in a breath so hard she almost choked. Her stomach lurched, and for a second, she thought she was going to vomit.

She took another breath, then another until her pulse slowed.

Her living room had disappeared. Mayor had disappeared.

For several seconds, she didn't understand. "Oh, God."

A rush of heat rolled through her body as shock slammed into her. She'd space jumped from her condo to—to—she wasn't sure… Her pulse jumped and started racing again.

Avery couldn't make out much. Blinking into the darkness, she adjusted her eyes against the sudden lack of light. The moonlight from a sliding glass door also helped, giving her the impression she was on the main floor of a house. The place didn't have any furnishings. Maybe it was up for sale. From where she stood, she could make out a kitchen to her left.

She changed her mind. The place looked abandoned. Wires hung from a light fixture in what was probably the dining area, while a couple of cabinet doors in the kitchen were missing, and one hung half off its hinges. She turned around; the scrape of her heel against the dusty and littered floor ricocheted through the house. She peered at each exit, expecting the worst. When Mayor didn't appear, she still didn't relax.

For all she knew, she could have transported from one bad situation to one even worse.

She had no clue where she was. Frowning, she moved across the room with a tentative step. Then the yellow and orange polka dot drapes caught her eye. They looked familiar and unique. She walked over to a sliding glass door that contained a layer of grime, accidentally kicking a beer can lying on the floor. The can rattled across the floor, sending dust into the air while the smell of musk clung to the room. She wiped at her nose to stop the sneeze rising to her throat. She peered outside. The backyard also appeared so familiar…

Memories suddenly flooded her of another place and time, a time when she was a child, a time when she'd been happy. Janice and Gerald Pauley. They'd taken her in as foster parents, loved her unconditionally, and intended to adopt her. They'd even started the paperwork.

The family she'd always wanted but never got. Janice and Gerald had planned a trip to the city, to a highly reputable lawyer, and left her behind, telling her she would be bored. The trip had been their last.

They'd died in a fifty-car pileup on the interstate. Black ice.

Sudden and unexpected tears welled in her eyes. She hadn't thought about them for a long while. She'd tried to bury those memories with her childhood. They'd been too painful.

She wiped at her eyes with the back of her hand and walked from the sliding glass door to the front window, where she could make out the street and the rest of the neighborhood. Another house across the way looked equally abandoned. It seemed the area had gone downhill since she'd lived in the house.

She was stuck in another state. It seemed her wishes had come true. Mayor couldn't find her here. Hell, she didn't think she could get out of the neighborhood and get home without some serious help.

Avery said a couple of choice words under her breath. She grabbed her phone from her back pocket, already knowing it was useless. But she still double-checked. She almost expected the device to be mangled, smoking, or hot to the touch from her little excursion across part of the country in a fraction of a second.

Yep. Blank screen.

She was almost eight hours away from her home. Her thoughts turned to Clover. The cat could last a couple of days with both bowls full of food and water. At least that was something, but how the hell was she going to get back to Scottsdale? No phone, no one to contact. Ugh. There had to be a way.

Teleport. She'd gotten here and to the hospital. Then she thought of Luys' warning about how dangerous it was. She might be pushing her luck. The idea of her body turning into some morbid creature with mixed DNA from another species made her decide against it. She wasn't in danger right now.

She palmed her phone, nibbling on her lower lip. Maybe the time she'd shown up at the hospital by teleporting had only drained the battery. It could just need to be charged. From there, she could log into her app and get a ride. But she needed a recharge. She glanced over at the electrical outlets. That wasn't an option. The place probably hadn't had electricity for a couple of years. Maybe she could get it recharged somewhere. From what she could tell, the phone didn't look broken.

She stepped closer to the living room window and peered outside. The street appeared little better than the house. The neighborhood didn't look safe anymore. The unkept yards, chain-link fences, and bars on the windows on a couple of occupied houses told her walking around out there at night wasn't the smartest move. But she didn't have an option. Then she thought about going to a nearby house. Nope. That was probably a worse idea. She could get shot for trespassing. There had to be a convenience store close by, though, right? Maybe? They were everywhere in the city and probably safer than knocking on any one of those front doors.

But the idea of walking down the road with so few lights was intimidating and a tad scary. Well, it had to be done. Stepping outside, she crossed to the sidewalk, looked both ways, and decided to go left. Fingers crossed, she decided it turned out to be the shorter and the safest of the two routes. At one point, unease crawled across her entire body when she noticed a couple of shadowed figures down another street. Three men stood talking in a front yard. They grew silent as all of them looked her way.

I am not a victim. I am not a victim, she chanted to herself as she strode down the sidewalk. She glanced over to where they stood from the corner of her eye. They hadn't moved. When she crossed over to the next street, they disappeared from her sight. A few minutes later, she looked over her shoulder, and when she didn't find anyone following her, she relaxed.

A main road came into view. Breathing a sigh of relief, she found a store two blocks away.

She slipped inside and looked around for a charger. Crap. She didn't have the funds to purchase one. That was stupid to not have thought of it. Had she completely lost her brain somewhere? Sighing in frustration, she walked down a couple of aisles until she found one that would fit her phone. Stealing wasn't an option. That was just wrong. She'd done some crazy things when she was a teenager, but she wasn't one any longer. Sighing again, she pulled the charger from a hook and walked up to the counter. Right now, she was the only customer in the store. She eyed the cashier, a big woman with bleached blond hair, dark roots, and bright blue eye shadow.

The woman towered over her by a good foot. Avery suspected the raised floor on the other side of the counter gave the cashier a height advantage over anyone who walked in. "Um… I was hoping to get a charger, but I can't pay until my phone has some power. I don't have any cash, and I don't live in the neighborhood."

"And your point?" She snapped her gum with a loud pop. The crease between her brows looked like it had been there for decades.

Avery should have known she wouldn't get far without money. She'd had her head in the clouds. Her phone was the only option. She didn't know how else to get back home. She guessed keeping to herself and being completely anti-social was now biting her in the butt. She had no one to turn to for help other than strangers. "Well, I hoped that if I could borrow it and—"

"No."

"It would be for a couple of minutes until—"

"No."

Avery's eyes narrowed. She couldn't read what the woman was thinking with her map of deep creases. God, how was she going to get out of this one? Her shoulders slumped. "I understand." She picked up the charger and put it back on the shelf. She had to walk by the counter to get to the exit.

"Bad day, eh?" The woman snapped her gum again.

Tears welled in Avery's eyes. She couldn't help it. Having someone say it aloud just made it that much of a reality. She blinked until her vision cleared. "It's been rough. It's right up there with my worst."

The woman eyed the phone in Avery's hand. "I have a charger."

"You do?" Avery breathed on a soft sigh. "I'm hoping my phone just needs a boost and isn't broken."

"You can borrow mine and plug it in over in the corner there. I can't have you use something you haven't paid for."

"Thank you!" Avery wanted to hug her but decided the woman wouldn't appreciate it.

When she plugged her phone in, a faint red bar appeared on the screen. Thank God. She now had a lifeline. Technology. She hated and loved it at the same time. Avery tried not to pace as the phone charged but kept to the corner of the store as customers came in and paid at the counter. Some, she couldn't help noticing, reeked of alcohol or body odor.

When she reached 20 percent, she handed the charger back. "Thanks."

Her face still inscrutable, the cashier snapped her gum and nodded. "Just paying it forward."

Not knowing what to say to that, Avery nodded back and moved toward the double doors but paused. The newspaper's headlines screamed back at her.

Savage murder in upscale Scottsdale. The Butcher strikes again. She winced. She hated the name they'd dubbed for the murderer. It fanned paranoia and fear. She winced again. Ha. The truth was even stranger than any conspiracy theory out there.

She suspected word had traveled out of state because of the bizarre savagery of the killing. A simple stabbing or shooting didn't get headlines—pretty sad, really—but a bizarre ritualist killer that randomly found his victims stoked hysteria and fear.

The date was from today. But that didn't reveal how long the body had been decomposing before someone found it. It could be hours or weeks. After or before the police arrested Luys? The timing could mean everything. If Luys was innocent after all... She frowned. She didn't want to think about Luys.

She glanced over her shoulder and found the woman staring at her. Avery itched to grab the paper and run, but common sense stilled her itchy fingers. Instead, she flipped the paper over to read the rest of the article. The words *heart, ripped out, bloody* jumped from the page…

"We're not a library."

Pausing, she peered over her shoulder again at the cashier. The lines in the woman's wrinkled face had deepened. Sighing, Avery flipped the paper back to its original position and slipped out of the store.

She managed to get a ride through the app on her phone and didn't have to wait long. On the drive home, which was going to cost her a small fortune, she scanned through the stories in her phone's news feed, mindful of how much battery she had left.

There. Murder. Brutal attack.

Her hand tightened on her phone. The article involved lots of speculation as to the motivation and state of the body but no details other than another murder. No names, no specific location other than mentioning Scottsdale.

She leaned her head against the backrest and tried to get her pulse back to normal, as normal as she was right now. When it came down to it, she didn't know what normal was, not when it came to her body and the changes that had swept through her system. She didn't feel any different. She seemed to have a regular heartbeat. It didn't feel like it had liquefied or petrified.

Whatever was now flowing through her DNA had eradicated her cancer, and she should be thankful. But right now, she felt anything but.

The idea of going home filled her with dread. Mayor could be still inside her home waiting for her. Then there were Stephen's threats she couldn't exactly forget. She didn't feel safe in her place. Not now. Not when Mayor, in all her rage, was bound to show up at her condo again.

She'd have to find a place to stay temporarily until things calmed down or Mayor tired of looking for her. Yeah, she could try space jumping like this last time, but she could only run so long. Also, she was realizing time traveling was not so easy. She couldn't seem to do it with a thought or belief. There had to be an emotion behind it. Each place she'd found herself had been a deep and subconscious desire, a hunger for a person or place where she felt safe.

Avery's ride pulled into the parking lot of her condo complex a good hour before the morning's sun crested the horizon. She remained in the back until she looked through all the windows of the car for signs of Mayor. The area was quiet; it was early yet for people to be moving around on the weekend. She could still be out there, but Avery thought—hoped and prayed—after so many hours, she would have gotten tired and left.

Beyond exhausted, she fumbled from the compact car and, once on the sidewalk with the driver paid and driving off, she rolled her shoulders to get the kinks out of her neck. She walked over to the mail center, knowing Clover could wait a couple more minutes and delaying the inevitable moment when she stepped through her front door. She glanced over to her condo. The door was closed and looked like Mayor hadn't damaged the lock or jamb, unlike her brother. From the front window, lamplight illuminated the front yard. It didn't mean Mayor was waiting inside since she'd been the one to turn on the lights.

Even so, she wasn't going to just walk through that front door unprepared.

She didn't know if she should stay in her condo. It wasn't safe. Mayor could show up anytime. Avery wasn't the only one who could travel through space and time. Even though she was bone tired, her smartest move was to pack up Clover and some clothing and find a place to stay temporarily.

As she dug into the dark hole of her mailbox, a sound, almost like a low rumble, carried into the alcove from somewhere in the complex. She stiffened. Frowning, she pulled out several junk inserts and closed the mailbox door on a sigh, all the while trying to decipher the noise. She was getting creeped out, but she couldn't help it. Who wouldn't get all worked up after everything she'd been through? Damn it. Mayor could be playing with her right now, waiting around the corner, ready to attack at any second.

Avery curled her fingers around the mail and glanced over both shoulders. Nothing. Still…

Avery tensed.

There. Again. Soft but insistent. Someone moaning? Was a couple having sex close by? She wrinkled her nose. They should keep it behind closed doors. Frowning, she edged along the mailbox unit and toward the walkway between two residential buildings. She saw no one. Clouds covered the sky, deepening and darkening shadows. The rumble of thunder rolled across the night, melding, then obscuring the moaning.

She eyed her front window again, dread crawling across every pore of her body. If there was any hint of Mayor, Avery would break records getting out of the place. If there wasn't a sign of the other woman, she was going to slip inside, get her purse, Clover, and a week's worth of clothing, then she was in her car and driving off to somewhere far safer.

The moaning stopped. Sounds, far louder than before, followed. She detected possible grunting and shuffling. Avery wrinkled her nose again. The couple was really going at it. As she reached the sidewalk between both residential buildings, she glanced down the walkway.

Two figures seemed melded together off the pathway and in the bushes. Yep, a couple in a full-blown sex act. At least that's what she figured, but it was too dark to see much of anything.

With her gaze lingering on the couple as she moved toward her condo, she slowed to a stand and frowned. Something seemed off. A metallic scent drifted in the air. Blood? Oh, God, no… Heart pounding, she couldn't look away even if she wanted to as a different scenario hit her. The couple was not having sex like she first thought. One of the two seemed to convulse as gurgling noises carried across the distance between her and them.

Then both figures separated and the larger of the two lifted the other into the air—just like Mayor had done to her earlier. For a wild minute, Avery thought it was the other woman, but the shadow was larger, taller. Was the attacker like Mayor and Luys, even herself? Eternal and capable of inhuman powers?

She squinted against the shadows but couldn't make out if either were her neighbors.

Could it be Luys? Impossible. He was in jail. Unless he'd escaped…

She eased ever so slowly toward her condo, afraid any sudden move might alert the attacker.

The person holding the other in an effortless grip swiveled his head in her direction.

Avery sucked in a breath just as a cloud skated further across the sky, exposing the moon. The light briefly peeled back the shadows. Oh, shit. Just enough to reveal the attacker's identity. But far worse, the sudden moonlight revealed her own identity.

Her breath caught in her lungs. She knew him.

Not Luys. Not Mayor.

But Ben. Her neighbor.

Was he one of them? Was he working with Mayor? Were the two of them rampaging through Scottsdale and the surrounding area in a killing spree? He had to be tied to Mayor.

Damn it. He was a cop. Someone who was supposed to protect others, not kill them! He had to have been the one who murdered Noah Harris.

Ben dropped the body beside him and advanced toward her. The person on the ground didn't move and was probably dead or near death. She couldn't make out Ben's expression, but it couldn't be good.

She took several steps backward. Oh God. He was going to kill her. He had to after she'd recognized him. Pivoting, she dropped her mail, the letters fluttering into the air like dying doves, and raced toward her car. Her condo wasn't an option, not with the possibility of Mayor waiting inside. But she had a key to her car inside a magnetic holder in the wheel well. She'd just needed the time to get it, lock the door, and start the engine before Ben got his hands on her.

Luys. All this time the killer hadn't been Luys. They'd arrested an innocent man, and she'd believed the worst of him.

Oh, God. Now, more than ever, she needed his help.

The slap of her shoes on the cement rocketed into the night. Ben's feet thudded from behind. She needed to go faster, push harder. He was gaining on her. It would be a matter of minutes before he caught up to her. Her breath sawed in and out of her lungs, and a cry of terror sliced past her lips.

Her car came into view, a good 15 yards away.

Ben's footsteps thundered behind, increasing in volume the closer he got. He was gaining on her. She could hear his breath, feel the excitement rolling off him. She'd never make the car.

She veered to the left, back into the complex. It gave her added seconds, nothing more. But Ben quickly made up the distance.

His breath on her neck crawled across her skin as he grabbed her arm. Oh, God.

She was going to die. She wasn't a damn cat. She had one life. She'd escaped Mayor only to die from some sick serial killer.

She wasn't ready. Stupid, so stupid. *I'm so sorry, Luys, for doubting you! I wish…*

CHAPTER 25

I stand in the middle of the woman's living room in shock. She has vanished. But how? It is impossible. She has no experience, no knowledge of how to attain my powers and travel from place to place. Unlike us, she is like a baby with a child's mind. I refuse to believe otherwise. She cannot escape me.

But she did. She did because she knows how. She knows your secrets. She has been watching you, following you.

"Impossible!" I whirl around and face the room. "She knows nothing!"

I pace the floor, glance at the open door, and quickly close it. I don't want people looking in here, wondering what is going on. I don't need more trouble, questions, or attention.

I rub at my brow. My head throbs. Everything is confusing. I am overcome by the idea of the woman vanishing. Poof. One minute here, the next gone.

I pace again. Then I stop as fury roils through me. How could she have vanished? She is too new to be able to slip to another place or time.

But what if she is stronger than you?

Bah. Impossible. I'll not believe such a thing. Gabriel and Luys could never do what I have managed after centuries of perfecting my gifts. They are too weak and squeamish. They do not understand killing is necessary. Without the blood and organs of others, I'll lose my powers. The ceremonies require sacrifices; the dark forces demand it.

But what of the woman?

I hate the voices. Closing my eyes and covering my ears never keeps them away.

Maybe I didn't need to kill another. Maybe I was reborn with it. Which means all the death, all the ceremonies I did were for naught.

No. I cannot think that way. I will not think that way!

Pain cuts into my hands. I wince and look down. Bloody half-moons have appeared in my palms, and blood clings to my nails. I have dug so deep into the flesh of my palm that I've drawn my own blood.

The woman has done this to me. I smear my blood across the wall. Soon, I will make the woman bleed.

I need to find the woman, this Avery, first, but I know little else other than Luys found her entrancing. He was a fool to believe in anyone else but his family. We had been close once, believing in each other. I had hoped he would apologize and realize his mistakes and see me for the beautiful sister I am. No longer. Yet again, he has tossed me aside, considered me no more than refuse forgotten on the side of the road. No more. We are too different today, with little trust between us.

Again, a woman has ruined another brother. I glare at my blood on the wall.

Avery. She lies about Luys. She is responsible for his disappearance. Luys is too good a man to be arrested. If she has hurt my brother, I'll make her scream and beg for a quick death. I'll not be merciful. She does not deserve my mercy.

Gabriel is gone. Luys is gone.

Abandoned again.

Alone. Always alone! For the love of Christ!

You are alone because of her. She has ruined your life, has done something awful to your brother.

"Yes! Yes, she has!" She lies. I know this! Why would the police take Luys away? There is no reason! He doesn't call attention to himself; he doesn't hurt the humans.

"Ahh!" This Avery has done this. She has caused me too much pain. I gave her the world, and she was thankless. Frustrated at her, at Luys, at Gabriel, at these estúpidos humans, I lash out, smashing my hand against a nearby floor lamp. It crashes to the floor.

The rage builds inside me. I let it consume me. I enjoy the heat of it. I attack her furniture, the precious knickknacks. She will be sorry. I'll make her sorry.

Finally, I am spent and look around. There are holes in the walls, pillows thrown to the floor, and pictures flung from their hooks. The devastation has not made me feel better.

My anger quickly dissolves, and despair sinks through my being.

I cannot go back to this new home I have taken as my own. The walls are too silent, the rooms too empty. I will suffocate. The building feels more like a cage the longer I stay. It amplifies my feelings of want, of loneliness. I can't go back there.

My gaze narrows. The woman has powers. But not for long. Only me. No one else has my abilities. I'll not stand for this woman to be stronger than me.

But she is. She can go from place to place, vanish into the air without killing, without hurting another. All your hard work calling on the dark powers of the gods has meant nothing.

You are not worthy of your brother and of this woman… They have not performed the unspeakable deeds you have done.

Enough!

I put my hands over my ears to stop the voice. I hate that voice. It makes me doubt myself.

This Avery is evil. Dangerous. More dangerous than I could have thought.

Tears stream down my face in sudden despair.

My daughter. I want my daughter back.

CHAPTER 26

Saturday, September 1ˢᵗ – 4:32 am

Luys' eyes snapped open. With both palms beneath his head, he remained frozen against the length of the thin, stiff mattress. He stared up at the ceiling. Light from the hall illuminated his room through the one rectangular window on his door. Something had woken him. The cellblock had quieted several hours ago—as quiet as a prison could get.

He remained frozen, listening, knowing something was off. There…

Breathing, quick, agitated.

Luys tensed.

A shadow moved to the side of him. He jerked up and around, standing with both feet planted to the floor, ready to attack, his mind still filled with memories of the last time he'd been jumped.

"Jesus!" Luys cried out against a choked gasp before saying in a harsh whisper, "I could have hurt you, even killed you. What are you doing here? It's dangerous."

Avery stood in the middle of his cell. Auburn hair framed her pale face. A pair of black leggings hugged her hips and thighs, and a gray sleeveless shirt clung to her breasts and waist. God, he'd forgotten how stunning she was. The sight of her filled him with a mix of fear and elation. He wanted to wrap his arms around her, hold her, feel her warmth and curves against his body, but the way they'd left kept him where he stood. Instead, he should be angry at how she'd been so quick to believe the worst of him, but, in all honesty, he probably would have done the same.

Then he realized that her usually well-groomed hair was unkempt and ragged in places and what looked like dirt clung to her neck and throat.

He stepped toward her and whispered, "What happened? Are you okay?" He kept his hand to his side, but the temptation to touch her was overwhelming. "Did someone hurt you?"

"Couldn't be better."

Luys frowned. Sarcasm didn't suit her.

"You can tell me, you know."

Her face tightened. "What's done is done."

He bit down on his inner lip to keep himself from volleying questions. The idea of someone hurting Avery sent a wave of anxiety and fear roiling through his body. With it came rage. If someone touched her, he wanted to wrap his hands around the person's throat and squeeze until they passed beyond this Earth. He curled his hands at his sides, shocked at the strength of his anger.

He looked toward the door as he played out 'what ifs.' He was powerless in prison, unable to protect her, watch over her. She was in trouble because of him. He'd made a mess of her life. He should have left her alone, kept far away from her. But he couldn't have turned away that fateful day when he had seen her in obvious distress. At least there was one consolation and only one. Mayor had saved her life. Otherwise, Avery's cancer would have eventually taken her.

He needed to do something, anything to stop this sense of powerlessness. "I can't stay here," he muttered. "The next opportunity I have, I'll get out of here."

Avery's gaze widened. "What? You can't be serious. And where will that get you?" Her brow dipped. "Back in prison, shot at or on the topmost wanted list on the news. You can't risk it. It's too dangerous."

"What you just pulled showing up here was just as dangerous. You could still be arrested if you're found out. You could have easily appeared in another part of the prison."

"But I didn't. I think me focusing on you and not the location did the trick."

Hoping to clear his head, he put some distance between them. He sank back onto his bed, but Avery followed. She sat down beside him, her scent wrapping around him. She was the nicest smelling thing he had experienced in days. God's teeth, he'd missed her. He was coming to love her.

He took in a ragged breath. "I want to apologize for everything. If you hadn't met me, you would be living your life and not be encumbered with my psychotic sister."

"But I'd be dead in several months," Avery whispered as she placed a tentative hand on the back of his.

"Did you see the doctor about your cancer, then?"

She nodded with a half-smile. "It seems I'm cancer-free. A miracle, according to the doctor."

He turned his palm up and twined his fingers with hers. The feel of her flesh sent his pulse roaring. She spoke the truth, but still, Mayor's way of healing her by an ancient ritual deeply troubled him. He didn't think the guilt would ever go away. He bowed his head. It was amazing she would forgive him when he could not do the same.

"Before I forget, did you take Clover?"

Her face softened. "I've got to get back to make sure she's okay."

He frowned. "Why did you come here when you know how dangerous it is? You can't get much worse than appearing in a building filled with murderers."

"Believe me, the plan wasn't finding myself behind bars. Far from it." Her chuckle turned into a groan. "I got myself into a situation I needed to get out of and thought of you."

His gut twisted. He knew she was making light of her predicament. But at the same time, he was touched she felt compelled and safe enough to come to him. He shifted on the bed to face her and caught her self-deprecating smile. "Planned or not, you're lucky I am not sharing a cell with anyone. They just moved my roommate yesterday and have not replaced him yet."

"Yes, well, anything was better than where I was."

"What do you mean?"

"Well..." She rubbed the back of her neck and stared back at him silently.

He waited not so patiently.

Finally, she cleared her throat and said, "Your sister's a threat. I can't argue with that. But there's much more going down than Mayor. I've got threats from all sides now, and I can't figure out how all the pieces fit together."

"What threats? What happened? If it's not Mayor—"

"Ben. It was Ben all this time. Not Mayor like I thought."

"What do you mean?"

"Sorry, it's just I'm so amped up with everything that happened that I can't think straight." She jumped off the bed and paced. "I came across him at the complex. He was killing someone. Right. There. In. Front. Of. Me." Then her face twisted as she glanced over to the cell's door. She lowered her voice. "He saw me. He started coming after me. That's when I—

"Ben the cop?" Luys whispered, mindful of how the cement and concrete amplified everything. "The one who arrested me?"

"Yes," she hissed.

Luys frowned, trying to make sense of Avery's news. He rose quickly to his feet and walked to his cell door to peer out the one window slot, but he couldn't see anyone or much of anything other than the cells across the other side of the block. He could break the window, pull the door off its hinges.

"Don't!" Avery crossed the distance between them, guessing his thoughts. "Don't be an idiot. If you rush out there now, there's no way your powers will get you beyond the prison's perimeter. You may think so, but bullets will slow you. They'll hunt you down. They might even find out what you are."

"I…"

"Please, Luys. Promise me."

"I can't."

"This is what Ben wants. Can't you see that? He wants to expose you. I can't see any other reason for why he would frame you."

"But why?"

"I don't know. But he's got to be like you and your sister," she murmured as she turned away from the door and him and sank down on the bed.

"That's impossible."

"Why?"

"Because…" He thought back to his life centuries before. Some things were so vivid: the atrocities, the horror. But time had scoured away the memories of everyday life, daily rituals, and habits. He couldn't seem to remember the people he had associated with during that time. Their faces and identities had melted away. In the beginning, when they'd been first captured, there'd been so many of them. Everyone had been crammed into cells, barely able to stand, never mind sit. He closed his eyes, hoping he might pull something tucked away deep in his brain, but it was pointless. Long ago, when the nightmares made him useless and unable to function at some points, he'd intentionally tried to stuff his memories into the dark corners of his mind, hoping eventually they would seep into nothingness.

He'd thought the three of them were the only ones that survived those years. No one he remembered had fled the village with them that fateful night.

"It was the three of us. No one else escaped. They'd killed others they'd created with their rituals."

"But you don't know what happened after you left? There could have been others, right?"

"Yes, I guess." He again searched for memories of a man with Ben's features, but a blank wall came back to him. "I don't know why he would try to frame me. There are no motives."

"Obviously, he's got something against you."

He shook his head, disgusted at his inability to find a tie between Ben and himself.

"Maybe you inadvertently hurt him and just don't know it or remember it."

"That might be possible." But he had doubts.

"Well, why else go to the point of making sure the police arrested you for murder? There's something there."

"Sorry, I'm of no help. There's nothing I can think of that would make this man hate me enough to send me to prison."

"Maybe Mayor knows. If I talk to her—"

"Don't!" he said in a harsh whisper. "Promise me you will keep away from her."

"I—"

"Avery, promise me." When she still prevaricated, he said, "Give me a little more time. Gabriel is looking into my release."

"Do you think Gabriel knows something?"

"It's possible."

"Luys, you're fighting against a police officer. They have power."

"I know that. But if the court system fails with the help of the lawyer Gabriel's hired, I'll find another way. Your justice here takes too long." He failed to keep the frustration from his voice.

"There's a reason for that. Democracy might not be perfect, but it keeps many an innocent person from being jailed for speaking out against that system." Her eyes clouded. "You just happen to be the exception."

"Why are you doing this?"

She stilled. "Why?"

"Yes, why."

"Because…" She searched his face. "I care about you. You've done some cruddy stuff, but I know you're good inside. You wouldn't have tried to help me when I was down. Other people would have pretended that I was drunk or high on something." She smiled, but her expression looked anything but happy. "And to be honest, I can't kill this connection between us, even if I wanted to. I have feelings for you. But more important than anything else, you need help."

Even with the dim lighting, he read the sympathy in her eyes. He wanted more than her sympathy, though. He wanted…her passion, her love. Talk about the worst timing. But he'd take what she called this connection between them and whatever feelings she had for him. It was enough. For now anyway. She was everything he'd ever wanted in a woman.

Taking in a shuddering breath, he sank down on the bed beside her, cupped her cheek, dipped his head, and brushed his lips against hers. When she didn't draw away, he did it again. Strange how when one's life was in chaos and things couldn't get much worse, life sent a glimmer of hope, of humanity.

She sighed into his mouth before she kissed him back, her lips feeling like crushed velvet. She caught his hand resting on his thigh, her fingers small and delicate against his. Her lips firmed, grew bolder.

She tasted better than any erotic dream he could imagine. Before he became lost in the kiss, he took a shuddering breath and broke away. But her passion gave him a bit of hope—something he hadn't had in a long while.

"Bad timing all around?" Avery joked.

"I think that's an understatement."

"I have one good thing going for me I didn't have before." She squeezed his hand; her gaze remained soft with a hint of passion. He was coming to realize she could easily seduce him with a look or a word.

"And that is?" He stared at her lips.

"I didn't think I might live out the year. Now I'm healthy. As healthy as anyone my age, and I have years, so many more years than I ever could imagine." She bit her lower lip. "But I can't be invincible. No one is. I would think you and your family have some type of vulnerability."

"We're far from invincible." He only had to think back to what had happened to Gabriel in the last year.

Her smile turned sad once again as she twined her fingers between his and looked down briefly, seeming to find their clasped hands fascinating. When she next looked up, she searched his face, curiosity in her eyes. "You've mentioned we can live decades, even centuries, without dying, but we must have some type of weaknesses. What are they? I need to know. I would have been more prepared with Ben."

"It's something I should have told you, but with everything happening..." He rolled his shoulders, suppressing the urge to ask more questions, particularly about Ben. "There are several things that can kill you. We've witnessed a few during the Aztec's reign. You can die by what would fit in your standard horror movie. I guess folklore is rooted in some truth. Beheading, being engulfed in fire, a spear, or any sharp object embedded into the heart.

Avery wrinkled her nose. "I'm sorry I asked."

He squeezed her hand. "But we've survived shootings. I've had a bullet or two. Same with Gabriel and Mayor. Knife wounds. We recover easily with the last."

"I guess that's something." Avery didn't sound overly enthusiastic as she slipped her hand from his. "I'm sure you still feel the pain of any wound."

"Yes, there's no avoiding that. Some wounds are far more painful than others. One is worse than anything else. When this particular element contacts our skin, our demise is rapid and excruciating. But unlike everything else that can kill us, mercury's impact can be reversed."

"Mercury? Like the silver liquid that they used to have in thermometers way back when? It's poisonous to humans too."

"Yes. But with humans, mercury's lethal power is far slower. What takes decades with humans takes minutes with us." He rose and stepped away. Focusing was hard when she was close enough to touch. "In Tlacopan, one of the priests, who was considered more of a magician or witch doctor, favored using mercury in several of his ritual offerings. Cipactli and several other priests in the city believed mercury came from Xiuhpillim, or the great turquoise ruler, considered the most powerful of gods. The element had the power to give life and take it away. Through *Cochehua*, the awakening ceremony, he would drip mercury on the beating heart of the person. From there, they became a *nagual*, shapeshifter."

"So this happened to you?"

"Yes," Luys admitted. "But others were not so fortunate. They would randomly pick slaves, captives, the spoils of war. Before the person had time to realize they hadn't died but had been transformed into a *nagual* or had become *cochehua*—awakened—the priest would use mercury again and smear the victim's back. The element quickly kills naguals, not humans. Within seconds, the stench of burning flesh would fill the air. It still turns my stomach thinking of it, even though it's not any worse than other ceremonies I have witnessed. I believe once they perfected the ritual on their slaves, they used it on the citizens of Tlacopan." Tension crawled into his muscles and joints. He stared at the wall in front of them as images flashed across the concrete. Having witnessed how the Aztecs were experts in pain and torture, he should be immune to the horrors after so much time. Their imprisonment had been soul-crushing. It was through the grace of God that he, Mayor, and Gabriel had escaped before it was their turn to face their final death. Until Avery had entered his life, he'd tried to avoid thinking of those times. But Avery needed to know some of the history to understand her own awakening. "Once mercury touches the skin of a *cochehua*, nothing—almost nothing—will stop it from killing them. Death is painful but rapid. The silver will eat through flesh until it reaches the bone. Until, until—"

Avery winced. "Yes, I get the picture all too much. It sounds awful."

"My brother almost died accidentally after having come into contact with mercury. Because of some higher power or luck and a woman with steel for guts, he was spared the final death."

"How?"

He paused, knowing again it would sound fantastical. "Holy water."

She frowned. "Okay, you've had me at this point, and that's because I've witnessed enough craziness as it is, but what does holy water have to do with an Aztec ceremony? That's a Catholic sacrament and blessed by a priest and so far removed from the Aztec beliefs."

"The Spanish and Aztecs despised each other. When they learned the Spanish were killing *nagual* Aztecs through mercury, Cipactli and the other magicians took their holy water, a sacrament they found silly and useless, and made it into something far more powerful—at least to their way of thinking. They created an elixir to save *naguals* from the Spaniards. I think they chose holy water because, knowing how much the Spanish hated them and considered them heathens and evil, they knew it would horrify the Spanish if they used a Catholic sacrament and something the Spanish believed was holy and from their God.

"I always found it strange that the Spanish considered the Aztecs savages when their behavior wasn't better. The Spanish would feed the natives to their dogs, burn them alive, bash the brains of babies, impale women and children by throwing them into pits filled with stakes. I could go on… This was, of course, all in the name of their God. Or the blessing of the church."

When Avery dragged in a deep, rattling breath, Luys realized how horrifying he must have sounded to her. God's teeth. He talked too much, but he had not shared his past with anyone else, and once he started, he spilled far more than he should have.

"I don't know what to say to all that." She grimaced, hugged herself, and rubbed her arms. "Other than what you've just said explains everything. Noah Harris was murdered because he knew too much. He had done all this research. And I didn't know why Catholic crosses and Aztec rituals were tied together until now. It's all so gruesome."

"I'm sorry. You don't need all that detail."

"I guess when you think of it, it's just as bad as today, but differently. We have our serial killers, massive gun shootings, and a lack of compassion for our neighbors. Maybe one day, we as a species will grow. But I don't see that in the foreseeable future."

"I wish I could say you're wrong."

Avery dropped her hands to her side and straightened. "Okay, other than sharp objects to the heart and other scenarios you've mentioned, I guess I need to be careful if I decide to use mercury for enemies like myself unless I have holy water nearby."

"Even then, it can be dangerous for you. Lead or another heavy metal has to encase the element. If you remember, I had that metal cross displayed beneath glass in my condo? There is a vial of mercury hidden behind the stone, and a small latch will open to a compartment inside where I have it stored. I keep a small sample of mercury on hand if I ever need to use it. But I make sure I never hold the medallion for long. Mercury's power will slowly deplete your strength and send you into a catatonic state."

"How do you know? Did that happen to you?"

Did he lie? Should he? No, he couldn't do that. He had lied enough already with Avery. "No, but Gabriel and I put Mayor in such a state. She'd grown too powerful, too filled with hate. Our only option was to kill her or keep her captive in a deep, secluded cave."

Avery's eyes widened. "Oh, my God. That's horrifying. Why would you do that to your own sister?"

He searched her face but could not find any judgment there. Even so, the heat of shame burned his face. "We couldn't find it within ourselves to end her life. We didn't have an alternative. In time, we were hoping to fix her."

"Fix her?"

"I suspect she has schizophrenia, though she'd never been diagnosed. The Aztecs offered her daughter to Quetzalcóatl, the god of wind and rain. She was never the same since, and her condition worsened. Her rages became frightening. Every time they happened, someone ended up dead. We could not allow her to kill another human. It was too much for us to bear. When we imprisoned her, there was no medication for her condition. And she has this belief…"

"Belief…?"

"That if she eats the flesh of a human, it will strengthen her powers."

"Do you believe this?"

"I did at one point," he admitted, "because she was so much stronger than Gabriel and me. Her abilities were beyond anything we could conjure. But then, when you recently became a *nagual*, you turned out to have the same ability as Mayor to travel through space and time, something she could only do."

"Is that why she hates you? I always got that impression even though she gave me as a 'gift' to you from her. She's got this love/hate relationship and is conflicted about how she should feel about you."

"Yes."

"I'm finally able to put some pieces of the puzzle together, but I still don't know how Ben fits into all of this."

He tensed. "Don't go near Ben."

Avery wrinkled her nose and didn't meet his gaze. "I didn't say I would."

"You don't have to. I see it in your face."

"I'm not going to confront him. I'm not that crazy. I don't know what he's capable of." She wrapped several strands of hair around one ear as she searched his face. "So, there have been others like you?"

"At the beginning, when they started experimenting on us, there was a good dozen of us. They kept us in line with mercury, but I am only aware of the three of us that escaped from the pen."

"But could you have left Ben and others behind?"

"I don't know. It was so long ago." He didn't like the sudden blank look that crossed her face. "Please, stay away from Ben. I can't stand the idea of him doing something to you."

"I'll be careful." She got off the bed and backed away from him until a foot separated the two of them. "I'll find a place to hole out until some of this blows over. And I'll take care of Clover."

"I—"

"Trust me."

He wanted to argue. Then he forgot to when her lips caught on his, and she kissed him, sliding her hands up his arms to the back of his neck, where her fingers twined into his hair. Her tongue slipped between his lips, and he groaned.

Suddenly, silently her body dissolved in his arms,

and a swirl of mist enveloped him. Then he was alone in his cell, with the scent of her lingering on his skin, the taste of her mouth still on his lips.

He stared at the empty cell. His throat tightened, and he fisted his hands at his sides. He didn't dare let her go. She was in danger. He stepped toward the door and eyed the hinges. He could break himself out. Several bullets might stop him for a while, but if he focused hard enough, used his brain along with his muscle, he just might escape with his body intact.

"Trust me." Her words echoed in his head.

He stilled by the door.

Did he dare?

CHAPTER 27

Monday, September 1ˢᵗ – 9:00 am

I pace the confines of my small living space as I pluck at the sleeves of my blouse. I pivot again and pace the floor. I am at a loss. Where is the woman? Days now, and I have yet to see her.

I look out the window. From my vantage point, I can see the parking area of the complex where the woman lives, even to the empty spot where she usually parks her car. I picked this place because I can see Luys come and go from his home.

Luys is nowhere to be found. I have traveled to the nearest prison and found the chain link, the barbed wire, the armed guards, and the brute force of the men within the walls daunting.

They are puny humans. But there are many of them and only one of me. If I try to go in, I will more than call attention to myself. They will learn I am unlike any of them. Word will fly between them all, and they will make a point of hunting me down because I am different.

You are being weak. A coward of all things!

Since when have I shied away from humans? I use them until they are useless husks. They give me strength.

But do they? Do they really? Avery has the same ability.

She is an anomaly.

But is she?

Enough!

I glare out the window.

Your daughter is human.

That is different. She is part of me, born from my loins.

My lips curl. My daughter will not remain human for long when I find her. And I'll find her. I'll change her, turn her into something far better than any human, into a superior being as she deserves.

First, I need to find Gabriel.

I frown. Soon, I will remove myself from Luys' life. He is not turning into the brother I had hoped. Sudden rage flows through me. He has betrayed me, and I still go back to him like a whipped dog.

I close my eyes against the pain. But he is my little brother. I love him. I always have.

He wants you to get help. He says they have medication to help you think clearly.

He's lied before. He might be lying again to trap me, to make sure I don't bother him or Gabriel again. To keep me away from who is rightfully mine.

The medicine might be a way to convince them you are fit for your daughter.

No. Never. Taking modern medicine and agreeing with him screams that I am weak.

I pause in the middle of the room. Being inside this box of a building makes my skin crawl, and the rage swirling inside me is not abating. I need to feed the fury. Only a hunt for an undesirable will appease it.

In a swirl of mist and fog, I disappear from the room.

Monday, September 1ˢᵗ — 9:46 am

Avery sat on the edge of the bed of her hotel room. How she landed safely after leaving the prison, she didn't know. Kissing Luys had been distracting as hell. But she'd focused on her hunger and the place she loved to frequent. Somehow that focus had sent her to her favorite pizza restaurant blocks from her condo. Maybe, just maybe, she might be getting a handle on crossing long distances. She just thanked God no one saw her 'appear' out of a mist on the side of the property.

Beyond shocked, she stared out the window. She was on the third floor of a weekly vacation rental and six miles away from her condo. Far enough, hopefully, to be unfindable from Mayor, but close enough if she had to run back to her condo. But the only way she would show up at her home again was if her life depended on it.

After landing at the restaurant, she'd ventured back to her condo, needing a week's worth of clothes, some essentials, her computer, and of course Clover. When she'd stepped through the front door, she nearly cried at the disaster. Upended cushions, fist-size holes in the plaster, kitchen chairs broken and upended. Her gaze narrowed on the wall opposite the front door, and she found herself unable to turn away as she moved forward on unsteady legs. The air was dry and cold against her skin. Blood smeared a random path across the wall. Her nose wrinkled. But whose blood? Did she even want to know? She hoped the stain was from Mayor and not someone else.

Clover! Panicked, she hurried through the living room, checked the kitchen, and found no sign of the kitten. Oh, God. She prayed Mayor hadn't hurt the cat. Only when she stepped into her bedroom did she relax. The kitten sat in the middle of her bed. On Avery's entry, Clover sauntered across her bed toward her, her tiny mew a relief to hear.

She packed up as quickly as she could and smuggled everything into her car. She paused at her door. Damn it. The lock was ruined—the second time in less than two weeks. She'd have to call a locksmith, but she'd wait until she was far enough away from her condo first.

Once safely ensconced in one of the Grove's weekly rentals, she knew she couldn't continue on this route, though. She'd asked for an emergency time off at work, and they'd agreed to give her two weeks, but it was out of the question for anything longer unless it was a medical emergency. Her funds would eventually run out. Staying at a hotel and paying rent at the same time wasn't in her budget. She had to do something; she couldn't remain inactive for long.

Earlier, even though Luys had mentioned Mayor had since moved, she still found herself driving through Mayor's old neighborhood and past the house where Mayor had held the party she'd attended, which seemed like months ago now, but the home looked like it was occupied by a young couple. Avery drove by several more times to double-check. When she saw the woman in the yard another time, Avery stopped her car long enough to ask if she knew where the previous renter had moved to. She hadn't been able to give Avery any answers.

So where could Mayor have disappeared to? She had to be nearby, watching, waiting for an opportunity.

Rolling her shoulders, she decided she needed answers before she did anything else and called the police department.

Finally, after what felt like an eternity and three transfers, a woman answered. Avery asked, "I was hoping to see if my police report was filed with the right department or wherever it's supposed to go."

"Name?"

"Avery Fleming." She waited several minutes until the woman reconnected. "Can you give me your name again?"

"Avery Fleming."

A long pause followed, and for a minute, she thought the clerk disconnected the line. "I can't find anything by that name. Could it be under your maiden name?"

"No. I'm not married."

"I'm sorry. I can't find anything. Do you remember the officer you talked to?"

"Ben Atkins."

"Let me do a cross-reference." Another long pause. "Sorry, still nothing. You'll have to come back in and file another report."

"Thanks."

Avery hung up and swore under her breath. The bastard. Here she'd thought she could trust him, and he'd betrayed that trust. Of course, he'd betrayed it! He was a freaking murderer! He'd ripped people's hearts out. A shiver raced across her arms and the back of her neck as images from the other night with Ben and his victim flashed across her vision. She blinked several times to get the pictures out of her head.

The idea of walking away, leaving town slipped into her head but just as quickly slipped out. She couldn't leave Luys in prison for a murder he didn't commit. He was the only person who knew the new her. The only one she had a connection to. Too long, she'd kept people at bay. She hadn't with Luys. At least near the end, she hadn't.

The one thing going for her right now was that Ben didn't know that she'd turned into—what had Luys called it? A *nagual?*

But how could she fight a police officer? He was the law. Who was going to believe her over a cop? But he wasn't the only law out there. Her mind segued to Hatcher, the detective who had shown up at the hospital with Ben. But did she dare go to him? Did she dare trust him? Weren't they partners? Wasn't there that code of silence between cops?

Her stomach roiled. If this pace kept up, she was liable to get an ulcer, among other ailments, if that was at all possible now with her *nagual* condition. Groaning, she sank down on the edge of the bed. Her nerves were shot; her mind was a mess. She needed to focus.

The key to everything was Ben. Why frame Luys? There had to be a reason, and she suspected that reason was inside his condo. But even if she couldn't find an answer to the tie between Ben and Luys, she might just find proof of a connection between her murdered neighbor, Noah Harris, and Ben.

Had they worked together? Why were they in the same complex? There were too many unanswered questions.

Then there was this latest murder. She'd seen Ben toss the body to the ground. The victim had been dead or near dead. They had looked lifeless from her vantage point. Yeah, there had been shadows, but there had also been moonlight. There was no way she hallucinated the attack. Especially when Ben saw her and went after her. But where was the body? She hadn't read anything in the newspapers or online.

Oh, God. She needed proof. But what type?

She flopped back on the bed and stared at the ceiling.

Proof…

The only place to find it would be at his condo. She winced at the idea of going anywhere near the complex, what with Mayor also running around. The idea of going into Ben's place was even more cringe-worthy. But what choice did she have?

She sat back up and made a quick call to the police department again.

"Yes," the operator said. "He's in today. I can ring him through to his desk."

Avery quickly hung up and sighed. The last thing she wanted to do was talk to Ben. The name alone sent her pulse skittering and her skin to grow clammy. So… if he was at work, that meant his condo was empty. That meant she could get into his place undetected through her new abilities.

All she would need was a good hour, right?

And what if she found something? Did she even want to find anything? She cringed again. She *needed* to find proof. Okay, so say she actually found evidence of him being a murderer? What then? Call Hatcher?

After rummaging in her purse for Hatcher's card, she sank back down on the bed and flapped the card against her thigh. She bit down on her lower lip. She wasn't in her condo, so even if she confided in Hatcher and he was somehow tied to Ben, he couldn't get to her. Ahh, but he could. They could put a bogus warrant out for her arrest. After all, they knew her home address, her driver's license number.

Oh, God, she was screwed.

But she had to do *something!*

Grumbling under her breath, she flipped through her phone and started doing some research. She needed to protect herself if, for some reason, she got caught in Ben's condo. Mercury was out, but Luys had told her there were other ways. Phone in hand, after flipping from article to article and eyeing anatomy pictures, she stepped into the kitchen and then palmed a couple of knives from the butcher's block. She settled on a long, narrow wicked-looking blade. It would have to do.

After fifteen more minutes of research, she pocketed her cell in her back pocket, held the knife in one hand, and closed her eyes. Focus. Think of Ben's place. She waited, breathing slowly, trying to calm her heart. She opened her eyes. She was still in her living room.

"Damn it!"

The air left her lungs, and a powerful force flung her body into a black void. Then a kaleidoscope of color swirled around her, blinding in intensity. She gasped for air, but it didn't matter. She didn't need air. She was weightless and without form.

Another violent blast thrust her to the side and down. Avery crashed into Ben's kitchen. In the process, she smacked the side of the kitchen counter. She sucked in a breath. Her legs buckled as she slammed to the ground. A wave of nausea roiled through her.

She lay on the kitchen floor for several minutes as her breath calmed, but the pain lancing into her eyes stabbed at her again and again.

More breathing. Slow, steady. She needed to get

control of her body. She didn't know how much time she had to search Ben's place.

She pulled herself from the floor with the help of the counter, looked around, and glanced through the partition to the living area. A sectional in black leather with a chrome and glass table filled much of the space, and a large-screen television rested against one wall. No movement or sound came from any of the other rooms.

Her knife. Oh, shit. She didn't see it anywhere. It looked like it hadn't made the trip. She checked her hands and body just in case she'd cut herself with it. Nothing. She leaned against the counter until the muscles in her body stopped vibrating and contracting. The idea of leaving now wasn't an option. This last trip had been far more difficult and taxing to her system than any of the others. She needed to get some semblance of control over her body.

Still hunched over the counter, she pulled her phone out of her back pocket to check if her phone was still working. It was, but she didn't like how the battery was down to 10 percent, but there wasn't anything she could do about it now. She'd also missed a call. She didn't recognize the number and whoever hadn't left a message. She'd look into it later when she was safe.

Several minutes later, after gaining her equilibrium, she rummaged in the kitchen drawers until she found a twelve-inch blade. She wrapped her fingers around the handle to test its weight.

When she rounded the kitchen into the main area, she froze. She hadn't seen the side wall in the dining area until now. She moved further into the room and around the dining table, unable to take her gaze away from the items displayed on the wall.

Weapons. Guns, knives, spears, machetes, axes—all ancient and all deadly looking. The knife by her shoulder was unadorned of feathers. The handle, made of some type of jade or turquoise, looked like someone had carved an image of an Aztec god into it. The blade, possibly onyx, was pitch black with a primitive serrated edge. She ran a finger carefully along the flat of the blade, noting how razor-sharp it was, and wondered if it was a ceremonial knife when the Aztecs ruled with fear and blood.

Had Mayor used one similar on her? Had she stood over Avery and incanted the words of the old ones?

Avery shivered and turned her focus from the morbid idea.

There weren't too many places to search. She checked the coat closet by the front door, looking for boxes or storage containers where he might hide important information. She eyed the tablet on the coffee table with little hope of finding anything. Two seconds later, she found the screen locked. She couldn't find any computer or laptop.

The bedroom didn't reveal anything other than Ben was a slob. Strange that the main living area of his place was immaculate, but his bedroom was anything but. Socks, shorts, and underwear littered the floor. There had to be something! Next, she moved into the closet and flipped on the interior light. Something smelled awful. Her nose wrinkled. Not wanting to, but knowing she needed to, she shoved the clothing on the hanger to one side.

There. A garbage bag. Her hand tightened on the handle of the knife, and she took in a deep, rattling breath. She didn't want to look inside, but she had to. She didn't have options if she wanted answers. Rolling her shoulders and taking in a deep breath for courage, she untwisted the top of the bag and peered inside.

Clothing. Smelly at that. A gym room in a bag. Actually, the whole bedroom smelled of a gym bag.

She twisted the bag back in place, not sure if she was relieved or disappointed that there hadn't been any other incriminating evidence inside. From the bedroom, she walked into the bathroom and froze. Blood. On the shower curtain, on the tile by her feet, and probably on the dark clothing flung to one corner of the room.

Evidence screamed back at her. But could she get Hatcher here before Ben? It would depend on how close the two men were. But how was she going to explain why she was in Ben's condo? Did she dare lie? It didn't matter right this second. She'd think of the logistics later.

She backed away from the room, careful to make sure the soles of her shoes didn't come into contact with any stains or evidence. Once in the bedroom, she pivoted, rushed from the room, down the hall, and into the living room. She stumbled to a halt. The front door stood open, with Ben blocking the exit.

Oh, shit.

Talk about bad timing.

"Well, well, well." Ben closed the door behind him without breaking eye contact with Avery. "Did you really think you'd get away with breaking into my place?"

"How…you couldn't have known that—"

"The ever-efficient Clara." He flicked the lock

with a click. "She worried that one of my calls didn't go through and gave me the number of the caller. It doesn't take a genius to figure out that you were up to something."

Avery thought back to her brief conversation at the police precinct. She should have known they would have a record as to the calls that came in. Damn it. She should have used a burner or public phone. But she hadn't thought. She hadn't— Oh, God. The missed call. It could have very well have been him, and she wouldn't have known it unless she'd taken the time to find out who belonged to the number.

And here she'd thought she'd been so smart. Her powers had blinded her to her fallibility.

Ben stepped toward her, his movements measured and slow, which felt far more threatening than if he'd rushed her.

"This saves me from a huge headache."

She lifted the knife in the air, trying to focus, to remember how to protect herself against someone like him. "Keep away from me."

He arched a brow and eyed her weapon with an amused smile. "Really?"

"Yes, really."

His smile dropped as he took another threatening step. "Where's Mayor? She's been holed up somewhere, but I haven't been able to find out where."

"Mayor?" she parroted like an idiot, but the question was the last thing she expected.

"Yes."

"I don't know who that is."

"I'm not going to tolerate your lies."

Her lips tightened.

"Why would you protect her?"

Avery didn't know why she was protecting her. The woman had nearly killed her. Maybe it was because she was Luys' sister. Or that she'd learned of Mayor's vulnerability when it came to her daughter. The woman was capable of love in a sick, twisted way. Unlike the man in front of her. "I don't know her."

"I don't have much patience when it comes to you." He took yet another step toward her as she backed into the dining room, her hand fisted around the blade's handle. There was one other exit: the sliding glass doors at the back of the dining area. "You've made my life far too messy, and I don't like complications. I get rid of them. Quickly."

He rushed her. She didn't have time to do anything but react. She should have used her powers to disappear, but she was afraid her body wouldn't take it. She flung herself around the dining room table toward the sliding glass doors, then pivoted back around to face him. She slashed the knife side to side. He dodged the blade, swept a hand in, and punched her in the gut.

She grunted and doubled over. Her vision blurred. He was far stronger than she'd imagined. As light flashed and sparked along her peripheral vision, she sucked in air, trying to gain her balance. His other hand slammed across her wrist. She bit back a cry. Pain cut across her bones and tendons, but her grip held steady on the knife. Straightening, she shoved at his shoulder with her other hand, trying to get enough leverage between them to use the knife. He stumbled backward, his eyes widening. Somehow, strangely, she had a strength she hadn't possessed before. Maybe she was acquiring new powers beyond what she already had. And just maybe she might get out of this alive.

Curiosity flashed in his eyes. "I can't believe you're one of us."

Suddenly, he pivoted, twisted at the waist, and kicked a foot out to connect with her wrist and the weapon. At his unexpected move and the lash of pain that drilled into her arm, she dropped the knife. Breath hissing into her lungs, she pressed her hand against her stomach, willing the pain and numbness to ease as she retreated around the dining room table and along the wall with the weapons.

His gaze narrowed. "How did Mayor turn you?"

She wouldn't answer him, but it sounded like he knew too much already. He had to have been the one with the listening device in Luys' condo.

"What ritual did she use?"

He lifted a hand until his palm hovered over his gun belted to his waist.

"Or was it Luys?"

Her heart rate kicked up a notch at the mention of his name.

"I didn't think he was as strong as his sister." Ben cocked his head to his side. "Where's Mayor? This is the last time I'm going to ask."

Her pulse pounded inside her head.

He'd shoot until she was incapacitated. Then even if she had some type of superior strength from what Mayor hadn't given her and bullets wouldn't kill her, she would need time to recover, time to get enough strength to fight back. It would be too late. He would finish her off.

She felt useless, foolish, incapable of beating him.

"You made it so easy. You're in my place. An intruder. With a knife, for God's sake."

Wearily, she watched him as she backed through the dining room, forcing herself not to look at the weapons to the right of her on the wall. He followed, edging even closer as he pulled the gun from its holster.

Avery had one option and only a second to act.

She had to do it. She needed to do it. Her life depended on it. She sucked in a breath and let fear and anger propel her forward and from the room. She fell into space, sucked into another dimension for seconds, minutes, she didn't know. Just as suddenly, she was yanked back with savage intensity. She reappeared behind Ben and right beside the Aztec blade on the wall. Fighting back nausea and dizziness, she grabbed the knife from the hook as he turned. Without hesitation, she plunged it into his body at an angle, through his ribs, and into his heart, just as she'd envisioned after reading and viewing picture after picture of the human anatomy on the internet.

Eyes widening, he stared at her as if in shock. He hadn't expected such a move from her. Silent, he glared down at her hands around the blade, grabbed at her wrists, struggled to pull the weapon from his body. For several heart-rending seconds, they battled over the blade. But Avery held on with both hands, willing herself for more strength, knowing her life depended on it. As his hands weakened around her own, she found a renewed energy and determination. Ever so slowly, the stunned look on his face evaporated. His expression slackened as his fingers slipped from her hands. She jumped back as he tumbled to the ground.

Body shaking, breath sawing in and out of her lungs, she backed away from Ben and latched onto the edge of the dining room table, afraid that if she didn't grab something for support, she'd land on the ground beside or on top of him.

She waited, staring at his prone body lying on its side. Nothing. No movement, no sound. She waited longer. And still nothing.

His body didn't shrivel up into a husk of its former self. He didn't evaporate into a mound of dust. He lay there, the fabric of his white dress shirt darkening around the protruding knife.

Unable to take being inside, she stumbled from the condo and stood outside. It had been self-defense. The police would have to see that. Wouldn't they?

With a shoulder against the side of the wall, she grabbed for Hatcher's business card in her back pocket with a trembling hand. He'd given the card to her just a little over two weeks ago. Hard to believe it wasn't that long ago when he'd first shown up in the hospital with his initial questions with Ben. It felt like years since. She grabbed her phone from her other back pocket to call him. But then she paused.

911 first. Then Hatcher. The more police, the better. They couldn't all be like Mayor or Ben. When she finally got the shaking under control, she called the emergency line and waited outside of the condo.

"Avery!"

Her entire body jerked in reaction. She spun around. Her friend, Cristina, trotted down the walkway toward her. "My God. Where have you been? You've had me so worried!" She stumbled to a halt in front of Avery, her voice ratcheting up a notch. "I tried calling you. Even left a couple of messages. You didn't call me back. I showed up at your condo too, and nothing either. Why? I thought we were friends!

"I seriously thought of calling the police. I've been afraid for your life. I know Luys was arrested, but still. There are so many wackos out there."

Avery rubbed a thumb across the surface of her phone again and again as she fumbled for an answer. She'd completely forgotten about Cristina. She'd been so focused on her own drama. "I've been staying with a friend over at the Grove. She's visiting from out of town with her husband, and there wasn't enough room at my place for everyone," she said, surprised that once she started, how easily the lies came.

Gaze narrowing, Cristina backed up and paused long enough to look over Avery's face and body. "Something wrong. What is it? You look like hell."

Avery opened her mouth—she couldn't help herself—and blurted out, "It's not good. Not good at all."

She'd known there would be questions. Many questions. Not just Cristina's but the police's.

But her answers?

Well, it was simple. That she knew. She'd have to lie.

CHAPTER 28

Wednesday, September 3rd – 12:45 pm

"You're out."

"What?" Luys stared at the open door of his cell, where a guard stood with a hand against the door frame and above his head. He snapped a piece of gum between his teeth.

Luys had seen him before. Except for the shock of white on the top of his head, the rest of his hair was shaved on all sides. He had yet to see anything on his face other than a frown. Polanco. Luys now remembered his name.

"Come with me."

Dread buried into Luys' gut as he followed the correctional officer from his cell and down the hall. Whatever was happening couldn't be good. Had they moved him to a facility with more violent criminals?

"Where are we going?"

"You're being released."

"What? Why?"

The guard arched a brow and snickered—the first smile Luys had ever gotten from him. "Haven't a clue. They don't pay me enough to ask questions."

When they reached the property room, another guard with close-set eyes and thick, black-framed glasses dropped a clear plastic bag onto the counter. "You need to go over to the next building through the double doors to the right. First, trade out your uniform with your clothes. There's a basket in the bathroom," he nodded to the door across the hall from him.

"Don't come back. Next time I might not be so nice," Polanco threw over his shoulder with a smirk as he disappeared through the double doors, and Luys quickly changed into his clothing in the locker room.

When he went through the double doors, a clerk handed him a stack of paperwork. Several signatures later, he was done. "Is that it?"

Were the guards going to let him walk out? Just like that? "Do I need to speak to anyone?"

"Nope." The clerk arched a brow. "Did you want to hang around here longer?"

"No, of course not." He looked down the hall to the single faded yellow metal door and hesitated. Outside waited, but he had no clue how far a drive or walk it was to his home. "I need to call for a ride."

"Behind you. But if you're calling for a taxi, there's no need. You have a ride waiting for you."

"Oh." Gabriel, of course.

Once he stepped outside, he blinked, adjusting to the sun's blinding rays. He looked around at the few parked cars in the lot, but he didn't see any sign of his brother. He then noticed a woman leaning against the side of a compact car. The sun's rays caught her hair and shot metallic highlights into the strands.

At the sight of her, he felt his chest expand and a wave of relief wash over him. Avery. She was safe. And she hadn't given up on him. After she vanished from his cell, he'd had Gabriel check on her, but his brother had found her car gone and no answer at her condo. What had stopped Luys from going completely mad was that Gabriel had checked all the hospitals and morgues and found her in neither. When his brother couldn't find her car in the complex's parking lot, they both believed it was a good sign she had hidden out somewhere safe.

Avery waved, and as he drew closer, it felt wonderful to see the welcome smile on her face. He stood in front of her as she grinned up at him. "Well, are you going to kiss me hello?"

That's all he needed to hear before he swept her up in his arms, holding her tight for a long moment before catching her mouth in a deep, slow kiss, savoring the taste and smell of her. After a few moments, and when both were breathing heavily, he forced himself to break off their kiss and look down into her twinkling eyes. "You're the best thing I've seen."

Her lips twitched. "That's saying a lot about how long you've lived."

Finally, reluctantly, he unwrapped his arms from around her and stepped back, but he had to touch her one last time by sweeping a strand of hair that had caught on her eyelash before curving it around her ear. "Why? I don't understand."

Her brow dipped as she searched his face. "You mean your lawyer didn't notify you?"

"No."

"They dropped the murder charges against you."

"How? I don't understand. What happened?"

"They found the person who really murdered Noah Harris. Your sister isn't the killer."

He trailed a hand down her arm to catch her hand in his. He could not stop touching her. She felt too good, but he needed to focus on the reason behind his release. "Was it the plainclothes officer who arrested me? The one you mentioned earlier? This Ben?"

"Yes."

"But how? Did they get evidence from his latest murder? The one you witnessed?"

"Not the last one I witnessed. I checked all online sources, and there's no news on a brutal murder. Maybe he cleaned the area and disposed of the body." She slipped her hand from his and bit her lip. Something was off from her guarded expression. Her next words confirmed it.

"Let's talk in the car. I have a lot to catch you up on, and here isn't the best place."

Once behind the wheel and out of the parking lot, Avery explained what had happened after she left him that day in his jail cell. A chill washed over him as Avery confessed to going into Ben's home to find a way to prove Luys' innocence, how Ben had found her inside and she'd been forced to kill him before he did the same to her. She also explained how she'd found blood and fibers in Ben's bathroom that tied him to Noah Harris' murder.

He was humbled, ashamed, and… "I don't know what to say…." But then he thought of what she had gone through, the danger, the possibility of dying because of him. "I really should be furious that you jeopardized your life for me."

"How about a thank you?" She arched a brow at him.

"Of course. Words feel inadequate and can never repay you, not for all you've done for me." He glanced over at her profile, taking in the sweep of her glossy auburn hair, her upturned nose, the strong but elegant line of her jaw. He didn't deserve such a woman in his life. "Thank you."

"You're welcome," she said, her voice turning husky and sober. "I have to admit there were a couple of moments where I didn't think I'd be able to outsmart or outrun Ben." She rolled her shoulders. "Thank goodness that's done. But now I'm in Mayor's sights. She trashed my condo. I guess she was unhappy I escaped and took it out on my furniture and walls. She's the main reason I can't go back home. I'm pretty sure she wants me dead."

"I don't know how yet, but I'll repay you. Of course, I'll reimburse you for any damages done." Luys knew that was little consolation or compensation for having someone laying waste to a person's private space.

"We can worry about that later." She shrugged, her voice turning wry. "There are more important things to consider right now."

Her words humbled him further. He didn't understand how one woman could turn his life into something unrecognizable in the course of weeks, not months. His chest tightened with a deep, all-encompassing emotion he couldn't remember experiencing for the longest time. Love. Could something so profound have entered his life after so many years of emptiness? "Where have you been staying? I'm curious. Gabriel looked for you. When he couldn't find you, the only thing keeping me sane was the knowledge that you were smart enough to keep away from your home."

"I'm renting over at The Grove. They're weekly rentals a couple of miles from the condos." Her hand tightened on the steering wheel. "I don't think it's such a good idea to go over to your place right now. At least, not for any length of time."

"I do have to get a change of clothes if nothing else."

"Okay, we'll make it quick."

When they reached the complex, she backed the car into a parking slot. From this vantage point, she could get a good view of the complex and anyone coming or going. She kept the car running. She wasn't about to venture into any building right now, even if Ben was dead. There was still Mayor. The last time they'd met, the woman had tried to kill her. She needed to talk to Luys about her. They needed to figure out how to work with her sister, whatever that meant. But right now, she wanted to avoid anything to do with Mayor and her penchant for killing people, including the possibility of herself.

"Do I need to get cat food for Clover?" Luys paused after opening his door.

"No, I've got her covered. She's all safe where I'm staying."

"Okay, I'll be right back."

Avery waited tensely, locking all doors with a click of the button. She eyed the other cars, the walkways. Even with no sign of Mayor, she didn't relax. That was fine. Really. Paranoia was good.

Finally, Luys appeared with a backpack over his shoulder. After Avery unlocked the car, he slipped into the passenger seat. The minute he was situated, she clicked the locks again and drove out of the lot. Only then did she feel the tension ease from her back and shoulders.

With the idea of Mayor far away somewhere, she relaxed even further and her thoughts segued in a far different direction. She glanced over at Luys. His long legs brushed up against the dashboard, and his large body and wide shoulders filled far more than his section of the front of the car. Memories of them previously flooded her mind. His hand on her breast. The feel of him inside her. She shifted in her seat as a wave of longing pooled in her belly. He was a selfless lover.

The air between them thickened with awareness. Or was it just her? But there was a definite something to the silence, and it was growing pretty lengthy.

"Are you hungry?" Oh, hell, not a good question. She needed to rephrase that. "Did you need something to eat? I have very little in the fridge."

"No, I'm fine," he said, his voice wrapping around her in its husky baritone.

Hands tightening on the wheel, she shivered and glanced quickly over at him. He met her gaze, and something in his eyes made her body feel that much hotter.

"Okay," she managed, finding her words far too shaky with need, and she suspected he could hear it in her voice.

When she rested her arm on the pad between the seats, Luys caught her hand in his and twined his fingers around hers. "I've never been able to forget being with you. How you tasted. How you felt."

Her fingers tightened around his before she whispered in an equally husky voice, "I haven't either."

There had been times she'd wanted to forget. She'd been furious with him when she'd found out his secrets. But now, how could she? She'd killed a man. Granted, she was protecting herself, but she knew the danger she was putting herself in when she went into Ben's condo and that someone could end up dead. She'd been lucky that she hadn't been the one who had died. Immortality, or the next closest thing, kind of put a stop to her death. But it was more than that. He had been trying to protect a sister. Yes, lots of gray, but the meaning behind his actions was understandable. She didn't know what she would have done in the same situations.

Every move after—even though neither one of them touched each other—from the time they left the car and walked across the parking lot and up the walkway to the rental, she was hyper-conscious of the way his body moved, how he dwarfed her height, the inches or feet that separated them. She felt like she was about to self-combust at any second, and she'd only touched his hand!

The moment they stepped into the rental and Avery closed the door, Clover meowed and charged toward them. Luys picked her up and scratched her behind her ears. Her purr, a loud rumble for such a tiny cat, increased in volume, and Luys rubbed beneath Clover's chin. "I'm glad to see I've been missed."

"She's a sweet little thing. I'm sure she knows she's got it pretty good. It has to beat living out of garbage pails and scrapes from fast food wrappers."

He placed Clover back on the ground, where she wound herself around both his legs. But she quickly lost interest and trotted over to the window by the sofa and jumped up on the ledge. Luys' smile of affection deepened when he turned his gaze from the cat to Avery. His brown eyes turned to dark chocolate. "I wonder if I can make you purr as loudly as Clover?"

She barely had the chance to take in a shivering breath of excitement before Luys had his hands in her hair, his lips on her mouth. With fumbling fingers, she got the door locked before her brain turned to mush and her insides reacted with a wave of intense sexual need.

Sighing into his mouth, she kissed him back, rising to her toes and pressing into the immovable wall of his chest. At the feel of his erection and how it dug into her stomach, her legs started shaking. Knowing that he wanted her just as badly made her want him that much more.

She toed her shoes off, broke off their kiss just long enough to pull her t-shirt up over her head and toss it on the ground. Luys followed with the same. He then tugged her toward the bed, picked her up, and dropped her on the sheets. A second later, he was on top of her, still in his jeans. Even so, the heat of his body burned into her, his cock nestled between the juncture of her legs. She lifted her knees and pressed into him, sucking in air at the hunger that raged through her body to grip at her belly. Her breasts tightened with need.

He lifted himself, rested both elbows on either side of her, and looked into her eyes. The heat of his gaze scorched through her skin and into every cell. "Thinking of being with you like this while I was in jail was the only thing that kept me going. I was terrified for you."

"Well, I'm fine now." She lifted her neck until her breath fanned his lips. "I don't want to think about anything but now." She flicked a tongue across his lower lip. "We're together, we both want each other, and that's all that matters."

"You're right," he whispered against her lips before sliding a palm along her neck to brush a thumb over the pulse point below her ear. She groaned as his mouth replaced his finger, and he laved the lobe of her ear and cut a path down the sweep of her neck and to the ridge of her collarbone. Still lower he went. He paused at the edge of her lace bra, but for a second. Then he enclosed his mouth over her nipple.

She gasped, arching toward him, curling her hands into his hair, and pressing his head against her breast. He suckled her for several long, toe-curling moments. Avery forgot everything but the heat of his mouth on her, the dampness of his tongue, and the way his hands stroked restlessly up and down the sides of her body.

Then he moved back to her lips and claimed her mouth again. When his kiss grew hotter, more demanding, Avery lost it. She opened her mouth wider, brushing against his tongue with her own, delving beyond his lips. She wanted to consume him.

The need got so bad she started squirming beneath him. "I can't take much more. I. Need. You. Bad."

When he drew away, she clutched his biceps while the pit of her stomach twisted with excitement. She wanted more than kisses.

"Maybe this isn't a good idea after all," Luys whispered, his face flushed, air sawing in and out of his lungs. "I've got baggage like no other."

He didn't have to mention her name. They both knew he meant Mayor.

"Don't," Avery breathed. She ran her hands down the hard muscles of his shoulders and upper back. "We both deserve a moment to find pleasure, a bit of happiness."

At her words, something inside him seemed to crack, and his tense muscles eased beneath her palms. This next time, there was a subtle difference when he kissed her, almost as if he were savoring each touch, each caress with a new depth.

With his mouth still on hers, he slipped both hands down over her arms to clasp her hips to tug her even closer. He thrust back and forth. The friction of their jeans against her sex stoked her desire, making her feel out of control. The room filled with heavy breathing, moaning. Then she realized in shock that it was herself. He made her feel alive. It was both terrifying and intoxicating.

Avery sucked in a breath. "I can't take it any longer..."

She didn't have to say anymore. He slipped off the bed. With quick, efficient hands, he pulled his pants, socks, and underwear off until he was naked at the end of the bed. Lifting up on her elbows, she eyed his scar on his chest briefly before dipping past his flat stomach to his erection. He was big. Thick. The idea of him inside her, flexing, pumping, moving flooded Avery. Her sex quivered and tightened.

She couldn't get the rest of her clothes off fast enough. He helped her, his hands deft, warm, lingering on her skin until she was naked, and he pulled her further down on the bed where he stood between her legs. Bending, he clutched her hips and wrapped them around his waist as he slid into her, inch by electrifying inch. With both feet flat on the mattress, she lifted her hips up to meet his body until he was flush to her. The hunger, the need was all-consuming. Too quickly, he'd branded her body, her mind, her thoughts. She didn't question the well of emotions flowing through her. Now wasn't the time.

Fully impaled, she sucked in a breath with a loud whoosh. They stared at each other for a heated moment, both breathing heavily as he moved inside her. Her legs tightened around his waist, locking her ankles around him, and he pushed them both along the length of the bed while still embedded in her. His fingers curled into the thick waves of her hair until he cupped her skull in both hands to hold her steady as his tongue mated with hers, and he began deepening his strokes.

He shifted beneath her, tilting his hips in a way that deepened his movements. Avery groaned into his mouth, savoring the way his body fit into hers. Thoughts fled. Sensation took over. Breaking off the kiss, she gripped his shoulders, ran her hands into his hair, curling the strands between her fingers and tugging until he gave her his neck. She licked at his throat, scraping her teeth along the corded muscles as she arched into him. Both their bodies were slick with sweat. An oncoming orgasm wound tighter and tighter through her body, unrelenting, savage, until it broke free and barreled into every muscle, every fiber of her body, as her insides clutched tight around his cock.

Luys gulped in air, grabbed her hips, and shuddered above her. He came long and hard. His grip on her didn't loosen until he was spent, and his body's weight sank onto hers.

Gasping, she came down from her orgasm, slowly, effortlessly. The rough texture of his cheek against her neck, jaw, brow highlighted every sensation that still encompassed her body.

"I didn't hurt you, did I?" He drew back and searched her face.

"No, not at all," she whispered, unable to stop looking up at him with wonder. "I…"

He stared down at her, waiting.

"Thank you."

"You thanked me last time." His brow dipped as he trailed a finger along her shoulder and over the indentation above her collarbone. "We're both giving each other pleasure."

Heat flared into her face. How did she say what she wanted to say without coming across as cheesy? She guessed it didn't matter, not with what they had both gone through so far. "Yeah, but it's more to me. I've never felt this connected with someone else. It makes being with you different, far more… I don't know how to say it. With you, I feel out of control, like my body isn't my own. The pleasure. It's so intense. Nothing before compares to what this is between us."

His lips grazed her temple. "I know. I feel it too. It's scary and exhilarating at the same time."

When he wrapped his arms around her and pulled her along the full length of his body, she rested her head against his arm and took in the moment, relished the sensation of his breath against her cheek, how the hair on his calves and thighs brushed her skin when he entwined his legs with hers.

After a couple of minutes of silence, Luys' lips

curved against her brow before he murmured, "I hate to say it…but I'm hungry. This time for food."

She drew back and eyed him with a smile. "Well, I guess that's better than falling asleep on me."

"I can always hold off for another round. I could have a bite of you right now instead."

The wicked gleam in his eyes and his innuendo made her body clench in reaction. "Don't tempt me." She kissed him and scrambled from the bed for her phone. "If you want another romp in the sheets, I'm going to need some energy. Pizza sound fine?"

"Yes, anything other than anchovies."

"Perfect. Glad to see we're on the same page." She grabbed her cell phone on the nightstand and did a quick order through her app. Then she picked up her clothing scattered around the room.

"I think we are on the same page on many things."

She hugged her clothing close to her body, feeling suddenly self-conscious with Luys staring at her with those dark, fathomless eyes. Trying to shake off the feeling, she teased, "Hmm, hopefully, you don't have any darker secrets hidden away. I don't think I can take anything more. Like loud, break the door down snoring. That's something I won't tolerate!"

A look of mock shock crossed his features. "I would never do that."

"Only time will tell," she said and immediately realized how she'd taken the next step between them for granted. She backed up toward the bathroom.

"Yes, it will," Luys agreed, his gaze softening. "I would like to spend all my nights with you, not just my days."

She paused, still holding her clothing against her middle. "I just realized your job and how you must have lost it. I'm sorry."

"Before everything, I was well regarded, so I'm sure I'll have it back. If not..." He shrugged, though he looked somewhat pensive. "I should be able to find another."

"Do you enjoy your job?"

"Sometimes, but I was researching on the side and trying to find solutions behind Gabriel's, Mayor's, and my ability to live beyond a normal human's lifespan. Gabriel would like an ordinary life with his wife. Amanda isn't like us. She'll grow old. After several decades, people will think she's his grandmother, not his wife."

"That would be hard." Her clothes bunched between her fingers. "And Gabriel wants to be normal? After all this time?"

"Yes. He's tired, I think." Luys slipped from the bed and sauntered naked toward her. He stopped a foot away and looked down at her with a sad smile. "I believe the love he has for his wife is strong. So strong the idea of living after her death is not an option he wants."

The idea of not having Luys in her life stung. She wanted him longer than a week, a month, or even a year.

They took a shower together. Washing each other quickly turned sexual, and they made love with the mist and water around them. Luys was tender one moment and fierce the next. Feeling completely relaxed, she dried off and changed. God, it felt good to feel so alive, even happy. Yeah, there was Mayor, but hopefully, things would calm down. Maybe Luys could talk some sense into her. With the three of them in a room together, just maybe Mayor could see that Avery posed no threat to Luys.

As she pulled her t-shirt over her head, the doorbell rang. "I got it."

After paying the pizza delivery driver, she closed the door and carried the pizza over to the kitchen as her cell phone started ringing. She grabbed her phone on the counter, saw that it was Cristina, and thought of letting the call go to voice mail, but then her phone turned silent. Two seconds later, Avery's phone started up again. Cristina again. It wasn't like Cristina to hang up and call again. She usually left a message or text. Something was off.

"What's wrong?" Avery asked. "Are you okay?"

"No! I'm scared. So damn scared." Cristina groaned and started crying. "Is Luys with you?"

"Yes," Avery answered, her voice thickening in alarm. "Why?"

"It's Stephen. I need help. He's gone crazy. Luys is big enough to stop Stephen if he tries anything." Cristina sniffled and took a deep breath as if to get a hold of her crying. "I can't go to the police. He threatened he'd kill me if I did. I don't know where to go. You're my only friend."

"Where are you?"

"Home, but I don't have much time until Stephen comes back."

"What about his brother? Can he help you?"

"No. He's been gone all day. And he hasn't a clue about what's going on between Stephen and me."

"We'll be right there."

CHAPTER 29

N o," Luys argued after she rushed back into the bedroom and told him about her phone call with Cristina. He shrugged into his jeans and zipped up his fly. "You're not going anywhere with her husband nearby."

"I can take care of myself. I have abilities—"

"I don't care. Passion can make someone far stronger than they normally are."

"But she's my friend," Avery argued, disliking the stubborn slant to his jaw.

"It's too dangerous, Avery." He grabbed his shirt, pulled it over his head, and shoved his arms through the sleeves. He smoothed down flyaway strands the shirt had mussed up. "Let me go alone, be the one to check on her. Even with your new skills, Stephen might be able to overpower you."

Avery wanted to stamp her foot in frustration and overtake him at the front door, even knowing he was right. Instead, she followed him to the living area and kept her mouth shut.

When he rose from tying his shoes, he looked down at her. Inches separated them. Heat radiated from his body and warmed her chilled skin. Her chest tightened. "Be careful. You don't know what you are walking into."

"I will."

He bent down, and she caught him midway, her lips molding over his, her hands clutching his biceps. Maybe she was overreacting with all the horror of the last couple of weeks, but she feared for his life. In all honesty, she was falling hard. She was starting to care deeply for him in a way that scared her. She didn't want to think that this might be their last kiss, their last goodbye.

He must have read the fear in her face because he said in a husky voice, "I'll be fine. I'll call the minute I've figured out what's going on and have Cristina in a safe place."

"Promise?"

"Promise."

She closed the door with a ragged sigh and watched from the window. Two seconds and he was gone from view.

She waited on the edge of a chair, not paying attention as she scrolled through the news, her social apps, and emails. At least the hours after Ben's death had been less horrifying than the death itself. Hatcher had arrived quickly, taken one look at the bathroom, and her account of self-defense had held up well enough that she'd walked out of the precinct that same night—shaken and hollow, but free.

Eyeing the time on her phone, she jerked to a stand. An hour. The temptation to call Luys was overwhelming, but she hauled back the urge. Now wasn't the time. She could interrupt the situation and distract Luys, which could be the last thing he needed.

An hour and fifteen.

An hour and thirty-three.

An hour and forty-six.

Two hours.

She called his cell. When she didn't get an answer, she tried Cristina's. All she got was her voice mail. Then she called them both again and left messages.

Something was seriously wrong.

She grabbed her car keys, phone, and purse. At the front door, she paused and glanced over her shoulder. Clover rested curled up on the top of the sofa by the window. The kitten had enough food and water for the day.

Avery took in a deep fortifying breath. "I'll be back as soon as I can."

The cat blinked.

"Promise."

Pain pounding into his skull, Luys woke up with a jerk and blinked once, twice to clear his vision. He frowned, then winced as a new wave of pain stabbed into his head. It took him a moment to realize he sat in one of the chairs in his living room.

How? He didn't remember getting there, only that he had stepped through the door. He tried to rise, to move his hands. Something kept him bound to the chair. His hand rested uselessly on his thighs; his legs wouldn't respond to the simple command of rising.

Confused, he glanced around his condo but was unable to thoroughly look around because a strange weight kept him from being able to move his head in any direction. He realized he wasn't alone. Legs crossed at the ankle, Stephen sat on the farthest end of the sofa from him with an arm slung over the top as he watched Luys with unblinking eyes. Slowly, Stephen uncrossed his legs and sat forward, leaning an elbow on one knee.

Luys tried to rise again, but his body wouldn't obey. Had Stephen drugged him? "What did you do?"

"Just made the playing field even." He waved a hand.

Glancing down in the direction he pointed, Luys searched his arms and the rest of his body, thinking zip ties or cords bound him to the chair somehow. Then he noticed the medallion, the one he'd kept in a glass case by the dining room, resting against his chest, its weight and power binding him to the chair. A locket contained a vial of mercury beneath the roughly faceted and thumb-sized ruby in the center of the cross. The thick tempered glass case had kept the mercury from harming him, but now it lay against his body, feeling like a crushing and suffocating weight. One drop on his skin would eat through his flesh, ravage his body, and kill him.

How could Stephen have known about the mercury hidden within the medallion? Was he working with Mayor? But that didn't make sense. She could have enlisted Stephen's help long before.

For a moment, he thought Stephen must be like Gabriel, Mayor, and himself, but that wouldn't explain him calmly sitting so close to him and the medallion around his neck. The mercury's proximity to him would eventually drain his strength. Stephen must have learned it from someone else, then, someone very much like his siblings and himself.

A buzzing came from beside Stephen, the tone familiar. Luys then noticed his cell next to another one and a gun on the cushion beside the other man. The screen lit up as Luys' phone continued to ring.

Avery. It had to be. She needed to stay away. Stephen could be capable of anything.

"Why me? I've not done anything to you." He hadn't had the opportunity to confront Stephen or find Cristina. When he knocked on their door and got no answer, he'd peered in the windows but hadn't found either one of them. From there, he'd decided to get a change of clothes at his condo and regroup. Cristina had sounded terrified enough to have already fled on her own.

"Your sister."

"What? Mayor?"

"Don't look so shocked. The woman is a menace. She's ruined lives because of her selfishness."

Luys could not help but be surprised. He couldn't think of any link between his sister and him. "I don't get it. Why me? For what purpose?"

"To get to her. She's given us few options, with her being so elusive. We knew she had two brothers. When we found you, we knew she would eventually turn up. We put a bug in your place, thinking that might help. Every damn time anyone of us spotted her or heard that she was with you, we couldn't get to her fast enough. Since then, nothing. We'd grown impatient."

He gestured toward Luys' phone. "A text from you begging for her help should get her here."

"You don't know that."

"True, but what's that saying about blood being thicker than water? She'll come, but I need the element of surprise. She's too dangerous, otherwise. I'm very much human and nothing like you or her. But if that doesn't work, we'll be more forceful and barter for your life. That should make her move faster."

"You're wasting your time. Mayor can't stand me."

Stephen frowned. "I don't believe you. According to what we've managed to hear from our recordings, she might be furious, but deep down, she wants to reconcile with you."

"Believe what you want. That's your choice."

"If that's the case, you're of very little use."

"You plan to kill me?"

The idea of death had always terrified Luys because of what he had become. He had no idea if he had a soul or would end up in purgatory. But he'd always kept all that in the back of his mind, thinking the possibility of his demise near impossible. The reality of it hit him like a sledgehammer to his body. What shocked him about his response was not the idea of his passing but of him dying before he could keep Avery safe.

Luys searched his memory for some type of link between Mayor, Stephen, and the murders. "Does this have to do with Ben Atkins?"

"You have no idea, do you?" He snorted and picked up the gun beside him. "Ben moved into the complex because of you. Just like me, he was also waiting for Mayor to show up. I thought he was invincible until Avery killed him. His death isn't going to go unpunished. Avery's going to have to pay for his murder, and

Mayor? She's going to die for her sins. I hope it's slow and painful."

Rage and impotence roiled through Luys, urging him to move his hands, his body, anything to lash out at Stephen's snide expression, but his body remained frozen to the chair. He couldn't do anything to stop him from hurting Avery and took a moment to calm himself and made a point of adding a thread of indifference to his voice. "She was only defending herself. He was going to kill her, just like he did Noah Harris.

"I don't understand Atkins' motivation or the connection. Why Harris? And why frame me?"

Stephen's lip curled. "It was all Ben's idea. He thought for sure implicating you in a murder would smoke Mayor out, and with you framed, no one would look at me, Cristina, even Ben as the suspect."

"And Harris?"

Stephen eyed him in distaste. "Ben didn't have much choice."

"How so?"

"Harris started sticking his nose in other peoples' business. He was putting it all together. The murders, the Aztec rituals." Stephen ran a thumb across the metal barrel. A silencer was connected to the muzzle. "He knew about people like you, Mayor—"

"So you and Ben killed him?"

All this time he'd been suspicious of his sister, even though Mayor had been quick to tell him how he always assumed the worst of her. And she'd been right.

"What else were we supposed to do? Don't tell me if you found out your cover was going to be blown, you wouldn't have stopped Harris."

"I wouldn't have killed him!"

Stephen stopped caressing the metal. "So self-righteous. Your sister learned the ways of the high priests, honoring and sacrificing to the Quetzalcóatl. They had such power! Such respect!"

"And death. Everything they stood for was to create terror amongst their enemies."

"You're blind to their ways. It's such a shame. Death is an instrument of life. Without death, there's no life." His gaze narrowed. "Your sister. She's far worse than you, and she'll pay for her sins."

"What did she do?"

Stephen shook his head, his voice thick with disgust. "It doesn't matter now. Soon she will become no more than dust."

Luys glanced down at the medallion resting on his chest, its chain like a venomous snake wrapped around his neck and squeezing the energy from his body. If only he had the strength to pull it off. Focusing all his energy, he struggled to lift his hand until his fingers shook with the effort and sweat on his brow chilled his flesh. Gasping, he released the muscles of his arm. He'd managed but a centimeter of space between his palm and his leg.

"Mercury really does keep you in line, doesn't it?" Stephen eyed him across the room before setting his gun back on the cushion beside him. Next to the two phones, he picked up another item Luys hadn't noticed until now. It looked like a clear tube, about an inch high and half an inch wide. Between his thumb and forefinger, Stephen moved the vial upside down and back again. Mercury rolled back and forth from within the vial.

He'd come here with the intention of helping Cristina, but he'd screwed everything up for her, his sister, and Avery.

"Where's Cristina? What did you do to her?"

"Do?" Stephen laughed. "She's busy right now."

Stephen set the mercury on the cushion and picked up Luys' phone. "Love. Such a powerful motivator. I bet you I can get Mayor and Avery here because of it. Mayor's taking her sweet time, though. I think she needs more of an incentive. Hearing a loved one's screams tends to get a person moving."

CHAPTER 30

The doorknob turned easily in her hand. Taking in a deep breath and trying to ignore the wild beat of her heart, Avery eased the door open to Luys' condo and paused. She'd tried calling a couple more times on her way to the condo complex. Luys hadn't answered. Neither had Cristina. Once she'd pulled into the parking lot, she'd immediately gone over to Stephen's and Cristina's place but hadn't gotten an answer. She'd found the door locked and all the blinds closed. Calling out for both hadn't gotten her anything but silence.

Something was definitely wrong. Cristina would have answered if she'd been able to. Same with Luys. With both Luys and Cristina missing, her thoughts veered to Stephen. Could he have hurt them both? Luys was the larger of the two men, but Stephen could have caught him unawares and disabled him. But there had been no signs of a struggle around Cristina's condo.

The only thing she could think of was that Luys had found Cristina and hidden her over at his condo.

Avery stood to the side of the doorway to Luys' condo as lights from the sidewalk speared a path across the living area and toward a figure slumped in a cushioned chair. There was enough light to distinguish the man's thick brown hair, firm jaw, and high cheekbones.

"Luys?"

He didn't lift his head or move from his position in the chair.

Opening the door wider and peeling back more shadows, she edged deeper into the room. Movement in the corner of the living room made her turn. She tensed. Someone else was in the room. A flash of metal, a loud cough. A bullet slammed into her shoulder. She grunted and jerked backward at its force. She hit the side of the doorway with her arm and twisted around and out of the condo before the person had shot off another bullet and hit her again.

Gasping against the pain, she lurched away and down the sidewalk before glancing down. She touched her shoulder, lifted her hand, and came away with blood on her fingers. A dark stain appeared against the navy blue of her t-shirt. She inhaled sharply. A shiver of shock rushed through her. Oh, God. She'd always wondered what a bullet felt like, and now she knew. It felt like hell. The pain was excruciating. Taking in deep, steady breaths, she tried to focus on what to do next. Luys needed help. He could be dead already.

Panic bubbled through her insides, and she ruthlessly pushed it back. Now wasn't the time to let emotions control her. She needed to think, to act, to help Luys however she could.

She glanced up as someone rounded the corner of Luys' condo.

"Cristina. Thank God! We were so worried about you."

Cristina smiled and spread her hands wide. "I'm good. Sorry. I panicked."

Avery struggled for words. She didn't know how much blood she was losing. "Someone just shot me."

"Oh, no!" Cristina hurried over, brows shooting up and eyes widening. "What happened?"

"Something's wrong with Luys. He's inside with someone else, but I didn't have time to see who it was."

Cristina moved closer, glancing briefly at Avery's wound before grabbing her hand and urging her back to Luys' condo. "We need to help him."

But Avery remained rooted to the sidewalk. There was no way she was going back in there until she had some type of plan. Tears blurred her vision. She tried not to think that she might already be too late for Luys. Then she noticed Cristina's neck. "You've got new bruises."

"Yes, well. Those don't matter right now."

"I've got to call the police." With her good arm, she reached behind her for her phone in her back pocket, but Cristina caught her arm in midair. She frowned and looked down at Cristina's hand around her wrist. She tried to pull away, but the woman was much stronger. "What are you doing?"

"We're going inside."

"Are you crazy? Someone just shot at me!"

She pried at Cristina's fingers, which tightened until she thought her wrist might snap from the pressure. Then she noticed the coldness in Cristina's eyes, the rigid thrust of her jaw as she pivoted around Avery and dragged her toward the front door. Avery bucked, twisted back and forth, tugged harder, tried every maneuver, but she couldn't break the woman's hold. The power behind Cristina's grip was crazy.

Then Avery realized maybe Cristina wasn't who she appeared. Maybe her friend really wasn't a friend but someone like Mayor. Someone who had been turned like Avery. Someone who had motives Avery could only guess at. She couldn't think of the woman's betrayal. Not when her life depended on survival.

Cristina shoved her toward the open door. The force propelled Avery over the threshold, where she landed on her knees in the entranceway.

She struggled to her feet and glanced over at Luys. He remained motionless, his chin against his chest as if in defeat or something even worse. Please, God, don't let him be dead. She eyed the medallion. She didn't know how quickly it took hold, but Stephen didn't seem worried, and neither did Cristina as she stepped into the condo and slammed the door behind her.

Deciding not to wait to find out what they planned to do to either of them, she rushed over to Luys. A muscle pulsed by his jaw, and he blinked. The emotions in his eyes hit her in the gut. Despair and desperation. Biting back a cry, she clung to him, shielding her hands with her body. He had mentioned the mercury was hidden beneath the stone. If she could just get a hold of it for a minute, then get rid of it. She fumbled for the clasp. A smooth cylinder fell into her palm as she snapped the empty locket closed.

Someone grabbed her from behind and flung her across the room. The mercury slipped from her grasp as she tumbled backward. Her hip hit the wall, and for several minutes she lay there, stunned, trying to regain her breathing.

"Touch him again, and I'll kill you now!"

On her side, Avery cringed against the wall. Cristina stood over her, face blotted in shades of red, veins lifted against the skin of her neck.

Avery avoided her gaze. Beneath lowered lashes, she swept a glance across the floor and spied the mercury she'd dropped near Stephen's feet and under the end table by the sofa. She prayed it was far enough away for it not to affect her and Luys, but it would work its power on Stephen? His foot was less than twelve inches away from the metal.

Cristina turned back to Stephen, who held a gun in one hand. "Do I always have to clean up your mess?" Cristina bit out. "What were you thinking, having her run off like that?"

Stephen's face grew slack-jawed. "Are you serious? What was I supposed to do? You wanted me to wait here until Mayor showed up."

All this time, Avery had thought Stephen had been in control of their relationship, but it looked like Cristina was the one with the power, which didn't explain the bruising, the possible beatings.

"Mayor?" Avery asked. "I don't understand. Why? Why her? Why try to kill Luys and me? And what does she have to do with you?"

Cristina closed her eyes as if the questions pained her. "You got in the middle. I'm sorry for that."

From the hard edge to Cristina's eyes, Avery didn't think Cristina was sorry in the least.

"Are you like Mayor?"

Her gaze turned furious. "Don't ever think it, never mind say it! I may have become a *nagual,* but I'm nothing like her!" Her hands fisted at her sides. "She has hurt me like no other."

"How?" Avery asked.

"She killed my babies! If not for her, Madelena and Juan would still be alive!"

"I never knew you had children."

"Why would you? I have trouble even now thinking of the loss, the pain, even though it's been centuries. The Aztecs believe there is no death, that it is just a cycle, and a person moves on to Mictlan. They lie! My children are forever gone! They were killed because of her. She put her own needs above everyone else. She convinced the priests that her child was feeble and unworthy. They chose my two children instead. Their death and tears were offered to Tlaloc, so he could release the rain and stop the drought."

"But didn't Mayor's daughter also die?"

"Don't question me!" She pounded her fist into the wall. Flecks of plaster and paint landed on Avery. "I deserve my revenge. I've lived and breathed for it for as long as I can remember. If it wasn't for her, they would have looked somewhere else. They took twelve children that year for Tlaloc, but they didn't touch her child!"

While avoiding looking anywhere in Luys' direction, Avery searched for a way to keep Cristina from killing either of them. She needed more time to heal. There was also Luys. She'd removed the mercury from around his neck, but did it matter? No, Avery needed to think positive and pray the metal had kept him a prisoner and hadn't killed him. But how long did it take for it to stop working? She could stall for minutes, but hours? That was impossible.

"And Ben? Was he the father?"

Cristina closed her eyes again as if in pain. "Ben was someone I could trust, someone who believed in me and I in him. He became nagual, like me, centuries before. He hated Mayor, sometimes more than me, because he knew how she ruined my life and killed my children. He helped me again and again in my quest to find Mayor. When we discovered her brother here in Scottsdale, we moved in and waited for Mayor to show up. With Ben nearby, he strengthened my desire to seek vengeance and made me feel powerful. We are friends, lovers, family."

"But Stephen? I thought you were married?"

"We are. His family's money keeps us comfortable. He does things to me few men will do; he gives me the pain I crave to ease the guilt, even if it's a moment. And if he proves himself, I will ensure he becomes like Ben and me." Cristina swooped closer until her shoe bumped into Avery's knee and her face was a foot above Avery. "You should never have killed Ben."

Her swallow caught mid-throat.

"You had no right!" Cristina snarled.

"He was going to kill me!"

"And you killed him instead!" she spat out.

Avery tensed, ready to duck and pivot, knowing she was no match for Cristina. Only when she knew she had no other option would she vanish from the room. She'd been lucky her timing had been perfect when she reappeared behind Ben and used the knife against him, but if she tried teleporting again, her odds showing up at the ideal place and time were far from guaranteed. There were too many people involved.

A blast of wind and clouds barreled into the room. A shadow appeared within the thick haze, and Mayor materialized in the center of the room, mist evaporating in her wake.

"Get her! Stephen, use the mercury. Use it on her!"

Stephen dropped the gun on the sofa and picked up something on the cushion to his right. A glass vial with silver liquid inside. Mercury. It glittered in the artificial light as it moved within the vial, harmless to Stephen and deadly to everyone else in the room.

As he rose from the sofa and opened its top, Avery scrambled to her feet. Her back to Stephen, Mayor stood between him and Cristina, but she turned as if in slow motion toward him. He raised his hand to fling the contents at Mayor.

Avery reacted, flinging herself toward Mayor, ramming her shoulder and entire weight into the other woman's body. She connected, muscle against muscle, and propelled them to the side and away from the liquid's trajectory.

On the ground, out of breath, Avery glanced down at her hands, her arms, her legs but saw nothing had struck her. Then she looked to Mayor, who lay on the floor facing her. Eyes swirling with rage, the other woman stared back at her, and she knew any second Mayor was going to do something involving her body parts.

Oh, God. Avery was dead. It wouldn't matter from whom. Mayor, Stephen, or Cristina. Three to one— terrible odds.

A scream erupted into the room. She swiveled her

head around as chaos erupted. Cristina writhed and convulsed on the floor. Mayor sprang to her feet and launched herself toward Stephen. He crawled across the sofa to get away from her, but she kept coming. As he tripped over the sofa's arm and onto the floor, Mayor launched herself after him. Avery scrambled backward on her butt, afraid of getting in the path of Mayor and Stephen.

With one hand, Mayor grabbed him by the back of his shirt. Material tore. She used her other hand to grab him by the shoulder. She flung him across the room. He hit the wall and slid to the ground, leaving a trail of blood on the paint in his wake.

Then Mayor swiveled on her heel and faced Avery.

This was it.

Still on the floor, Avery closed her eyes and focused on her condo. Now. She needed to vanish.

She opened her eyes.

Mayor was closing the distance between them.

CHAPTER 31

Slumped in his chair, Luys focused on his breath, his muscles, his senses, the voices, and movement around him. The powerlessness of earlier and his inability to help Avery had lashed at his soul. His fingers twitched on his lap, and slowly, ever so slowly, he struggled to raise his head. Finally, movement. The cobwebs inside his skull retreated. The last few minutes, with each thump of his heart, the numbness slowly receded while his frustration continued to mount.

He'd never felt so helpless as the room erupted into chaos. So much violence, so much rage. He sat helplessly, horrified at his inability to act and protect Avery. Moments later, the air cut into his lungs at the sudden silence and stillness. The room lay in ruins.

Avery lay sprawled on her side, alive, gasping for breath.

Arms flung on either side of her head, Cristina lay on her back. A section of her neck and arm had been eaten away by the mercury, revealing bone. Luys didn't want to know what her clothing hid.

She was dead.

Stephen's body lay crumpled on the other side of the room. Blood crept across the floor from beneath his head. Sightless eyes stared back at the room.

Flexing his fingers, Luys felt their strength return as well as the muscles in his thighs, shoulders, and back.

Then Mayor, with predatory and deliberate steps, advanced toward Avery.

No!

Luys sprang from his chair, shaking his head to clear the last of the fog from his brain, and launched himself between Mayor and Avery.

"Not another step," Luys warned.

"Why? She's hurt you. Made a fool of the both of us."

"She's done nothing but help me. If it wasn't for her, I'd still be in prison." Luys clasped Avery's hand, helped her up, and stepped in front of her. Tension clutched at every tendon and muscle in his body. "Touch her, and I'll kill you!"

"You can't kill me, Luys!" She laughed, moving toward them. "I'm stronger than you."

"Try me!"

Mayor paused and cocked her head to one side. "You care for the woman, yes?"

"Yes, of course I do!"

His sister's gaze shifted. "I'll not touch her if she means so much to you." She arched a brow. "But I don't understand. Why did she save my life after all I've done to her?"

Avery stepped from behind Luys, though he retained a hand on her arm, afraid if he let go, something dire would happen to her.

She eyed Mayor warily. "I don't know. It was a knee-jerk reaction. Maybe because you're Luys' sister. I didn't want him grieving over your death, even though I would be fine with it."

Mayor frowned. "I don't know why these two wanted me dead."

"It goes back to your past when you were Aztec captives," Avery answered, her hand clutching his as if for strength. "Cristina said you were to blame for her children's deaths. Something about convincing the priests your daughter wasn't a worthy sacrifice, so they turned their focus on Cristina's son and daughter. It sounded like they had been offered to this Tlaloc."

"The rain god," Mayor murmured. Her brow knitted while a faraway look darkened her eyes. "I don't understand why she would think I had any control over what our captors decided. We were all powerless."

Luys could see that Mayor believed her own words, but he wasn't so sure. He'd lost trust in his sister long ago.

"Well, she blamed you for their deaths and wanted revenge."

Luys followed both women's gazes to Cristina's lifeless form. Such hatred. And what did it give her? Nothing.

When Mayor looked up and met Luys' gaze, her blue-silver eyes had grown bright with unshed tears. She shook her head, a look of uncertainty flashing across her features. "I wouldn't kill someone's child. I may have done many crimes, but not that, never that. Luys, you must know that's the truth with how I feel about Maria."

Mayor's gaze softened, even turned vulnerable. It was shocking. Maybe there was something in his sister other than the hatred and rage that had always fueled her for so long.

Luys urged, "Mayor, get help. There's medication now that can ease your pain. You don't have to live the way you do. You've been so focused on the death of your daughter. Let it go. Concentrate instead on getting yourself healthy, of finding happiness. It is possible."

Mayor's gaze narrowed, and she lifted her chin proudly. "I might. Only because of my daughter."

He inhaled sharply. Having her admit to getting help was a first, but again, her motivation involved her daughter. Always her daughter. Mayor needed to move on if she was ever going to heal. "When will you drop it? Maria is dead. She died, and there's nothing you can do about it."

"But she lives on through Nicole! She is Maria's incarnation." The softness in her face dissolved. Fury and outrage flared back in her eyes as she slashed a hand through the air. "Where are they?"

"Who?" Avery asked.

"Gabriel and that woman. They have Maria. They call her Nicole. Such an estúpido name they gave her. It's all that ugly woman's fault I can't find her!"

The anguish in Mayor's eyes threatened to soften his resolve. Pity wouldn't help Mayor or anyone else. "They must have moved to protect her."

"Why would they do something like that?" A tear pearled on Mayor's lower lash and slid down to her cheek.

"You know why." Luys' gaze narrowed. "You're dangerous. They know you want to turn her like you've done Avery. They don't want that for her. It's too dangerous."

"But I did it to her!" She eyed Avery with narrowed eyes.

"Luck. It could have been that and nothing more. Like I said, it's too dangerous. You could kill Nicole."

But Mayor wasn't listening. "I will find them. It will only take one mistake, and in time, I will be there waiting. I deserve to have my daughter with me."

"She doesn't want to be with you. Mayor, why else would they move? The girl is terrified of you."

"You lie. She *knows* me. I took care of her as best as I could. I cherished her. She *remembers*. She knows I would never hurt her."

"You don't understand, Mayor. You're different than the woman or girl you were when we fled Spain. She doesn't know who you have become."

"I am the same woman I was then." She lifted her chin. "You and Gabriel disgust me! Your superiority is revolting!" Her face darkened with fury. "No one will keep me away from her!"

A gray-white fog formed, swirled around Mayor, and then thickened. The hem of her dress rippled as the smoke billowed around her, faster and faster until it obscured her from view. Suddenly the mist exploded in all directions.

Luys stood frozen, momentarily stunned. But he shouldn't be. Mayor always loved being dramatic and leaving a mess behind her for others to clean up.

Avery clutched at Luys and barreled into his chest, wrapping her arms around his waist and resting her head against his shoulder. "She's gone. I never thought it would end. I was sure you and I would die."

"She's out there still, but she'll be careful, knowing

Gabriel and I will try to track her to ensure Nicole's safety."

"But she's done with us."

Luys thought about it for a moment. "For now. But Nicole is out there. I must protect her from my sister. She wants to make her like the both of us, and it must be Nicole's choice. Mayor may have turned you, but I'm pretty sure you were the first. You could easily have died because of her experiment." He looked down at her upturned face, his breath catching in his throat. "And where would I be without you? You've brought me something I thought I'd forever lost."

She searched his face. "What's that?"

"Love. Something simple but something more powerful than anything else."

Her arms around his waist tightened, and she seemed to relax against his body. "It can get people through many things. Even today."

He glanced around the room as Avery stood in the circle of his arms. So much death and destruction. They would have to call the police. Cristina and Stephen's deaths would have to be explained. They didn't know how yet, but between the two of them, they would have to find a way.

Strange how Cristina's life had paralleled his sister's. Their rage had clouded everything, eradicated any possibility of happiness or life's small wonders.

There might be others like him, but he didn't care. He had Avery; he had a life that held promise. Ahead would lead to obstacles, but with her, he felt he could overcome anything.

That included Mayor.

CHAPTER 32

Wednesday, October 15ᵗʰ — 7:55 pm

Clover jumped up beside Avery on the sofa, where she sat with her feet curled beneath her and Luys by her side. Her head rested against the hollow of his shoulder while his raised arm lay on the headrest behind her. She winced as the kitten kneaded her leg, claws stabbing and retracting into her flesh, before curling into a ball on her lap.

She slipped her fingers through Clover's silken hair, the act soothing. Having Luys beside her was even more calming. "It's hard to believe how our lives have changed. A month ago, I didn't know if I was going to live or die, you hadn't entered my life, and I had no clue the way my world was going to upend."

"Everything could have ended far differently," Luys murmured against her brow as he cupped her shoulder. "It worked out okay, at least for us."

"Yeah." She sank deeper into Luys' side. "We were lucky. For a while there, I didn't know how we were going to explain everything to the police." The police had found the bullet from Stephen's gun that had passed through Avery's shoulder. The physical evidence pointed to Cristina as the person who had killed Stephen. They'd eliminated Luys and Avery as suspects for both murders.

Their DNA didn't match, and neither of them had any markings to indicate they were the assailants.

Cristina's death was initially attributed to a severe allergic reaction but was later recorded as undetermined. Neither one of them was going to explain how dangerous mercury was to a person like Cristina. The police wouldn't believe them anyway, so they both remained silent. Somehow, they'd walked away from the police station. But innocent people had died, and Mayor was still out there.

They later learned the police had uncovered correspondence between Stephen, Cristina, and Ben, tying them to the string of killings in the area. Ben's death had required the most explaining — or rather, the least. A dirty cop with a body count had a way of redirecting the department's curiosity away from how he'd died and toward what else they'd missed while he was still breathing. Detective Hatcher had explained that Avery and Luys had unknowingly gotten mixed up with a group of cult members. Avery suspected he still had his doubts about Luys, but without proof there was nothing he could do.

"Do you think there are others like you, Gabriel, Mayor, and myself?"

"I could pretend the likelihood is low, but I'm a realist. I'm sure there are. Mayor figured out a way to turn you. Cristina or Ben could have done the same. Mayor might try again."

"With Nicole?" She glanced up to catch his eyes darkening with unease.

"Yes, unless Mayor somehow changes, she'd do it. But that's if she finds Nicole. And Gabriel and I are going to make sure that doesn't happen."

"I feel for Nicole—the anxiety of constantly looking over her shoulder and wondering when Mayor will show up."

Avery rolled her shoulder where the bullet had entered and exited. It felt like nothing had happened. She placed a palm against her chest and thought back to that fateful day when she'd woken to find someone had operated on her. Who would have thought Mayor's ancient ceremony would end up saving her life? Against her palm, her heart drummed, steady and strong. All her physical wounds had healed. She had survived, stronger, wiser, carrying internal scars, ones that would eventually heal.

Both had survived and were settling into a relationship that felt new, exciting, and filled with possibilities. She'd persevered and made it to the other side, wholly alive.

She lifted her hand from her chest, twined her fingers between his, and squeezed, finding herself captivated by the heat and strength in his grip. Her chest tightened. She would never take for granted his incredible gift of love.

He gave her a questioning look.

"Loving you is incredible. And I'm just happy. Really happy. Actually, more than happy. I can't remember a time when I've ever felt this overwhelming joy for the life I have. And the future. Hell, I didn't think I had a future."

Luys dipped his head and brushed his lips against hers in a slow, tender kiss. "This is only the beginning."

The End

A KISS BEFORE DYING

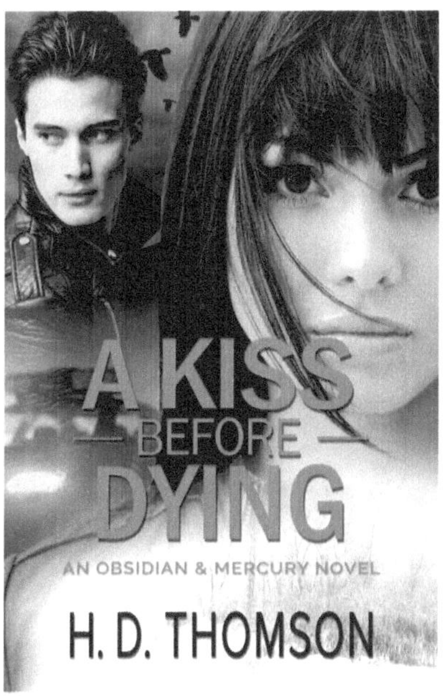

ANXIETY

"There is mystery and suspense and underlying it all is a romance that will melt your heart."

"Different tones keep us guessing in this suspense murder mystery/romance. ...I'll just say that this plot is incredible and unpredictable and I highly recommend it."

THANK YOU!

Thank you for reading *A Long Kiss Goodbye*. I hope you enjoyed it.

I need to ask a favor. Reviews are hard to come by these days. You, as the reader, have the power to make or break a book. If you are so inclined, I would love a review of *A Long Kiss Goodbye*. Let me know whether you loved it, hated it. Any feedback is greatly appreciated.

You can find all my books available at major online storFor news on latest releases, contests and other news, you can signup for my newsletter on my website. Also, if you feel like contacting me, you can always catch me on Facebook, or you can email me at bellamediamanagment@gmail.com. I'm always excited to hear back from readers.

Again, thank you for taking the time to read *A Long Kiss Goodbye*.

With gratitude,
H. D. Thomson

BIBLIOGRAPHY

https://www.smithsonianmag.com/history/discovery-secret-tunnel-mexico-solve-mysteries-teotihuacan-180959070/

https://en.wikipedia.org/wiki/Tlaxcala

https://www.houstonculture.org/mexico/tlaxcala.html

https://www.aztec-history.com/aztec-empire.html

https://www.latinamericanstudies.org/aztecs/aztec_human_sacrifice.pdf

https://rubens.anu.edu.au/raid1/student_projects97/aztec/ACosWorldView.html/World1a.html

https://en.wikipedia.org/wiki/Spanish_conquest_of_the_Aztec_Empire

https://aztecsandtenochtitlan.com/aztec-names/aztec-boys-names/

https://mexicounexplained.com/three-martyred-children-tlaxcala/

https://www.thoughtco.com/hernan-cortes-and-his-tlaxcalan-allies-2136523

https://www.cs.cmu.edu/~kvs/heraldry/spanish16/
male-given-alpha.html

https://www.cs.cmu.edu/~kvs/heraldry/spanish16/

https://www.bcmj.org/premise/history-bloodletting#4

History of Mercury

https://www.dartmouth.edu/~toxmetal/mercury/
history.html

https://www.rt.com/news/252985-mexi-
can-tomb-king-mercury/

https://www.dailymail.co.uk/news/article-3054296/
Hunt-ancient-royal-tomb-Mexico-takes-mercurial-twist.
html

https://www.history.com/news/7-unusual-an-
cient-medical-techniques

ABOUT THE AUTHOR

H. D. Thomson moved from Ontario, Canada as a teenager to the heat of Arizona where she graduated from the University of Arizona with a B.S. in Business Administration with a major in accounting. After working in the corporate world as an accountant, H.D. changed her focus to one of her passions—books. She owned and operated an online bookstore for several years and then started the company, Bella Media Management. The company specializes in web sites, video trailers, ebook conversion and promotional resources for authors and small businesses. When she's not enjoying small-town life in Ryderwood, Washington or heading her company, she is following her first love—writing.

HDThomson.com

What they're saying about H. D. Thomson's books:

"My applause to the author on an entertaining read." – *Romance Novel Junkies*

"Author H.D. Thomson does a great job of keeping the reader guessing." – *Paranormal Romance Party*

"Bravo H. D. Thomson!" – *Writer's and Reader's of Distinct Fiction's Top Read.*

"Thomson's writing is spot on…" – *Confessions of a Bibliophile*

COMPLETE LIST OF TITLES

ROMANTIC SUSPENSE

SMOKE & MIRRORS SERIES

ANXIETY
DUPLICITY
IDENTITY

PARANORMAL ROMANCE

ONYX & MERCURY SERIES

A KISS BEFORE DYING
A LONG KISS GOODBYE
A KISS THAT KILLS

SHADES SERIES

DEADLY SHADES #1
SHADES OF HOLLY #2
KILLER SHADES #3
SHADES SERIES BOX SET - BOOKS 1
THROUGH 3

CONTEMPORARY ROMANCE

THE LONG ROAD HOME
PROTECTING KATIE

NONFICTION

WHAT I WISH I'D KNOWN: 100 AUTHORS
REVEAL WHAT THEY WISH THEY'D TOLD
THEIR YOUNGER SELVES

WRITER'S SECRET WEAPON